are also published by Sphere.

*Praise for Lucy Dawson*

'Funny, dark and very surprising – a compulsive new breed of chick-lit'
*Louise Candlish*

'This isn't your standard chick-lit fluff – and for that we're very grateful . . . This tale is so deliciously dark, you'll be left craving the next twist of dubious events ★★★★'
*Heat*

'This dark, compelling tale is a warning for every female with a new friend'
*Sun*

'Chick lit with a sinister twist'
*Elle*

'Totally gripping ★★★★'
*Company*

'[An] intense and gripping read ★★★★'
*OK!*

'Darker than your average chick lit, you'll be engrossed from the first page. A compelling, excellent read with a twist'
*Candis*

'Lucy Dawson spins an intriguing tale . . . A break from the black-and-white morality of the chick-lit genre'
*London Lite*

'A claustrophobic and compelling tale, with a lethal eye for the strains and terrors that can lie beneath the surface of a friendship'
*Waterstone's Books Quarterly*

'Most definitely a cut above, [this] reaches dark places which other novels in the genre would steer well clear of, on the way to a thought-provoking ending'
*Peterborough Evening Telegraph*

# THE ONE THAT GOT AWAY

Lucy Dawson

sphere

SPHERE

First published in Great Britain as a paperback original in 2010 by Sphere

A CIP catalogue record for this book
is available from the British Library.

ISBN 978-0-7515-4252-3

Typeset in Bembo by Palimpsest Book Production Limited,
Falkirk, Stirlingshire
Printed and bound in Great Britain by Clays Ltd, St Ives plc

Papers used by Sphere are natural, renewable and recyclable
products sourced from well-managed forests and certified
in accordance with the rules of the Forest Stewardship Council.

**Mixed Sources**
Product group from well-managed
forests and other controlled sources
www.fsc.org  Cert no. SGS-COC-004081
© 1996 Forest Stewardship Council
FSC

Sphere
An imprint of
Little, Brown Book Group
100 Victoria Embankment
London EC4Y 0DY

An Hachette UK Company
www.hachette.co.uk

www.littlebrown.co.uk

For Mum and Dad

## *Acknowledgements*

Thanks to Sarah Ballard, Jo Dickinson, Rebecca Saunders, all at United Agents and Little, Brown, James and my family and friends for their encouragement and support. I am very grateful to you all.

Thank you to those who offered me practical advice, in particular Patricia.

And finally thank you to DS for being the person who once told *me* the joke. Despite the trouble it's caused.

# Chapter One

As I fling the wet door of the car boot open, my fingers slip and one of my nails bends back, making me yelp and drop my overnight bag. I grab the offending digit and examine it carefully for any signs of injury; it's throbbing, the nail bed has gone a bit white, and there's a line where it *might* have snapped, but didn't. Nevertheless, hot tears prickle my eyes . . . great . . . I'm not only late, but I'm going to cry too. Brilliant.

I take a deep breath, blink furiously as I try to gather myself and then determinedly pick up the bag from the soggy drive. Shoving it in the car, I slam the boot firmly shut and make my way round to the door. Once I'm in, have clipped my seat belt on and adjusted my mirror so that my own eyes are staring back at me, I clock the violet shadows and the concealer already starting to settle in the creases. I got very little sleep last night.

Last night. I remember my husband, looking at me incredulously across the bed, stunned by what I had just said.

I twist the key in the ignition, trying to ignore the rush of shame that accompanies the memory. Jerking my head round – as if I'm trying to jolt the picture out of my mind – I look over my shoulder and start to reverse sharply. I *wanted* to say sorry to him this morning. I was going to – I would have said it last night except he insisted on sleeping downstairs. And anyway, how am I supposed to apologise if he's just going to bang out to work like that? How does that help anything?

I slam on the brakes, just shy of hitting the bank behind me, and crunch the gears into first before lifting my foot up too crossly, lurching inelegantly out of the drive and on to the road. I love Dan more than anything, but being curt when he could see I was trying to make it up to him, deliberately not kissing me goodbye? OK, he's not usually like that at all, which means he is *really* angry . . . and hurt . . . but still – it was a mean thing to do.

Leaning forward I switch the radio on and mutinously put my foot down in anticipation of the speed bump that Dan always tells me I go over too fast. It gives me a brief moment of satisfaction to fly over it in the manner of Daisy Duke, but I can't help wincing at the God-awful noise the suspension makes when I land; that actually doesn't sound good. I tense up and listen, worried that the bottom

2

of the car is now about to drop off – just to cap it all – but nothing happens, and by the time I pull up at the red traffic lights, my anger has begun to dissipate and I'm not gripping the steering wheel quite so tightly. In fact I feel suddenly tired and very sad that for the first time ever, we've had a barney that has lasted into another day.

I should have just kept my mouth shut. I'd be angry with me if I were him; I like to think I wouldn't have slammed out of the house like *he* did, but I can see why he's outraged.

'You didn't just say that?' I hear the echo of his disbelief. 'But I'm your *husband*!'

I get another stab of remorse, staring unseeingly at the brake lights of the car in front of me while we all wait for green. The sound of Elbow's 'One Day Like This' fills the car and I begin to listen to the lyrics attentively. I can identify with every single word.

Well, except there's no morning sun – it's a day that could do with wringing out if anything, commuters are scurrying towards Brighton station, with cold hunched shoulders as they hurry past, but yes – why *did* I behave that way, saying things I didn't mean to say? I swallow hard. I know Dan doesn't realise it, but oddly, last night DID happen because of how much I love him and in some ways, maybe this is a good thing: we don't normally hold things back from one another, he and I are usually very good at saying how we feel. Now at least we both know we have a problem, and we'll be able to do something about it.

I exhale worriedly. The trouble is . . . the trouble is how do I tell my husband that I have realised I'm scared of doing something everyone else seems to find second nature? That yes – I wish someone WOULD tell me how to feel, because I am genuinely, honestly confused.

I did not see this coming. I really didn't. You think when you're younger that you will grow up, fall in love, get married and have children – simple as that. It's what pretty much everyone does, it's certainly what I thought I'd do, and yet last night I accused my husband – one of the kindest, most honourable people I have ever met – of trying to trick me into getting pregnant.

And the worst thing is, it wasn't the alleged duplicity I was particularly worried about, it was simply the very real prospect of being pregnant that freaked me out. I wasn't happy but nervous, or excited and scared . . . just plain and simple, grade A, no lies terrified at the thought of actually *having a baby*. And I mean all of it; the no turning back, the pregnant bit, giving birth, being responsible for a small person for ever – end of life as I otherwise know it. Yet up until now, it is something which I have always assumed I would do and – more importantly – would want.

HOW can I not ever have properly thought about this – just assumed it would work somehow? Dan by comparison was so excited; busily talking about new adventures, next stages . . . What if – and seemingly overnight – my husband and I have become completely incompatible?

My eyes widen with fear at the thought of actually being without Dan – and panicking, I fumble for my phone.

4

I'm just going to ring him now, ring him and say I'm sorry unreservedly. Because whatever my own feelings about this, I shouldn't have accused him of doing something so underhand, no wonder he—

But before I can dial, an angry honk behind me tells me that the lights have finally changed and everyone wants to GO! I pull away, dropping my bag back down on the seat as a caffeinated DJ crashes in over the remainder of the song and begins to blather on about roadworks in a city centre I am nowhere near.

And just like that, I miss my window without even realising it.

I will look back on this moment. I will remember nearly calling my husband and saying sorry and I will wish with all my heart that I had taken my chance while I had it.

It would have changed everything.

It might even have saved a life.

# Chapter Two

I don't want to go to this sales conference in Windsor today. And I shouldn't be staying away tonight either. I need to be coming home to Dan, not doing small talk with my colleagues at the hotel bar, before cautiously inspecting the sheets of a bed that will smell faintly of the cigarettes people used to be allowed to smoke in it.

Chewing on one of my nails, I picture sitting down in our kitchen instead and talking things through with Dan, explaining my unexpected worries and fears, which is what I should have done last night instead of having my completely crazy moment . . . but in my defence, the last couple of days haven't exactly been easy.

Not that I'm trying to make excuses for my behaviour; but I do HATE the way you can be having a really nice time of it one minute – genuinely happy with your lot and wouldn't change a thing – and then the next moment it's as if some malign force has noticed you skipping around minding your own business and pointed a finger at earth, blasting down a beam that messes everything up completely, apparently just for the hell of it.

Saturday was when everything started to swing out of kilter. I had been having one of those random, relaxed lunches with Joss and Bec in town, where the only rush is one of occasional spontaneous warmth that makes you say happily to the others 'this is *nice,* isn't it?' at which they smile back understandingly and say 'very'.

We chatted about this, that and absolutely nothing – the way you can when you've all known each other for ever. We were simply enjoying each other's company and, if truth be told, eating quite a bit more than we probably should have been; the rapidly impending Christmas party season was already going to necessitate industrial Spanx. I was secretly undoing my top button under the table when Joss sat back contentedly and patted her still somehow flat tummy, which, unfairly, wasn't even vaguely straining at the waistband of her jeans.

'How do you do that?' Bec said enviously. 'How do you *eat* that much and still be so skinny malinky?'

'Worms?' Joss shrugged.

Bec smiled indulgently. 'Do you think it's because you're taller?' she said after a moment's consideration. 'Tall people really have to go some before they look properly porky, don't they?'

Joss looked a bit taken aback at that and I grinned.

'What I mean is,' Bec said hastily, smoothing out her dress, which had rucked up slightly, 'you've got more leeway than a shortarse like me. If you and I ate the same amount of cake for a week, I'd look fatter sooner, because I've got less height to spread it over.'

'But wouldn't Joss also burn off more cake than you anyway *because* she's taller?' I looked at her doubtfully. 'Like men need more calories a day than women . . . not that I'm saying you're mannishly tall, Joss. Certainly not Brigitte Nielsen freaky big—'

'Thanks.' Joss wrinkled her nose. 'I think.'

'If you were a model, five foot seven would actually be quite short,' I pointed out, reaching for one of the biscuits that had come with our coffees. 'And you're not a Weeble either,' I turned to Bec reassuringly. 'You're both lovely just the way you are.'

Bec wasn't listening, she was still looking at Joss. 'I've got a question. Suppose you met a man who was wonderful in every way, and I mean *perfect*; funny, kind, optimistic, great with children, great in bed, bought you treats without being asked . . . BUT he was considerably shorter than you; would you still go out with him?'

'Well he wouldn't be perfect then, would he?' Joss said bluntly. 'If he only came up to my armpits. Who wants that?'

'Really?' Bec was fascinated. 'You wouldn't date him?'

'No,' Joss insisted. 'I wouldn't. Why is that a surprising thing? You want to be able to look up – or at least across – into your bloke's eyes. Not down. Never down. Urgh.'

She shuddered and her long corkscrew curls shook with disgust.

Bec turned to me. 'Would you have gone out with Dan if he'd been shorter than you?'

'But I'm only five foot five, Bec,' I smiled. 'You're talking seriously short for a bloke.'

'Like Danny DeVito,' Joss said, reaching out and snaffling the last biscuit before Bec could get there. 'Tasty,' she smirked through a mouthful of crumbs.

'Would you?' Bec persisted.

I thought about it for a moment. 'Probably not,' I conceded.

'NO!' Bec was amazed. 'You wouldn't have gone out with Dan? I don't believe it!'

'Well I wouldn't have known what I was missing out on, would I?' I explained. 'I just wouldn't have found him as attractive, we probably would have only chatted for a bit and then I'd have gone on my way none the wiser.'

'Yeah right!' Joss scoffed. 'You two were a done deal from the word go.'

But Bec's eyes had widened. 'Seriously? All that happiness, all that love, you'd never have taken the chance of discovering it? You would have not married the love of your life, THE ONE, if he'd been three inches shorter than he is? I'm shocked at you Molly Greene. Shocked and disappointed.'

I deliberately paused for a moment. 'Bec,' I leant forward in my seat and lowered my voice to a secretive whisper. 'There's no such thing as THE one.'

Bec yelped in horror and Joss nudged me. 'Stop it,' she grinned. 'Don't wind her up.'

'I mean it!' I said quickly. 'What Dan and I have is unique to us, there's one *him,* but if he died—'

Bec looked like she was going to faint with horror and slip under the table.

'—I would be devastated, of course I would, but I know Dan wouldn't want me to live the rest of my life alone if he couldn't be with me any more.'

I watched Bec hesitate.

'It's like friendship,' I continued. 'You don't have one shot at that for the whole of your life do you? Lots of people can bring you happiness. I think there are probably lots of "ones".'

'All right – I get it,' Bec said ruefully. 'I should keep an open mind to all opportunities life throws at me. You're right.'

'That's all I'm saying,' I smiled at her.

'Would you want Dan to meet someone else if you popped it then?' Joss asked slyly.

'Of course I would,' I said quickly. Then I thought about it a bit more. 'But not for at least a year and I'd want her to be fatter than me.'

'Oooh. Talking of people *departing* – Joss,' Bec cut in, 'I did a visit to one of my mums the other day – she's just had twins and they're *so* sweet – and I was walking past that salon you used to have that Saturday job at.'

'Judy's Garland?' Joss muttered darkly, narrowing her eyes. 'I hated the bloke that owned that place . . . sausage fingers and all those gold rings, *and* his vile long man nails. Two pounds fifty an hour he paid me to wash those skanky old women's hair. I wonder what happened to him?'

Bec stared at her. 'Well, he's died. Surely you could see where I was going with that? The salon's closing down.'

'I can't believe it was still going! He was old even back then!' I exclaimed. 'Do you even remember his hair?'

'Canary yellow!' Bec giggled. 'That can't have been his natural colour.'

'It wasn't.' Joss gave a snort of amusement. 'He used to whip the wig off in the back room and flap it around when all the dryers and the overhead heaters were going because he'd get so sweaty and hot . . . although that was more down to his leather trousers I think.' She shuddered. 'Every time he lifted his arm up to put a curler in, his belly would flop out over the top of the waistband, all red and crisscrossed.'

'Urgh!' Bec and I exclaimed in unison.

'He was like a walking rolled pork joint,' Joss continued relentlessly. 'The old birds loved him though,' she reached for her cup. '*C'est la vie* . . . or not as the case may be.'

'Joss!' I admonished as Bec gasped so loudly she made us jump. Joss even spilt some of her coffee. 'Oh my God! *And talking of blasts from the past* . . . I can't believe I forgot to tell you THIS! You'll never GUESS who tried to add me as a friend on Facebook. Leo!' she squeaked excitedly, before we could offer any suggestions.

I paused. 'Leo, as in my ex Leo?'

She nodded.

12

'That turd basket!' Joss exploded in outrage. 'This is exactly why I refuse to go on Facebook or Twitter. You didn't accept him did you?' she glared at Bec.

'Of course not!' she said, looking insulted. 'What do you take me for? He's got an open profile though Moll; I looked. He's married now!'

'You are *joking*.' Joss was appalled.

'That's nothing – I think he's got kids too!'

And to my surprise, I felt something inside me pause, like the small hand of a clock losing time for just a second, before resuming as normal.

'Is he married to *her*?' I heard myself ask calmly.

The girls shared a look and then Bec said uncomfortably, 'Cara? I don't think so, no. The woman I saw looks at least our age and Cara was younger wasn't she?'

'She had peroxide blonde hair.' I picked up my cup and casually took a sip of coffee, even though there was hardly any left, and what was there had gone cold. 'Like Marilyn Monroe – hard to mistake. You'd know if it was her.'

Bec shook her head firmly. 'No then, it's not. This woman was a bit mumsy if anything; normal looking.'

'She can't be normal,' Joss said grimly. 'Not if she's married to him, poor cow.'

It was a slightly strange moment, realising that even though I no longer thought about Leo, he had of course been out there living his life anyway, meeting people, getting married, having children. It had all happened ages ago by the sound of it; I'd been none the wiser and neither had it made the slightest of differences to my life. Yet it was odd somehow to realise that he'd said the words I once thought we might say to each other, to someone else. I wondered if he'd felt the way I was feeling now, on hearing *I* had married.

Still, it was neither here nor there really. I pushed the thought firmly from my mind, smiled at the girls and said brightly, 'So, what does he look like these days then? Fat and bald hopefully?'

Bec snuck a quick look at Joss who was still glaring at her crossly and said uneasily, 'Pretty much the same as he used to.'

'Well that's annoying,' I said, seeing his slow, troublesome smile in my mind, ice-blue eyes staring brazenly back at me, intentions clear. 'He could have at least had the decency to let himself go.'

'So he hasn't tried to "be-friend" *you* then?' Joss said sharply.

I laughed. 'God no.'

'Well he wouldn't know your married name would he?' Bec said quickly. 'You're Molly Greene on Facebook. That's why I didn't accept him, so he couldn't see I was friends with you,' she explained earnestly. 'Or see any pictures of you.'

'Hmm. That was good thinking,' Joss said, thawing slightly.

'Thanks, Batman.' Bec looked relieved. 'I'm glad you approve.'

It had never really occurred to me before how bizarre that was; that an ex out there might potentially look at some of the most intimate snapshots of my life, occasions that were no longer anything to do with him: my wedding, birthdays, nights out . . . 'That feels a bit weird really.'

'It's just the surprise,' Bec said reassuringly, misunderstanding me. 'I'd feel exactly the same way if John suddenly popped back up out of nowhere too.'

'Which is exactly why I HATE Facebook,' Joss repeated. 'You're not supposed to know what your knobhead exes are doing. They're supposed to just vanish out of your life and that be that. All this so-called social networking is really upsetting the natural balance of things.'

'Bringing about climate change?' Bec teased. 'Disturbing the food chain? You really didn't like Leo and John did you?'

'I didn't dislike or like them,' Joss responded honestly, which surprised me. 'Not at first anyway. John was just spineless and a bit selfish. He didn't bring out the best in you Bec. He made you very needy.'

Bec looked a bit like she wished she hadn't asked.

'What I mean is, he didn't *add* anything to your life, he was always off doing his own thing, which made you very insecure. He was a bit nothing really. Leo, on the other hand,' she paused, 'could be a lot of fun, when he wanted to be. The trouble with him,' she began to get into her stride, 'was aside from turning out to be a cheating wanker, he was like that nursery rhyme; when he was good, he was very, very good – when he was bad, he was horrid.'

'—he wasn't the messiah, he was a very naughty boy.'
Bec added and they both laughed.

'You're thinking about that poem, the little girl with
a curl,' I said to Joss. 'Right in the middle of her forehead?'

She looked back at me blankly.

'Never mind. When I was about five I drew on my
bedroom walls with a felt tip.' I reached out and dotted
up a few leftover crumbs from the plate with my finger
and popped them in my mouth. 'Mum caught me and
I told her it wasn't me, it was my naughty hands, so she
told me if my hands felt like being naughty again, I should
sit on them. Leo should have spent some time sitting on
his hands.' I smiled at them both. 'In fact he probably
shouldn't have ever got off them.'

Joss grimaced. 'Imagine if you'd married *him* . . .'

'I wouldn't have,' I shook my head. 'Not if it had come
to the crunch.'

Neither of them said anything.

'I wouldn't!' I insisted. 'I know I got stuck there for a
bit, but he was never The One. I just thought he was for
a mad few moments.'

'I thought you said there was no such thing as The
One?' Bec said quickly.

'You're right,' I pointed at her. 'Well reminded. What
I mean is he wasn't someone who would ever have made
a decent life partner.'

'Too right. He should have been a three-month fling
at most,' Joss said. 'He just wore you down, that's all. He only

ever put up a fight when he sensed you were going off him. That's why blokes like him are such a headfuck. They're clever enough to sharpen up their game when they realise you might actually walk away . . . but then once they've hooked you back in and you start having perfectly reasonable demands and needs of your own – see you later! But what I *hate* him for,' she paused, 'is that he screwed you over when your dad was so ill. I still maintain he was a special kind of weasel to admit to shagging that bint when your dad had just had a heart attack.'

'If he were here,' I said casually, 'he'd say he had no intention of it happening like that, that he didn't know Cara was going to ring me and tell me what was going on.'

'If he *were* here,' Joss said quickly, 'I'd kick him in the nuts.'

'You're like an avenging elephant,' I grinned. 'Once wronged, never forgotten.'

'Yes I am,' she said loftily, not looking altogether displeased with that description. 'I'd trample anyone for you two.'

'It was a weird time,' I said, staring into the middle distance. 'I did everything backwards really, didn't I? I should have been out being unsuitable and living it up, not cleaning and cooking Sunday roasts aged twenty-five; trying to make it all fit when it was never going to.'

'It doesn't matter what you did or didn't do then,' Joss said firmly. 'You know where your head's at now and that's all that matters. I can honestly say that by and large my twenties were shit – I wouldn't have them again for all the tea in China. New shoes, pots of money, loud clubs and overpriced drinks; a bloke for that matter – all the things I was chasing; I just didn't need them. It's being able to do things like this,' she motioned between us, 'that makes me happy. And that's enough.'

'Here, here,' I said heartily. 'Although can I keep my husband please? I know I don't *need* Dan, but I sort of want him, if that's OK?'

'I'll allow that,' Joss said generously. 'Seeing as it's him. Are you still off to your mum and dad's for some fireworks later? Will Dan be allowed to light any of them this year or will Chris be in charge as usual?' she grinned, referring to my older brother who quite liked to take control of everything.

I laughed. 'My dad'll do it. Chris and Dan will be surveying carefully from the sidelines, while the girls will all be safely indoors with the children watching Stu enthusiastically heap too much rubbish on the bonfire, thinking it's a bit too near the back fence. Once a pyromaniac always a pyromaniac.'

'Stu's never going to grow out of his middle-child syndrome is he? I love your brothers,' Bec said fondly, 'in a non-sexual way, naturally,' she added hastily.

'Of course,' I replied. 'Been there done that eh?'

Bec blushed prettily.

'I'm joking,' I teased. 'It was what – 1990 or something? And Stu was *quite* the stud then with his baggy Vanilla Ice pants and bum fluff.'

'You know to this day I can't bear the smell of Cinzano,' Bec confessed.

I patted her hand sympathetically. 'Well, you both got a snog and it's provided me with endless teasing opportunities over the years, so everyone's a winner.' I reached for my handbag to get my purse out. 'I've had a lovely time today you two, thank you.'

And I had, although of everything we'd chatted about, it was Leo I found myself still thinking about on my way home, remembered hearing the surprisingly sharp voice at the other end of the phone line say:

'Hello, my name's Cara. I'm sleeping with your boyfriend. I thought you ought to know.'

Leo had just pathetically shrugged, almost helplessly, when I confronted him, saying – as if he couldn't quite understand it himself, like it was somehow beyond his control – 'the thing is, I think I might love her.' My furious questions had turned into crying and throwing things at him, all of which was met with an increasingly blank stare I'd never seen him do before. Just for a second, once he'd gone I almost wished I hadn't made him leave, even though I knew then and there it was over for good.

Joss was right. Boys like him were only built for infatuations.

And time really was a great healer.

I arrived home to find that Dan was still out, and having slipped my shoes off and made a cup of tea, I padded off upstairs to check my emails: one of the downsides of largely working from home as a medical rep was my

19

chronic inability to leave the computer alone come the weekend. There was nothing interesting pending at all, and so I ended up logging into Facebook instead . . .

And after hesitating for a moment I curiously typed 'Leo Williams' into the search bar.

I'd done a nosy search for him once or twice before in the past, but nothing had ever come up. That must have been because he'd only recently joined; surprising really given he worked in event management and was a total—

Well! I caught my breath as a tiny but recognisable picture appeared on the screen. There he was.

Laughing into the camera, his arms hugging a smiling dark-haired woman – *not* Cara – he looked very happy. This was certainly more interesting than a boring mooch through albums entitled 'randoms from my shit phone', belonging to someone I'd once gone to secondary school with . . . I peered a little closer and then clicked on to his open profile.

Bec was right. He didn't really look any different at all, just slightly older. He was wearing a dinner jacket, a good look on anyone, but particularly so on him. His almost-black hair was perhaps a little shorter than I remembered, flecked with some grey, but then it had been how many years since I'd seen him, four – maybe five? It must have been – it had all ended just before my twenty-ninth birthday. I scrutinised the picture, they were clearly at some sort of do, there were a lot of people surrounding them whose heads had been half cut off. It looked a bit like the kind of photo that might be found in the diary pages of a social magazine.

He'd added very little information – just his date of birth and that he was 'in a relationship'. When I opened his photos however, there were quite a few. Mostly just of him snowboarding and kite surfing, which were a bit, 'Yes, I'm as at home on the slopes as in the boardroom', although in fairness par for the course on a lot of blokes' pages. There were also a couple of an apparent holiday with the same woman, both of them sporting expensive sunglasses and tans as they clutched cocktails very close to camera . . . and just one with two young, slightly uncomfortable looking little girls stood in front of them, all smartly dressed. I frowned. What was Bec on about – calls herself a midwife – they weren't his, they looked about six and nine, way too old. I leant in closer, she was right about the wedding ring though; there it was, shining on his finger. I sat back and stared at them again. They looked just like any normal happy family. Leo was a stepdad. How very weird.

Even weirder, was it my imagination or did his wife actually look quite a bit like *me*? She was slightly older and Bec had a point, she was curvy, but in an attractive womanly way. It was the hair really – not a dissimilar style and colour to mine; mid-length with a long fringe . . . Still, most men usually went for a type; that was no news. She certainly looked determined – almost steely. Perhaps Leo had met his match.

I clicked back and stared at his profile picture again. I could practically hear his warm laugh, knew just what it would sound like . . . and those were arms that had once been round me, lips that had touched mine. How very strange. I'd posed for pictures just like that with him. I probably still had one or two of them buried away in a box somewhere in amongst old Christmas and birthday cards, graduation lists, friends' wedding invitations.

I scrawled through his list of friends . . . and straightened up as Cara Jones appeared on the list. No! He was still friends with her? Her profile was disappointingly closed, although it was quite satisfying to see from her picture that she wasn't ageing well.

Cara Jones. The last time I'd seen that face had been when I'd come back slightly too early from work and discovered Leo collecting the last of his stuff. She'd been leaning on her flash nippy little BMW, all smug, bouncy curls and crossed arms in her tight expensive biker jacket while she waited for him. She'd looked at me curiously as I'd walked straight past her, head down, into the building. I wasted some considerable time afterwards wondering if I should have gone back and punched her, and if not doing so made me a coward or the bigger person.

Thankfully, looking at her face no longer had the power to make me feel anything at all. I poked my tongue out at her − silly moo − and returned to Leo's profile.

And then, for no obvious reason whatsoever, I did something impulsively stupid. I stared at him for a minute and then I found myself clicking on 'Send Leo a message'. In the subject I put Wow! Typing quickly I wrote

```
I see you've been busy then! Congratulations!
Hope  you're  well.  Molly
```

And then I hit send.

## Chapter Three

Almost immediately I shifted in my seat with the uneasy feeling I'd done something stupid. But it was too late, the message had gone. It was out there on the loose.

Bloody Facebook – it was like being offered a manky chocolate you hadn't even considered eating, but somehow ended up scoffing anyway.

Well, I couldn't get it back. I shouldn't have even looked at his profile in the first place. I sighed. Perhaps it was just one of those foolish things best kept to myself – he'd probably just ignore my message anyway. Well, of course he would, this was Leo after all . . .

The front door banged downstairs, making me jump. 'Hello? Moll?' bellowed a voice. 'You up there?'

Dan. 'Hi!' I shouted brightly, deleting my email thread,

closing Leo's profile and clearing my history with a speed that surprised me.

When he appeared in the doorway a moment later, I was innocently clicking around on my own profile page.

'Hello!' he crossed the room to give me a warm kiss, his face still cold from an afternoon spent outside, cheeks ruddy. 'What are you doing?' He glanced at the screen, 'Ah, having a productive day I see?'

'How was the game?' I said quickly.

'Crap,' he said cheerfully, 'but someone got sent off and punched the ref which was quite funny. Look what I found in a shop on my way home though.' He pulled his hand out from behind his back to reveal several packets of sparklers.

'Oh well done! I completely forgot about them.'

He looked pleased. 'I thought you might.' Sitting down on the chair in the corner of the room he began to unwind his scarf before ruffling up his hat-flattened brown hair. 'I need a trim, I'm starting to look like a sheep.'

'I like sheep,' I said, as I shut the computer down.

'I like you too,' he wiggled his eyebrows suggestively, then his expression changed as he appeared to ponder something for a moment. 'I might give the hairdresser's a quick ring now, make an appointment before I forget . . .' he reached into his pocket for his mobile, ever the sensible planner. 'What time are we due at your mum and dad's by the way? Have I got time to— Oh! Text message,' he remarked, before I could answer. He frowned carefully at the screen for a moment and then his face lit up. 'Wow! Ed and Beth are going to have a baby!' he exclaimed, referring to our best man and his wife. 'Isn't that brilliant? I'll just give him a quick ring . . .'

'Mate!' he said, getting to his feet. 'Just got your text. Fantastic news! We're over the moon for you!' He rested his hand gently on my head and absently stroked my hair before breaking away to mouth 'tea?' to me.

'When's it due?' he continued as I nodded. He gave me a thumbs-up and began to amble off happily downstairs. 'Times they are a-changin' eh? I can't believe you're going to be a *dad*,' I heard him laugh. 'Your poor kid . . .'

'. . . I just hope it gets Beth's ears.' Dan was still nattering away about it in the car on the way to Mum and Dad's. 'No one deserves Ed's great lugs. Or his hair for that matter. You know he started losing it when he was twenty-two?' He shook his head with a chuckle. 'Poor bastard . . . Do you think *I'm* going any thinner on top?' he added after a pause, looking anxiously in the mirror. 'Maybe next week I should ask her to cut the sides but leave the top the same length? What do you think?'

'Eyes on the road,' I said gently, avoiding his question.

'So I AM going thinner. Let's hope our kids don't get *my* hair then . . . or my height and your feet. They'd fall over all the time.' He fell silent for a moment. 'Or your height and *my* feet. That would be even worse; a great big clown-foot baby,' he laughed. 'Scary eh?'

'Help me, someone!' I shouted. 'I'm so frightened!'

Oscar, my nephew, stopped growling and, balanced rather precariously on his scooter, pulled up his mask. 'It's still me!' he said delightedly as I flopped down on to one of the kitchen stools.

'Phew!' I said in mock relief, taking a sip of my tea. Oscar put the mask back on and scooted over to the other side of the room where his younger sister Lily was having an increasingly frustrating time of it attempting to lift her doll's pushchair over the lip of the kitchen step.

Oscar paused and assessed the situation coolly. 'You need a boy to do that,' he said and tried to lift it up for her. Lily however, under the impression he was trying to take it away, squawked loudly in outrage, to which Oscar, clearly deciding the job was more trouble than it was worth, dropped it and rode off, Lily glaring after him in a 'That's right pal, you jog on,' sort of way. Miscommunication between the sexes was apparently starting younger and younger.

While making his getaway, Oscar nearly crashed into Mum, who was attempting to clear up the kitchen. 'Er, it's getting a little crowded in here,' she announced in warning to the rest of us, most of whom were lazing around reading the Saturday papers.

'I'm on it.' My eldest brother Chris put down the finance supplement, unfolded his long legs and got to his feet. 'Right, time for a game of hide-and-seek before we do the fireworks!'

'I'll play, Daddy,' offered Oscar generously, looking excitedly up at him.

'What a good idea.' Mum whisked my half-drunk cup of tea away from under my nose and took it over to the sink.

'I hadn't finished with that,' I protested.

'Hadn't you? Never mind,' she said briskly. 'Off you go.'

'I shouldn't be surprised if one of these days *I* wind up on that draining board,' Dad remarked, keeping a firm grip on the review section and his own mug.

'Are you going to play hide-and-seek, Granddad?' asked Oscar.

'No, love,' Dad said regretfully. 'I've got a bone in my leg. I'll help you count though.' He looked at the rest of us expectantly, so my sister-in-law Karen and I began rather reluctantly to get up. My other brother Stuart continued to read the sports section, while his wife Maria looked relieved to have the excuse of giving my youngest nephew Harry his bottle. 'We'll go to thirty shall we, Os? One, two, three . . .'

'Come on Uncle Stu and Uncle Dan!' Oscar urged. 'We've started. You have to hide too!'


'We should cosy up in the dark like this more often,' Dan said in the spare room wardrobe, as he pinched my bum.

'I hope that was you and not Mr Tumnus,' I grinned as he leant in to kiss me. For a brief moment we started playing another game altogether until Dan reluctantly pulled back. 'I think we should probably stop now,' he said. 'But can we carry this on when we get home?'

'Yes please,' I murmured, then, hearing Oscar stomping up the stairs bellowing helpfully 'I'm coming to find you—' we both shut up. '—But I need a wee first!'

Dan snorted and I giggled. 'This may take a while, sorry.'

We waited patiently in silence for a moment. 'I hope they'll all play games like this with our kids,' Dan whispered.

'Of course they will!'

'I was thinking downstairs – you know Ed and Beth are having a baby? They got married *after* us. I know we said a while ago we'd wait until we'd bought somewhere – but why don't we just not?'

'What?' I said, confused. 'Buy a house?'

'No! Wait to have a baby. Why don't we just do it?'

'Finished!' Oscar shouted as the loo flushed. I put my finger to my lips and silenced Dan.

'What do you think?' he said eagerly.

'Shhh!' I said. 'He'll hear you! Let's not spoil the game.'

On the way back from my parents' house Dan was unusually quiet.

'You all right?' I asked, a little concerned, as he frowned at the road ahead of him.

'Hmm?' He shook himself out of his reverie and glanced at me before smiling briefly. 'Yeah, fine. Just a bit wiped out.'

'That'll be all those piggybacks you gave Oscar,' I reached out and squeezed his hand. 'You were lovely with him today, thank you – I'm not surprised you're tired though.' I yawned, a little weary myself. 'Early night for us tonight I think.'

But when Dan did climb into bed next to me later, he didn't seem to want to go to sleep . . .

Just as I was happily thinking to myself that we had to make the effort to have sex more often because we were really good at it, he said, 'Shall we not use anything?'

I came down to earth with a bump and completely caught off guard blurted, 'But I might get—'

'I know,' he said patiently, like I was a bit slow on the uptake.

'Oh I see.' We both went quiet for a moment and he began to kiss me again. But rather than feeling relaxed and slightly floaty, as I had been moments before, my heart sped up. We were actually going to do this? This was it? THE big moment? We were going to start – trying?

In five minutes' time I might be *pregnant*.

My heart gave another thump . . . with something that felt a lot like fear.

'Dan, shouldn't we talk about this?'

'You want to talk *now*?' He brought his head back up and looked down at me. 'Why?'

'Well about timings, that sort of thing,' I said quickly.

'Timings?' he repeated, clearly confused. 'I don't . . .'

'We ought to chat first,' I said, beginning to feel really quite panicky. 'It's not as simple as just doing it.'

'It isn't?' He was obviously thrown, but being Dan –

kind, caring and sensible to the core – he didn't want to get anything wrong, so, trusting me, he shrugged and reached for the condom box.

I was surprised and very unsettled by my almost instant sense of relief.

The morning after – we drove to Dan's parents' house in Chichester for Sunday lunch and it was my turn to be reflectively quiet. I was silently having a sensible word with myself over my reaction in bed the night before, thinking it was probably normal to feel like that – deciding to start trying was a huge step after all – being apprehensive didn't necessarily mean I didn't *want* children, for crying out loud.

Dan looked across at me and said, 'Don't chew your nails' before gently pulling my hand from my mouth. 'It's just lunch, Moll, we won't stay long if Dad's in one of his moods.' He smiled reassuringly at me. 'Tell you what, why don't you fill me in on these timing issues that I need to know about? When *should* we be doing it then? When you're ovulating?'

I shot him a look of surprise. I'd actually meant timings like getting pregnant in November would mean I'd be heavily pregnant in August which wouldn't be much fun . . . for a baby either come to that, having its birthday in the summer holidays for the rest of its school-going life. Ovulation? Since when had Dan been so clued up?

'You have a pretty irregular cycle though, don't you?'

he continued easily. 'Will that make it harder to work out when it is?'

My mouth gaped. 'Do we have to talk about this now?' I said faintly.

'Why not?' he said in surprise.

'Well, we're nearly at your mum and dad's house.'

'Moll,' he lowered his voice to a theatrical whisper, 'even my mother couldn't hear us from this distance, we're about six miles away.'

'Let's just chat about it on the way back,' I suggested and tried not to notice him give me a brief sideways glance.

'OK,' he said eventually. 'No probs. We can talk about it later.'

For once I was quite glad to arrive at Chichester. My father-in-law Michael was on unusually good form, proudly showing off his new nine-iron. Sadly though, it didn't last. Witty, charming and incredibly good company when he wanted to be, he could also – in the blink of an eye – flip into grumpy old git mode for no apparent reason. How Susan could stand being married to someone so temperamental was beyond me, but then in all the time I'd known her, I'd barely heard her swear and never seen her properly lose her cool. Maybe she'd become indifferent to him over the years, or perhaps she just didn't need to shout – once or twice I'd witnessed her utter a single, steely 'Michael!', making it clear he'd gone far enough, at which he'd fallen gloweringly but obediently silent. Then again, on more than one occasion I'd seen her embarrassingly left to pick up the threads of conversation after Michael had rudely stomped out of a room in a huff. Even after all this time, it was hard to work out who really wore the trousers.

As we sat down to eat, Dan mentioned that one of his school friends had been made redundant.

'Everything in your area is holding up though isn't it?' Michael said sharply.

Dan reached for the water jug. 'Well yeah Dad, it is, it's as safe as anything is these days. All our pay's been frozen though.' He shrugged and topped up his glass.

'Sorry?' Michael put his knife and fork down, sat back, wiped his mouth on a napkin and looked at Dan challengingly. 'Frozen? What do you mean frozen?'

My heart sank.

'I don't have a lot of choice in the matter, Dad.' Dan set the jug down with an unintentional clunk.

'Careful!' Michael admonished him. 'And don't be so ridiculous. Of course you have a choice. There are ways of negotiating tricky waters – I'm not saying there aren't – but you need to stay at the helm.'

Dan diplomatically said nothing, just reached for the bowl of roast potatoes and helped himself. Susan looked steadily at Michael but also stayed silent. I set down my knife and fork as I noticed her elderly dad, Dan's grandfather, had dropped his napkin on the floor but was unable to reach for it.

'Thank you, Molly,' he said softly as I passed it back

to him. His shaky hands reached out for the water jug Dan had absently set down.

'May I?' I offered quietly and he nodded gratefully. I refilled his glass and passed it to him. He glanced up the table at Michael and then subtly rolled his rheumy kind eyes as he looked back at me. I instinctively smiled and then discretely lowered my gaze as he returned to his food.

'You know I don't see that it can be that difficult to stand up to them,' Michael had started up again, his still-thick hair bouncing as he energetically sawed through a fat slab of meat. 'It's terribly simple actually. You go in and you say, "It's unacceptable that you are proposing to freeze my salary. Would you be prepared to accept this if you were me?" Honestly Daniel, next you'll be telling me you're expected to get in earlier and yet go home later.'

'Pretty much,' said Dan, 'but there it is.'

Michael shook his head in disbelief. 'Well, I tell you this,' he pointed his fork at Dan and I felt my temperature starting to rise. I stared back down at my plate, focusing on the pattern. 'I was always home no later than seven; I made a point of it. If you can't get everything done in that time you're either not working efficiently or your employers are trying it on. Do *not* become the man they all begin to wipe their feet on. Never run away, always stand your ground.' He jabbed a bit of beef in a liberal pool of gravy and then thrust it in his mouth. 'You're not at school now.' He turned to look at me, 'Do you know he legged it from his school at least three times Molly? The little bugger.'

'Really?' I said, trying to keep my voice steady, although of course I knew. Dan had been insufferably unhappy as a boarder and asked repeatedly to come home. Susan had wanted to remove him but Michael had put his foot down and told his eight-year-old son to 'take it like a man'.

'He couldn't even do that properly. Stupid child got on the wrong train and wound up in bloody Bristol.'

No one said anything.

'We had to go all the way down there and pick him up. He was snivelling in the lost property office when we arrived. Do you remember, Susan?'

I can't have been the only one who then imagined Dan as a small boy, frightened and alone, desperate for his parents to come and get him, but probably terrified of their arrival all at the same time. The protective, painful stab of empathy I felt also induced a brief flash of something close to actual loathing of Michael.

'Anyway,' poor Dan tried valiantly to get us all back on track, 'nothing would please me more than to have the kind of nine-to-five you used to enjoy, Dad, but it just doesn't exist any more. They'd laugh in my face if I said I needed to be home by seven every night.'

Michael snorted dismissively. 'Rubbish. I thought there were supposed to be advantages to all these IT developments you tell me are so potent and necessary. Weren't they all meant to make life easier, allowing you to have what I believe is referred to as "flexible working"?' he looked triumphant. 'Doesn't sound like it to me. You can't even get home at a decent hour and you work in IT, for God's sake.'

'Can you turn this music down a bit?' Dan was finally becoming tetchy too. 'It's really loud. Molly'll get a migraine and it must be hurting Grandpa's ears.'

Michael said nothing, just grabbed the remote, jabbed one of the buttons and turned it off completely, plunging us all into a pointed silence.

After a moment or two however, having not had the last word, he could contain himself no longer. 'That's the trouble with careers based on fickle fashions like information technology . . .'

I thought I saw Susan grip her knife a little tighter.

'. . . it all eventually comes down to simple supply and demand Daniel. You may think you know otherwise, but the rules haven't changed that much, I can assure you. There will always be a need for doctors, dentists . . . yet we could all still manage perfectly well without computers if you took them away tomorrow. I told you that a more traditional degree subject would hold its value, but you wouldn't listen, would you?'

'How is your knee after your operation, Michael?' I enquired, unable to bear it a moment longer.

'Much better, thank you,' he said, turning away from Dan. 'I was back at home after only a day! If it wasn't for this bloody weather I should think I'd be back on the course already.'

'It was supposed to be a week,' Susan said wryly, 'but thanks to this keyhole surgery . . . nonetheless, he does have to remember he's nearly seventy-three now.'

'Whole thing was a doddle.' Michael said, reaching for the peas. 'I really don't know what all the fuss was about.'

'It's incredible isn't it? They even do keyhole surgery for heart bypasses now,' I said innocently. 'A doctor was telling me recently that the surgeon holds tools connected to a computer . . .' Michael paused, serving spoon mid-air '. . .which interprets his movements and manoeuvres the instruments to eliminate any tremors in the surgeon's hands. So, they sort of work together to get the best results for the patient. I'm glad you felt the improvement in your knee so quickly.' I picked up my water as a grateful smile flashed across Dan's face.

Michael looked at me steadily, his eyes glinting. As I set my glass down he said, 'Not drinking, Molly?'

'Not today, no.'

'Oh?' he said dangerously. 'Any particular reason? You're not pregnant?'

'Nope.' I laughed lightly, thinking Oh just fuck off. You're going to have to try harder than that. 'I just don't fancy a *drink* drink – that's all.'

'You're not worried,' he sat back in his chair, hands resting on a remarkably flat stomach for a man of his age and appetite, 'that unless he gets a bloody move on,' he nodded at Dan, 'all the relative bits and pieces are just going to shut up shop?'

'Dad!'

'*Michael!*'

I should have left it — I should have let Susan do it — but as I stared at Michael, the urge to protect my husband mixed with outrage at how rude he'd just been; and maybe there was something else — a sensitivity or tension I wasn't even aware had been building up within me... they formed a fireball of defensive anger and before anyone else had the chance to speak, I heard my own voice say, 'You know I remember someone telling me that once men hit a certain age, they should never pass a lavatory without stopping, never waste an erection...'

Dan choked on a mouthful of Yorkshire pudding, looked at me in horror and grabbed for his water, the liquid jerking all over the tablecloth. Even Susan was stunned.

'... and never trust a fart. Would you say that's true, Michael?'

## Chapter Four

'Sunday lunch – and you start bandying erections about . . .' Dan struggled to speak, gripping the steering wheel fiercely '. . . in front of my *dad* . . . and my *grandpa*?'

'I know . . .' I couldn't look at him I felt so ashamed. 'I know, Dan. I'm so sorry; I lost it. I shouldn't have, you're absolutely right, but when he was picking on you like that, I couldn't bear it. What does he know about computers anyway?'

'Nothing!' shouted Dan, swerving slightly. 'That's the point. He knows nothing! He's just a pig-headed old man! You know the best way to handle him when he's in one of his moods is just to let it go.'

'But—'

'You played right into his hands by showing him he'd

hit a nerve with all that pregnancy stuff, charging in without considering the consequences.'

'He didn't hit a nerve,' I crossed my arms defensively.

'Yeah he did!' Dan said. 'I saw you. You looked furious.'

'Yes, because of what he'd said to you! I know I shouldn't have let rip and I *am* really sorry, but he *is* lucky they've made such big medical advances. When Dad had his heart attack they . . . can you slow down a bit?' I broke off for a moment. 'The roads are wet and I'd rather get home than not at all.'

'Right, that's it.' Dan exploded, pulling sharply left into a lay-by, causing the car behind to nearly wind up in our boot. Their horn blasted angrily as they flashed past.

'What are you doing?' I said, bewildered, as he jammed on the brakes, wrenched the handbrake up and turned the engine off.

'You drive then!' he said, unclipping his seat belt. 'Seeing as I can't even get that right!'

'Dan!' Amazed, I reached out and put a steadying hand on his arm. 'What on earth is wrong with you? It's just your dad being a prat, that's all.' I took a deep breath. 'I'll call him and apologise when we get back, OK? I'm sorry.'

Dan looked heavenward. I saw a muscle flicker in his jaw.

'And so what if work have frozen your salary?' I continued. 'At least we've both still got jobs, that's the important thing, because if—'

'How do you think it makes me feel,' he burst suddenly, 'listening to Dad have a pop like that, not knowing how

42

to defend you, what I ought to be saying, when inside . . .' He stopped and then took a deep breath. 'You heard what he said, "unless he gets a move on." And my mum made a good point on the phone last week; it's all well and good waiting to have our first baby until now – but what about the second and third?'

WHAT? I couldn't help my look of astonishment. And how exactly had that come up in conversation?

'We'll be ancient, we might not even be able to have them and I absolutely don't want our first to be an only child,' he said resolutely. 'It's not fair on them – I hated it. I still hate it now. Mum said she wished she'd kept on at Dad for a brother or sister for me.'

'You didn't tell me you'd talked about this,' I said carefully. 'And what happened with your parents was different, there was the age gap for starters . . .'

'They're obviously both wondering what's going on, and in a way Dad's right – it's not something we can keep dodging, Moll.' He ignored my point completely. 'You know what I've realised? This time *last* year we discussed starting to try and you said we should wait until we'd sold the flat. Well we have, and now somehow it's turned into we should wait until we're not renting . . . I wonder who else has started thinking "Come on Dan, be the man! Still no baby? Everything all right?" It isn't fair, because it's not me that's stalling is it, Moll?' He looked at me challengingly. 'Or perhaps they think there's some other problem, like you don't love me enough or something?'

43

My mouth fell open. It was so left field I didn't know what to say. We had never, ever questioned the way we felt about each other – ever. 'Are you worried that's what *they* think – or are you trying to say that's what *you* think?' I asked slowly.

He twisted in his seat so he could look me in the eye. 'You tell me! You've been acting weird ever since I tried to discuss it with you yesterday. You do actually *want* children, don't you?'

I almost couldn't speak for a moment. 'Of course I do! But Jesus, Dan, what's the sudden mad rush for? We've just been enjoying being married, having fun. What's wrong with that? And it's none of your Dad's – OR your Mum's – business what we do or don't decide to do. You shouldn't be discussing it with them anyway, you should be talking to me!'

Dan looked at me incredulously. 'What do you think I'm trying to do right now?'

'OK, OK,' I said, holding my hands up, trying to placate him; it wasn't like him to get so agitated. 'You don't need to shout at me!' He was completely overreacting; his dad had successfully wound him up and made him think there was a problem when there just wasn't . . .

I had conveniently forgotten my reservations from the night before.

'We will talk about this Dan, I just think—'

'But what's to talk about?' he exclaimed. 'We both want them, so let's do it.'

'OK, after Christmas—'

'Why after Christmas?' he said stubbornly. 'Why not now?'

'Dan, that's only another two months!'

'You're not exactly going to get pregnant immediately. How is waiting until then really going to make any difference in the grand scheme of things?'

'Well quite a lot for ME actually,' I said, starting to feel cross myself. 'OK, it *might* not happen straight away, but if it does, I'm going to be heavily pregnant right at the height of summer – I'd rather avoid that if I can, thanks very much. And I'd quite like to just enjoy my birthday and Christmas being able to drink too.'

'You could still have the odd small glass,' Dan looked out of the window. 'Well, probably . . .' He sighed, beginning to calm down, obviously considering my two-month deal. I should have just left it there.

'I've got to tell you though, putting pressure on me like this is not exactly making the whole thing fun,' I added tersely, and completely unnecessarily.

'Right!' he said triumphantly. 'So it IS my fault then?'

'It's not *anyone's* fault!' I shouted back, finally losing my patience. 'This is a completely pointless argument! All I'm saying is that we're never going to get this bit back again Dan. Can't you see that? Once we have kids, that's it. We'll be on a whole new adventure – and it'll be great, I'm sure, but please, stop wishing this part of our lives away. I just want to enjoy things as they are, for one or two more months. That's all.'

'That's what this is about?' He made a face. 'You just want to have a bit more *fun*?'

'Yes! What's wrong with that?'

'Well – we've been together four years.' He looked genuinely puzzled. 'How much fun do you want? I'm thirty-six Moll . . . I don't want to be an old dad.'

'You won't be!'

'OK, but is fun really *all* you're worried about?' he said, suddenly serious. 'Is there other stuff? Stopping working, that sort of thing?'

I hesitated. I'd not even considered that. 'Not really. I just like life as it is right now. I know it won't always be this way, but it'd be nice to have a bit longer of not needing to—'

'You've always said to me that it's important to work to live, not live to work . . .'

'Well it is, but that doesn't mean I don't get something out of having a job, Dan.'

'No one's saying you have to stop completely, you could go back part-time.'

'Yeah, I know, but when you're part-time you don't get given the good—'

'Both our mums would help out,' he cut across me eagerly. 'We wouldn't even need to pay for childcare; how lucky are we? I know we still need to buy a house, but the market's not exactly going to shoot up again, and it's not like we haven't got a second bedroom if it came to it.'

'You mean my office?'

He nodded. 'I know what you're thinking, but hear

me out. If we ditch the dining room table and move your desk in there, along with a proper sofa bed rather than that shit thing we've got at the moment, you'll still have somewhere to work *and* people could stay over if they wanted to. It'll be a better use of the space, in fact. Who has a separate dining room these days?' He had it all planned out.

I said nothing, just rested my head back in the passenger seat, suddenly exhausted.

'You don't seem very excited.' He looked deflated. 'Hasn't all of your friends – I mean your London lot, not Bec and Joss – having babies made you feel like you want one too?'

Hmmm. Well he hadn't been there when Rose announced her pregnancy and in the same breath said confidently, 'This won't change anything – this baby is going to have to fit around *me*...' I'd watched my sisters-in-law adjusting to motherhood for long enough to know that wasn't even vaguely how it worked. And so what if that's what they were all doing? Was it really that crazy of me not to want to swap lazy Saturday mornings for sleepless nights just yet? I wasn't saying *never*... was I?

Another car blasted past, making us rock slightly. We were both silent, I stared ahead at the wet road stretching out in front of us, feeling very confused. All I could hear was persistent rain on the car roof. I wanted to go home, back to our cosy house; shut out Michael and his nasty comments, shut out the world.

I reached for Dan's hand and held it. He didn't grip back, it sat loosely in mine.

'Please – I don't want to row like this.' I squeezed his hand. 'I love you.'

'I love you too,' he said flatly.

'Now say it like you mean it!' I joked. I really was only teasing, trying to lighten the tone.

'It'd probably be a lot easier if I didn't,' he retorted.

My eyes must have widened with surprise and fear, because he immediately looked like he wished he hadn't said it. Maybe it frightened him too.

'Sorry, I'm sorry,' he said immediately, 'I didn't mean that.' He reached across and pulled me towards him. We hugged awkwardly, the handbrake and seat belts getting in the way. 'Come on.' He kissed me quickly on the mouth. 'Let's go home.'

So given that we were already very much out of sorts, it was a little unfortunate that later – on going into our bedroom having removed my make-up and brushed my teeth – I found Dan standing by the bedside table holding a pin in one hand and a wrapped condom in the other.

# Chapter Five

I stood there, frozen to the spot, and stared at him.

He looked down at his hands, and then back up at me anxiously – but met my gaze directly. 'OK, in light of what we were talking about earlier I can see exactly how this must look,' he said, 'but I SWEAR on my life it's not. You know I would never, ever do something like that.'

It took about a half a second for a million thoughts to run through my mind: it would be completely and utterly out of character. Even if he thought I needed a nudge in the right direction – we were married, it was going to happen eventually, why not give nature a little helping hand? – he wouldn't do it. Dan was honest, straightforward, had never lied to me before and I trusted him with my life. It could only be appalling bad luck that I'd walked in as he was holding two such incriminating items. It was the events of the last few days that were skewing everything, making this moment appear more significant than it was. In isolation I would be thinking nothing of it. We'd be laughing — because after all, it was the kind of thing that happened in bad soaps, not real life, and it certainly wasn't something MEN did.

'So what *are* you doing?' I said eventually, and his shoulders visibly relaxed.

'Putting the condoms back in the box because you don't like leaving them out on the bedside table where anyone could see them. I was stuffing them back in and knocked a pin off the table — I honestly don't know what that was doing there,' he said sincerely.

'I pinned the new blackouts to the curtains on Friday—'

'You're so weird about needing it pitch black,' he smiled faintly. 'Anyway — I had bare feet and I didn't want to tread on it; I picked it up — and that's when you came in.'

'*That* was his excuse?' my ex-colleague froze — her baby held above her knees, mid-bounce — as she looked at me incredulously the following day. 'Tidying up?'

'It wasn't an excuse.' I tucked a stray piece of hair behind my ear. 'Dan does loads of stuff around the house.'

Anita raised an eyebrow as if that in itself was deeply suspicious. 'So let me ask you a question.' She settled her son down on her lap and handed him a breadstick.

'You walk into a room and someone's holding a gun and a dead cat: you're seriously telling me you think it's been run over?'

'That's my point,' I said patiently. 'Of course everyone would automatically assume it had been shot. It doesn't mean it actually was.' Hmmm, she wasn't seeing the funny side, I had misjudged my audience. 'It was just one of those weird things!'

Anita looked at me half pityingly and half like she thought I was completely insane.

'Okkkkayy,' she said. 'But you still made him fill all of the condoms with water, right?'

I hesitated.

'Oh you are *kidding* me!' Her mouth fell open so wide I could see fillings. Her little boy, as he sucked on his fingers, suddenly tired of our conversation and began to wriggle around on her lap emitting cross little squawks. I sympathised, I was beginning to feel much the same.

'Why would I have made him fill them with water?'

'Ah – *I* get it!' her eyes gleamed. 'You just bought some new condoms and threw the others away so he was none the wiser didn't you? You're right. Two can play at that game, can't they!' She nudged me.

It was my turn to look at her like she was crazy. 'I don't actually think Dan stuck a pin in the condom,' I said very slowly, so she understood.

There was a pause.

'You didn't throw them away either, did you? I don't believe it!' she exclaimed and then chortled with disbelief.

51

It was then that I realised this was going to be served up alongside the banana cake at her next mums' coffee morning: 'Don't say anything, because I really shouldn't be talking about it, but a friend of mine found her husband . . .' she'd pause for effect while everyone sat up, their appetites whetted; 'in their *bedroom* . . . pin in one hand, condom in the other . . . I know, I *know!*'

'Well,' she sniggered. 'I guess we'll find out in nine months.'

I sipped my tea glumly, wished I'd just not told her in the first place and wondered if it was too early for me to say I was going home.

'We're what, November now? Ooohh, a summer baby!' she teased.

Oh for God's sake. Since Anita had gone on maternity leave, it had become horribly apparent that beyond the bubble of medical rep gossip, neither of us – despite previously having been happy partners in work-related crime – actually had anything in common at all. Our 'catch ups' had become little more than me regaling the latest work dramas while she tried to look interested in people she no longer cared about and stared adoringly at her baby. I would then try to look equally fascinated by the very detailed updates on her son's sleeping habits. The visit had been looming in my diary like the Black Spot for weeks and I should have jumped ship a lot earlier. I could easily have blamed work being too busy, which actually wasn't far from the truth. But then it had sort of snuck up on me before I'd realised and by then it was too late to cancel.

'Can I ask you a question?' she said cosily. 'I don't mean to be nosy Moll, but—'

I braced myself, clearly she was about to be very nosy indeed.

'—why's Dan – taking matters into his own hands?'

I went quiet . . . but she was reaching to get a muslin and didn't see the look on my face. 'I just assumed you must be trying like crazy, you being – what – thirty-three? To be honest, I thought there was some *medical* issue and that was why it was all taking such a long time, but I didn't like to intrude. I thought you'd talk if you wanted to – nothing's worse than those insensitive types who say "So, when are we going to hear the patter of tiny feet?" every time you see them! *I* thought you and Dan,' she lifted her little boy up again and began to jiggle him about, trying to get him to use his legs, 'were one of the most sorted, together couples I knew. I did, didn't I? Yes I did!' She beamed at her son who regarded her thoughtfully and then poked her in the eye with the half-gummed breadstick. 'Whenever you brought Dan along to work dos and stuff, you both seemed so in sync . . . like . . .' she blew a raspberry on his tummy, 'I don't know, Paul Newman and Joanne Woodward.'

'Pre him dying I hope?'

'Paul Newman *died*?' Her jaw fell open. '*Nooo*! When was that?'

'About a year ago.'

'Oh how sad. I liked him. That's the problem when

53

you have kids,' she sighed heavily. 'You just don't have time to do stuff like sit around and read the papers any more.'

I bit my tongue. Thank God I'd scrambled like crazy all morning at home with unending emails and half a presentation just to make dashing over to hers possible. It had absolutely been worth it . . .

'So?' she said and waited.

'So what?' I tried to play dumb so she'd have to spell it out, but she had the hide of a rhino and wasn't the least bit embarrassed.

'Are you having problems?' She looked at me sympathetically. 'Going through a rough patch?'

'No. We're very happy.'

'Well, IS everything all right medically then?' she probed further.

'Yes!'

'But . . .'

'But nothing, I do want them, but I really like just spending time with Dan, we're in a rented place right now, work's tough and—'

'Moll, I'm going to stop you right there,' she interrupted with a deadpan look. 'There is *never* a good time, believe me. Dan's got the right idea,' she said, performing an astounding U-turn. 'Throw caution to the wind; just do it.'

'He wasn't *doing* anything!' I said, becoming exasperated. 'We will have them, I just want to have a bit longer as we are at the moment, that's all. It's probably a bit selfish of me but...' I shrugged and looked up at her. She had her eyebrow raised.

'Well, not really, if that's what you want,' she said eventually, clearly thinking I was very selfish indeed. 'Actually, I'm not that surprised – I mean, you don't exactly hide your light under a bushel, do you? Hmmmm,' she continued disapprovingly, lifting her son up and sniffing him. 'Has someone just done something a bit stinky?'

Yes, frankly, they had. I resisted the temptation to lean over, grab the breadstick and beat her with it. What did she mean by that? I was selfish *and* bolshy?

'Come and talk to me while I hose this one down. I think it's gone all up his back . . .' She stood up and carried her little boy out as I set my coffee cup down carefully on the table.

'So tell me then,' she mused loudly from the other room. 'When *do* you think you'll fancy getting all grown-up on us?'

My mouth fell open with astonishment and I mutinously booted a soft toy duck up the bum as I got to my feet. I didn't want to tell her *anything*. Except that I'd decided I didn't like her any more. Luckily my phone rang and, gratefully, I answered it.

'Sorry, Anita,' I said, appearing in the bathroom moments later as she looked up from the changing mat, 'but that was Pearce, he needs some background info for a meeting. I better get going.'

'Oh?' her voice became flirty. 'And how is the lovely Pearce?'

'Same old. Busy having his pick of the women. As I'm sure you remember,' I added tartly, before I could stop myself.

She wasn't remotely abashed though. 'Do I ever . . . if I wasn't married and with this one . . .' She raised an eyebrow and smirked. 'Say hi to him from me, won't you?'

I let myself back into the house an hour later, stomped upstairs and switched on my computer. Why didn't I fill them with water? – because I wasn't a freak, that's why. Stupid woman . . . She didn't even *know* Dan – and what was so strange about my wanting to have a bit more fun, for crying out loud? Surely that was a normal thing?

Several work emails appeared in my inbox. In amongst them was one that said

```
Leo Williams sent you a message on Facebook
. . .
```

What? NO! I opened it quickly.

```
Wow indeed! Hello! Have taken the plunge,
yes...Well - long time no speak! I looked
for you on here but didn't know your
married name! Life treating you well? Still
in Brighton?
```

My mobile rang. Dan.

'Hello!' I said chirpily, closing my laptop screen quickly

with my free hand, as if he were somehow able to see all the way from London.

'Hi.' He sounded a bit tired.

'You all right?'

'Yeah, not bad.' He sighed. 'It's been a mad day though. I dropped my roll on the floor by mistake at lunch so I just had to have soup and nothing else. My tummy has been making the most horrendous noises all afternoon, it's been really embarrassing. Like an angry bear growling.'

'Poor thing,' I sympathised. 'I'll make you something nice when you get home.'

'Thanks,' he said, sounding cheered at the thought. 'I'm so hungry I can't even tell you. Has the food been delivered then?'

'What food?' I said instantly.

'You did an online shop, didn't you?'

'No, what makes you think that?'

'Well, because all we've got to eat is a packet of Krisprolls and some Oatibix.'

'So *you* didn't do one then?' I asked, a bit confused.

'Me?' he said, surprised, like I'd asked if he'd done a lap of naked yodelling round the back garden. 'Well, I *can* do it if you ask me to, but you need to give me some warning. I can't just stop in the middle of a meeting and say to a client, "Sorry, I've got to go and—"'

'It's not a problem,' I interrupted, tentatively lifting the screen back up. 'I'll go to the supermarket in a bit.' Dan had a tendency to get slightly anxious when there wasn't plenty to eat in the house, even though we were still trying to lose the couple of comfortable pounds we'd put on during our summer holiday.

'Get healthy stuff though, won't you?' he said, as if reading my mind. 'No pies or biscuits. Or beer,' he added gloomily. 'Or those nice kettle chips . . . Oh God. I hate my life.'

'No, you don't.'

'I know,' he sighed again. 'I'm just feeling Monday-ish, that's all. Anyway, what you up to?'

'Finishing up some work,' I fibbed.

'Oh, sorry,' he said instantly. 'I'll let you get back to it then. See you later. Love you.' And then he was gone. I looked at Leo's message again, sitting there innocently.

Something told me to just delete it. But then wasn't it a bit rude to ignore his question? We were both grown-ups with new lives, we could be civil, couldn't we?

`Yes, still in Brighton. Good to see you looking so happy in your pictures. Take care`

There, that would sort it. It had a clear air of finality about it. Hastily, I deleted the thread and logged out. It was while I was getting rid of the email notification, just as I had done on Saturday, and from my BlackBerry too, that a tell-tale flickering began in the middle of my vision, a smattering of prickly bright lights. I blinked but when I opened my eyes again a blurred spot had appeared. I looked up and stared at the wall. Still there. My heart sank.

I got up and immediately took one of my tablets, then emailed my boss Antony to say I was sorry but I had a migraine coming on and that was me over and out for the day. Then I switched off my phone, went into our bedroom and lay down on the bed, closed my eyes and tried to stay calm . . . but as usual, the buzzing pain behind my eyes kicked in about half an hour later. No wonder I'd been so irritable at Anita's.

When I eventually woke up, it was dark outside and I was cold and ravenously hungry. I sat up stiffly and stared at the clock – *seven!* I hadn't had one this bad for a while. Dan arrived home ten minutes later to find me shuffling around our bedroom like Yoda, eating a biscuit and trying to find some PJs.

'You all right? Your phone's off?'

'I've had a migraine.'

'Oh, you poor thing,' he said immediately. 'I wonder what brought that on? Are you going to come down-stairs? Do you want something a bit more substantial than that to eat?'

'No thanks.'

'Have you been sick?'

'No. I just feel a bit drained.' I hesitated. 'I might stay up here for a bit.'

'I'll leave you to it then,' he said easily.

When I appeared downstairs later, he was eating beans on toast in front of the TV which made me feel a bit guilty, it wasn't much of a main meal given he'd been at work all day.

'Is that really all there is?' I nodded gingerly as I sat down next to him and leant my head on his shoulder for a moment. 'Sorry.'

He gave me a kiss. 'It's fine, don't worry about me. Bad luck about your migraine. What's the rest of your week like? Will you be able to make up today?'

I yawned as I straightened up. 'Not really. I've got that stupid sales conference in Windsor the day after tomorrow, haven't I?'

'Windsor's this week?' He pulled a face. 'I'd forgotten that. When are you back? Thursday?'

I reached for a cushion and lay my head down on the sofa arm. 'Yeah.'

'I hate to ask, but is there any chance you'll be able do an online food shop before then? I could get a couple of bits tomorrow to tide us over and you can get them to deliver it on Wednesday night? I'll be in.'

'I'll do it in the morning,' I said. 'I don't want to go on the computer again tonight.'

'Sure, or I can do it?' he offered. 'I don't mind?'

'Thanks but it's no problem, really.' Much as I loved him, we'd wind up with nothing but a million cans of beans, Guinness and some oven chips if he did it. I yawned again.

'I think someone needs an early night . . . and maybe I'll join you.' He flickered his eyebrows suggestively. The expression on my face must have given me away because he laughed. 'Or not . . .'

'Perhaps tomorrow,' I said weakly. 'When I'm feeling

a bit better.' Then as we both fell into companionable silence, I found myself thinking back to what Anita had said earlier and snuck a look at him.

No, she was wrong. Of course she was wrong.

He'd never do a thing like that.

## Chapter Six

Hang on! You didn't say how you are? So, married but ... Kids? Pets? House with roses round door? Living the suburban dream? X

Leo's new message arrived seconds before my mum rang. I was still scanning through it as I picked up the phone.

'Hello, love!' she said cheerfully. 'Having a nice afternoon? What are you up to?'

'Nothing . . .' I said, a little too sharply. 'Just working; the usual.'

'Is everything all right? You sound a bit tetchy.'

I rubbed my face tiredly and sighed. 'Sorry, I didn't mean to snap. I've had a testing couple of days.'

'Oh?'

I hesitated. 'I had a migraine yesterday after coffee with

this girl Anita I used to work with . . . she just wound me up a bit.'

'In what way?' Mum sounded concerned.

'She asked me if there was any biological reason why Dan and I haven't had kids yet and when I said no, she pretty much told me to grow up and get on with it.'

There was a long pause. 'I'm not sure I know what to say to that,' Mum said carefully.

'I know,' I said wearily. 'I didn't either, I just sort of insulted her back – which she'll no doubt think proved her point . . . I seem to be on a bit of a short fuse this week.' I thought uncomfortably of Sunday lunch at Dan's parents.

'Why? Has something else has happened?' Mum asked.

I told her what I'd said to Michael.

'Oh Molly . . .' Mum was appalled.

'I know . . . I didn't mean to – it just sort of happened.' I stared absently at the computer screen in front of me, Leo's message beginning to swim in and out of focus. 'Michael was being so cruel to Dan . . . and he *was* pretty rude to me too. Dan wasn't happy with me afterwards though.'

Mum sighed. 'Michael managed to push quite a lot of buttons by the sound of it. What you said was dreadful, but deep down, I'm sure Dan knows you were only trying to defend your patch, little terrier that you are. Do remember though, darling, that when you feel backed into a corner, you don't *always* have to come out fighting. I love that you're brave enough to stand up and be counted – but you have to bear in mind that sometimes people mistake that bark of yours for attack when it's defence,' she paused. 'It's all right to be frightened sometimes, you know.'

'Michael doesn't *scare* me,' I corrected her.

'I wasn't necessarily talking about him. Just give it some thought,' Mum urged gently. 'Have you got time to pop in tomorrow for a cup of tea?'

I shook my head regretfully. 'No, I haven't. I've got to go to Windsor for a sales conference in the morning – and stay up there overnight,' I added glumly.

'Never mind,' Mum said briskly. 'It'll be over before you know it. Come to lunch on Sunday instead then, I'll do a roast.'

'Thanks,' I was cheered at the thought. 'That'd be nice.'

In fact I felt much better for speaking to her and once I'd hung up quickly typed to Leo:

```
No pets, no kids. Renting since we sold
our place but now can't find anywhere we
like - suburban nightmare more like! X
```

It was only once I'd sent it that I realised with dismay I'd thoughtlessly added a kiss to the end of the message. A small warning bell went off in the back of my mind at the same time as a second email arrived with another merry Ping!

```
Facebook; Leo Williams has sent you a
message...
```

```
I know what you mean! We had to move last
year because of the girls' school — I've
got two stepdaughters now — CAN'T BELIEVE
I've moved to get into a better catchment
area...what has happened to me?!
```

I couldn't help smiling at that, and he'd ignored the kiss. Phew. I paused for a moment, relieved, my fingers hovering over the keyboard as I thought up an equally light response.

```
Tough being a grown-up eh? Do you also
have a 4×4 for school run? If so, trans-
formation is complete!
```

I pictured Leo behind the wheel in one of his sharp suits, important corporate 'access all areas' pass round his neck, but two kids in the backseat. Funny . . .

And yet my short-lived ease and the buzz of friendly banter began to drain away as I looked at the transcript of our exchange on the screen in front of me.

It wasn't that we'd said anything remotely inappropriate, we hadn't. It just didn't feel — quite right. It wasn't as if I was catching up with an old friend . . . it was Leo.

The fact that I couldn't bring myself to admit to Bec that I'd emailed him, when she called me later that night, just confirmed that I knew I'd inadvertently misbehaved. I decided then and there if he messaged me again I'd just ignore it. Instead I filled her in on the other events of the last few days.

'So is there other stuff you still want to do then?' Bec sounded a bit confused. 'Is that what's putting you off starting now?'

'Maybe,' I floundered. 'Dan and I have never worked abroad—'

'You're moving to another country?' she said, alarmed.

'No! We haven't even talked about it . . .' I trailed off. 'It's just once we start down this route—'

'Having children is a big decision,' she admitted, 'but I think it's great that you're going into it with your eyes wide open.' And then she ever so slightly slipped into professional mode: 'It's important you both talk about it, even if it does get a bit heated – it's the couples that don't you worry about.'

I fell silent.

'I've seen it so many times at work,' she continued, 'one of them is really overexcited about the pregnancy and the other one is totally disinterested – and you just know they're not going to last. Some of them split up before the baby is even born.'

The thought of being without Dan made me feel sick.

'Don't panic though Moll, it wouldn't be *impossible* if you left it another two or three years until you start trying, but . . .' she took a deep breath, 'if it were me –'

I winced. It was always hard to know if it was OK to talk to Bec about stuff like this, knowing that she very much wanted a baby of her own.

'– I'd get started in the new year. Facts are facts, Moll.

67

Nice though it would be, none of us have got a picture in the attic, have we?'

'Does it hurt, Bec?' I blurted suddenly. 'Giving birth I mean.'

She laughed. 'No Moll, fairies magic it out. Didn't you know?'

I laughed too, but slightly awkwardly. 'Right, I'd better go,' I said brightly. 'I'm going all wrinkly and the water's gone cold. Love you!'

'You're in the bath? Oh sorry – I'll leave you in peace. Love you too,' she said, and then she was gone.

'Did I hear you talking to someone?' Dan said when I walked back into our bedroom.

'Bec,' I hung my towel over the radiator wondering what he'd heard me say. Thank goodness I *hadn't* mentioned Leo's messages. I climbed into bed next to him.

'She all right?' he said.

I nodded. I just wanted to snuggle up to him, try and relax. I really didn't want to do any more talking to anyone about anything.

But neither it seemed did he.

It wasn't long before he was reaching to find a condom in the bedside table as I stared up at the ceiling feeling dreamily light as a feather and altogether much better.

'I can't . . . find . . .' he rummaged around and nearly knocked his water over. I heard some of it splash. 'Oh bollocks.'

'Leave it,' I said, eyes closed, starting to float back down to earth ever so slightly. 'I'll sort it afterwards. Why don't you just put the light back on so you can see what you're doing?' I yawned.

'Finally!' he said. I heard the small cardboard packet open and the tear of the wrapper. He was ready instantly. I wriggled under him but as he groaned happily, I opened my eyes in the darkness. 'Dan, is that on properly? I can't feel it.'

'Yeah, it's fine.' He breathed. 'Absolutely fine.'

I put my arms uncertainly round his neck and closed my eyes again as he kissed me briefly. I really couldn't feel it, but then did I notice it usually? Bizarrely I found I couldn't remember, ridiculous given the number of times we must have done it. But then nine times out of ten I saw him put it on, as we pretty much never turned the light off.

Which was a good point. Why had he turned it off? In fact why had he turned it off and then been ready to go at the speed of light? And why couldn't I feel it?

He *had* put it on, hadn't he?

But then why wouldn't he have?

Having said that, why hadn't he suggested NOT using one – like last time? If he was so eager to 'get started' why had he just happily reached for a condom . . . that I now couldn't feel?

And then I saw him in my mind standing there holding the pin and the condom.

I heard Anita's voice say 'taking matters into his own hands'.

69

Then I remembered him saying 'Everyone's thinking "Come on Dan – be the man!"' and 'I don't want to be an old dad!'

My eyes opened again in the dark.

'Dan,' I drew back ever so slightly. 'Seriously, I can't feel it. The condom. Do you think it could have,' I gasped, 'come off?'

'No, I don't,' he slowed down slightly. 'It's fine. It doesn't matter, just relax.'

*It didn't matter?*

Whoa, whoa, WHOA! Yes, it did.

I felt myself shrink away from him immediately. 'Just stop a minute.'

He didn't. 'That feels amazing.'

'Dan!' I shouted. And then I hit his shoulder, hard.

He stopped and then reached out and fumbled with the light switch. I winced at the look on his face. 'Did you just hit me?' he said incredulously.

'You weren't listening to me!'

'Because I told you it was fine! What's the matter with you?'

I hesitated, having a massive moment of self-doubt now that the light was on and he was looking down at me completely confused . . . 'You said it didn't matter, and it does.'

'I meant it didn't matter because it was all OK.'

'It's just, you were really quick putting it on!'

'Well it's not my first time, is it?' He exhaled heavily, propping his body weight up on his hands. 'That's successfully killed the mood.' He eased back, lay down beside me and stared up at the ceiling.

'Why did you want the light off? We never do that.' I said, my mind still racing.

'Yes we do!' he said, baffled. 'And so what if . . .' Then his expression changed. 'Hang on. What are you saying?'

There was a very ugly silence.

'I didn't see you put it on,' I said in a small voice. 'I couldn't feel it. I . . .'

'What, *exactly,* are you saying?' he said ominously.

'It's just . . . I saw you with that pin . . . and now suddenly I can't feel—'

'I *knew* it! Fucking hell!' He sat up sharply. 'Without meaning to be crude, don't you think you would have noticed afterwards that I hadn't been wearing one?'

'But it would have been too late by then, wouldn't it?' The words were out there before I could stop them.

He said nothing, just gave me an utterly disgusted look as he quickly threw the bed covers back, got up and left the room. I reached for my T-shirt as I heard him banging around in the bathroom, and then he came back in, towel round his waist.

'Stalling is one thing,' he said angrily, 'but this? Accusing me of stuff I would never do? All I wanted – heaven forbid – was to have sex with you.'

'OK, OK, I'm sorry.' Panicking slightly, I tried to calm him down. 'But Dan, you can't blame me for having doubts when—'

'Doubts?' he said incredulously. 'You didn't just say that! I'm your *husband*!'

I paused.

'I can't believe you think I'd actually do something like that!' He began to raise his voice.

'Dan! Shhh!' I hissed. 'They'll hear us next door.'

'I don't care,' he shouted, then he kicked the edge of the wardrobe in frustration and his towel fell off. All the moment needed was a comedy sound effect. He immediately bent to pick it up and ordinarily, if we'd been arguing about anything else, it would have diffused everything. I would have laughed, he'd have grinned sheepishly, and the argument would have ended. Instead I heard the unmistakable sound of a wail through our rented rice-paper walls. He'd woken up next-door's toddler.

'Don't. Say. Anything,' Dan pointed a finger at me warningly. He stomped round the bed and began to pull on his tracksuit bottoms.

'Where are you going?' I said as he marched out.

'I'm sleeping on the sofa bed.'

'Oh don't be such a baby!' I called after him, and then closed my eyes in regret at my crass but totally unplanned choice of words.

'Is that supposed to be funny?' He came straight back in. 'You think this is all a joke?'

'No, of course not. I just made a mistake. I meant . . .'

'Well try this one; my wife – who I love more than anything – doesn't seem to want a baby with me.' His voice cracked. 'Hysterical isn't it?'

72

'You're absolutely right I don't — not like this,' my voice was suddenly thick with unshed tears. The crying became louder next door and there was a warning thump on the wall.

'What is it you want me to do, Molly?' he raised his voice. 'Magic you younger? I don't understand. *Time is running out!* I don't want to be one of those sad OAP couples everyone calls selfish bastards, having IVF alongside our first hip replacements. You need to get a grip and grow up!'

He made for the door again, but then came back '—and I am *fucking angry* about what you've just accused me of,' he said furiously. 'We only use the bloody things full stop because you can't take the pill, thanks to your migraines! In fact, you know what? This whole thing is about you, not me. I can't believe you think I would do something so underhand; I love you! And now you're actually saying you don't want kids at all?'

'I'm saying—'

He didn't let me finish. 'At least that's more honest than the "next year" bullshit.'

'It's not bullshit!' I exclaimed.

He ignored me. 'I don't want to put it off any longer, Molly, I want to start trying for children NOW, OK?' he shouted. 'Not next month, not next year, NOW.'

I faltered as I looked at him. I could see he was completely serious, he simply wasn't prepared to wait any longer. For once I didn't go charging in, I'd already said enough; I was frightened of doing the wrong thing.

But he actually didn't wait for me to say anything.

'You know, I can't even look at you right now,' he shook his head. 'That you could think I'd actually do something like that . . .' he turned in disgust and banged out of the room.

Immediately I wanted to call out after him: 'Dan, wait. I'm sorry – it's because I'm scared!'

Because I'd realised I was. Scared of how it would change my life, what it would mean, what it would be like to actually have a baby. What if I was no good at being a mum? What if something happened to me or Dan? And what if – well, being a mum was crap? And lonely. Or changed things between Dan and me? Maybe they were things everyone worried about, it was totally normal, but what if it wasn't? What if I *didn't* want them after all? All that sitting there with Joss and Bec on Saturday smugly saying 'Yah yah, we know ourselves SO well now we're in our thirties . . .' but perhaps I didn't. Even worse, was this a part of me I had chosen to ignore?

Or were Dan and Anita right: I just needed to grow up. Maybe that was all it was, I was just being a selfish wuss. After all, everyone else seemed to manage it, Karen and Maria by and large enjoyed it. I tried to think back over the last year and a half, tried to remember all of the conversations we'd had about having children . . . perhaps Dan's comments about stalling *were* fair, but then surely the days of having to start trying for children the second you married were gone, weren't they?

I tried to take some deep breaths, attempted to stay

calm, but it felt like being stuck at one end of a fraying rope bridge; the ones that swing perilously over dark rocky gorges, or rivers of angry lava. Dan on the other side of the canyon shouting at me to hurry up, hand held out – and me not knowing if it was safest to run for it, to pick my way across . . . or stay put and make him come to me. One of us was going to have to cross to the other side – that much I did know. There was to be no meeting in the middle on this one.

I considered going downstairs to find him, saying sorry for my irrational outburst. I even got to the top of the stairs and listened tentatively – but the house was already silent. Perhaps he was already asleep? It *was* late and he'd be even more annoyed if I woke him up.

I decided I'd apologise in the morning.

But of course that didn't happen.

## Chapter Seven

I change gear and glance at the clock. Reaching Windsor on time for the start of the conference is not looking likely. The traffic has been *crap*. And so much spray everywhere – I hate driving when it's like this.

It had felt like I'd been asleep five minutes when Dan snapped the big light on this morning. I'd turned over to find him standing in front of the wardrobe in his towel post-shower, selecting a shirt. He'd rifled through the rack, grabbed one and stomped back out of the room.

He'd wanted to make the point that he was still angry, although sleeping on the sofa bed all night had kind of done that already. No one in their right mind would opt for it unless they had to, it's got a hump in the middle that makes it feel like you're sleeping on the back of a camel.

Then when I'd appeared downstairs twenty minutes later, dressed for work myself, his wallet, keys and phone were already on the side and he was rinsing his cereal bowl.

'Do you want a lift to the station?' I'd offered, trying to be helpful.

'No thank you.' He'd whisked his suit jacket off the back of one of the kitchen stools, pulled it on, picked up his bits and pieces and then strode out towards the sitting room. I'd followed him.

'You know I'm going away today and I won't be home tonight?' I had reminded him tentatively.

'Yup.' He began to rummage in the cupboard under the stairs for his overcoat.

I took a deep breath. 'Dan, about last night . . .'

'I haven't got time to talk to you about it now,' he said shortly, his back to me. 'I'm late, I'm tired and my back is screwed. I barely slept a wink last night.'

He wasn't going to make it easy for me. I sighed.

'What?' He re-emerged, looked at me confrontationally, pulled his coat on, then walked over to the front door. 'I really *haven't* got time. Thanks, though, for saying sorry.' He yanked it open. 'Oh that's right, you didn't, did you?' And then he'd banged out.

I change gear again defensively. I mean OK, I made a mistake, I get that. I really shouldn't have said what I did but equally this isn't just about him, and what he wants. What about me? There are two of us in this relationship; surely we have to make this next step *together*, or not at all. And as for everyone else sticking their oar in

78

– I've not even had chance to stop and think about how *I* feel about this. It's like having someone else slam a foot down on the accelerator; everything has sped up completely out of our control.

Still – it's not helpful thinking like that, getting uptight again. On the positive side – and there is always an upside – I can count on one hand the number of times we've properly argued; which is pretty good going for four years I think, never mind when you chuck a house move and organising a wedding into the pot. We will sort this, I know we will—

—Which is when I hear my phone start to ring in my bag. Pulling it out, I glance at the screen briefly – it's him. My heart softens. 'Hi!' I say quickly, 'Hang on – just let me hook the phone up to the hands-free.' I fiddle around for a moment. 'Sorry about that—' I begin, but before I can explain I was going to call him earlier he cuts across me tersely.

'What time is the food shop arriving tonight, please? I forgot to ask you.' There is no discernable hint of apology in his voice for slamming out earlier. If anything he sounds crosser than before.

Oh no. I forgot to order the food.

There's a long silence.

'You did do it, didn't you?' he says suspiciously. 'Remember I asked you on Monday? . . .'

'I can't do everything!' I exclaim. 'I'd just had a migraine!'

'So there's nothing to eat, again. *And* you've got the car? I said I could do it!'

79

'Dan – It's just a food shop! I'm trying to drive!'

'Fine.' He snaps. 'I don't want to talk to you if you're going to be like this anyway.' And then *he hangs up*.

I gasp and stare at the phone furiously, the only sound is the windscreen wipers bashing from side to side. Oh, he didn't just do that. The ONE THING he knows is guaranteed to send me into a fury in under three seconds. He has obviously thought better of it because the phone begins to ring again almost immediately.

I answer straight away. 'Don't you ever hang up on me again!'

'Um, okkkaaaay. I know it's been a while, and although that *does* sound like us' – there's a laugh – 'tell me you haven't really been holding on to that all this time?'

I nearly swerve off the road as I realise who the voice belongs to.

'Molls? Are you still there? It's me, Leo.'

## Chapter Eight

I can't think what to say. His voice sounds exactly the same. Slightly clipped and amused.

'I thought I'd give you a ring instead of us messaging back and forth,' he speaks easily, as if it hasn't been years since we last spoke. 'It occurred to me that you probably hadn't changed your number.'

'I'm surprised you still remember it,' I say truthfully, although it sounds like I'm fishing.

He laughs. 'Oh I know it off by heart.' He repeats it fluidly. 'See?'

There's a pause. I'm not sure what to say to that either.

'So, who hung up on you?' he says. 'Or shouldn't I ask?'

'Probably best not.'

'Want to talk about it?' he says simply.

It's then that I give myself a mental shake and realise what a bizarre conversation we are already having. Only Leo . . . the normal social rules don't tend to bother him.

'Not really, thank you,' I say lightly.

'Fair enough,' he says, still cheerful. 'I was only asking to be polite, I don't actually care. Is now a good time, by the way? You sound like you're on your way to some-where?'

'I'm driving to a sales conference in Windsor.'

'That sounds fun . . .'

'No it doesn't,' I can't help but allow a smile.

'Oh I don't know,' he says easily. 'It's hard to think what more *anyone* could possibly want from life than a conference in Windsor. So are you still working for – um –'

'MediComma,' I finish for him. ''Fraid so.'

'Nothing wrong with that,' he says. 'A good job these days is something to be proud of. But why Windsor, may I ask?'

'No idea, I expect they just got a good deal on the hotel.' I speed up to overtake the car in front, distractedly looking in my mirrors. 'Is that still your area of expertise?'

'What, lounging around in hotels?' he replies archly. 'Thanks very much.'

'No!' I correct him quickly. 'Corporate events.'

'Oh right. Yeah, it is. Which luxury travel lodge have they dumped you in then?'

I tell him and he gives a sharp intake of breath. 'That's bad luck.'

'Really?' I say in dismay as I pull back into the middle lane. 'Is it a hole?'

'No, I'm kidding – it's fine. It's got a—'

'Can you hang on a moment, Leo?' I cut across him, noticing that the traffic is slowing down very fast in front of me and I need to concentrate for a moment.

'OK, sorry about that,' I say as we come to a complete stop and I drop down into first. But there's silence. 'Leo? Hello? Are you still there? Leo?'

'Just waiting until you're ready,' he says smoothly.

I wrinkle my nose at the phone. I'd completely forgotten about that, his hating people interrupting him.

But then maybe he's actually being polite, because he cheerily starts up again: 'So tell me. What's your news? How about the lovely Bec and Joss, they OK?'

The car in front pulls away sharply, creating a large gap, even though the traffic is still moving slowly – someone is clearly in a hurry. I begin to drift after them as the phone reception goes a bit dodgy. When I glance over at the handset I notice the hands-free wire is wiggling loose.

'Although Joss'd hate to be called that, especially by me,' Leo says dryly. 'Which is completely fair, of course.'

I push the wire back in. 'Well, in her defence, she—' I look back up. 'SHIT!'

The BMW in front has stopped completely, yet I am still moving towards it. I hit the brakes but the ground is so wet that I simply slide. The BM's boot looms too large for me to do anything to prevent the surprisingly loud thud that results seconds later. My head jolts back on to the headrest. 'Oh fuck!' I gasp, fumbling for my hazard lights.

'Molly?' Leo says sharply. 'What's happened? Are you—'

The BMW's hazards flash on and I see the driver's door open . . .

'I've just hit a car,' I say in shock and then hang up as a very angry looking young woman starts to walk towards me.

She shouts some pretty choice things, and a few more once we are on the hard shoulder – other cars slow down to pass us, gleefully taking in the entertainment – and is far nastier than she needs to be. I know that the law will be on her side anyway, and am trying to explain that I'm the one with the crumpled bumper and smashed indicator, but she isn't having any of it. I end up shouting back at her, at which she gives me a disdainful look and says patronisingly, 'OK you're, like, clearly really *hormonal* right now. Just take my details and sort it out.'

I don't even have the chance to think of a devastating put-down as she flicks her hair at me and turns around on the spot before climbing back into her completely unscathed car and roaring off.

I get back into mine and just sit there for a minute in disbelief, which is when the phone rings again with a number I don't recognise. I pick up automatically. 'Molly Greene speaking – how can I help you?' My voice doesn't sound quite right even to me.

'Molly? It's me. What the hell just happened? Are you OK?' I can hear confusion and concern in Leo's voice.

'I'm fine,' I breathe. 'Just a stupid small bump.' But I wobble at the end.

'You don't sound OK,' he says doubtfully.

I don't know if it's just hitting the car, my row with Dan and the weirdness of talking to him, or shock, or frustration at the stupid girl shouting at me – but whatever it is, I burst into tears.

'Molly?' Leo is incredulous. 'Are you *crying*?'

'I'm so sorry—' I feel completely stupid. 'Leo, I should go.' I hang up quickly.

What a truly rubbish – and deeply surreal – morning this is turning out to be. I stare at the phone. He's going to think I've gone completely mad. I message him out of the blue and then hang up on him when he calls me. I shudder with embarrassment and then, so I don't have to dwell on it, hit one of the numbers I have on speed dial. A male voice answers with a terse 'Hello?'

'Hi, it's me.' I take a deep breath, this really is one of my worst Wednesdays *ever*. 'I've just had a bit of an accident . . .'

'Molly needs a top-up after the day she's had.' Pearce pours more wine into my glass. 'The important thing is, you weren't hurt.'

'Can you tell Dan that?' I ask. 'He gave me a proper telling off for not concentrating at the wheel.'

85

Pearce shrugs. 'Probably just worried about you, that's all. Cheers everyone.'

We all raise our glasses.

'Just to check,' Kirk, our newest and very junior recruit asks cautiously, legs spread rather too wide as he smoothes his Topman suit trousers down. 'We are now officially off-duty, aren't we? Whatever we get up to won't affect anything back at the office, so to speak?'

Pearce gives him a mischievous grin as he sits back in his chair. 'Nope. You can carry on getting ratted and behave badly Kirk, everyone else is going to. Sandra's already seen two people sneaking off upstairs who ought not to be.'

A small knowing smile passes about my colleague's beautiful glossy lips as she picks up her glass. 'This is your first conference then I take it, Kirk?' she turns away from Pearce and innocently sips her drink. 'The rules are, what goes on tour stays on tour, get it?'

We all watch Kirk falter under her Medusa-like gaze. 'Yeah,' he mumbles, loosening his tie and picking up his pint, obviously thinking how much he'd like to get it from her. 'Of course.'

Sandra laughs meanly and bats her long lashes at him, totally aware of the effect she's having. It's like watching a pike circle under the water as a duckling paddles hopelessly above. I'm about to step in and rescue him when my phone buzzes with a message: Dan.

we won't have to pay anything re car will we? Company insurance will pick it up? It

86

```
better - I don't exactly have money to
throw away right now.
```

I sigh. So that's why I got my lecture. I text back.

```
If any costs I will pay, but sure work will
sort. Leave with me.
```

Deciding to tease Kirk a little more, Sandra turns her whole body towards him for maximum impact. 'So, is this your first time then, playing—' she re-crosses her legs clearly imagining herself as Sharon Stone '—away from home?' All three men shift in their seat. Kirk nods. He's got hair like a greased baby hedgehog.

'Fun,' she murmurs in a sultry tone, but then turns away from him, to his evident disappointment. 'What's your room like Andy? Comfy?'

Andy takes too large a sip of his whisky. 'Very, thanks,' he says, and then ruins his cool by having to cough violently. 'You're welcome to come and have a bounce on the bed if you like.'

Pearce snorts with amusement into his drink. It's worse than watching dogs on heat.

'So you're married, are you?' Kirk nods at me, seeming to remember I'm still in the room.

'I think so.' I glance gloomily at my silent phone.

'Right,' Kirk says, dismissively. 'So it's down to the four of *us* to burn the house up tonight then?' He turns to the others, alcohol having lowered his inhibitions.

'Burn the house up?' Pearce laughs, glancing round the hotel ballroom. 'If you say so pal. Reckon you're going to like being a rep then, do you? Sure you've really got what it takes to be one of the team?'

He begins to give Kirk a pisstake interview as Andy gets some more drinks in. I sip my vodka, carefully chosen because I've had enough wine, and my guts twist sharply in response to another slug of alcohol; none of us have had very much to eat all day.

'So, next question Kirk.' Pearce is on a roll, amused eyes dancing. 'The boss rings and you know he's going to bollock you for not reaching your monthly target. Worse still, you cancelled your last meeting because you couldn't be arsed to drive all the way to Chatham and are in fact already at home having a cuppa, feet up in front of Countdown.

'Do you a) ignore the call and let it go to voicemail, leg it out to the car, get in, start the engine and call him back straight away telling him you're in a dodgy signal area between meetings, or b) pick up and say you're at home doing your paperwork because the GP cancelled on *you*.'

Kirk ponders this. 'B' he slurs slightly, before taking a big slug of rum and Coke.

My phone buzzes again. Dan?

It isn't. Two messages have arrived, but one is Abi reminding me that it's Rose's baby shower on Saturday the twenty-first in London and the other is Joss saying hello. I text Joss that I'm at a conference and I'll call her tomorrow night when I'm back.

'—and our survey says . . . uh oh! The correct answer is A. GPs never bother to ring and cancel because they think we are plebs, so he now knows you're lying. When in doubt, always pretend you're on the road, it looks proactive and you can cut him off if the questions about your missed targets become too hot to handle; shit signal remember?'

'Let's try again,' Pearce continues. 'You've had a heavy night and you feel ragged. Much like you're going to feel tomorrow,' he eyes Kirk drain his drink. 'You stink of booze and can't string a sentence together but you can't justify a day off sick either. Do you a) have a fat coffee, do your morning hospital meetings, but cancel the afternoon ones; b) cancel all meetings but drive to the hospitals anyway and nap in the car in the car parks—'

Kirk looks totally confused but the rest of us grin.

'—or c) put on a croaky voice anytime someone rings you and say you're tucked up at home with flu?'

'C?' Kirk hazards a guess. 'Because a doctor would know I was hungover and report me?'

'It's B,' Andy cuts in. 'That way you can get the tickets for the car parks that prove you were at the hospitals – they'll go through on expenses – but you won't actually have to bother with the meetings them- selves.'

Kirk looks gutted. My phone buzzes again. 'Some-one's popular,' Pearce remarks and Sandra narrows her eyes.

This time it *is* Dan.

```
Well will they or not? I need to know.
Can't just pull money out of nowhere and
neither can you!
```

Dan, I've said sorry! I take a deep breath – remembering what Mum said to me about getting angry when I'm defensive and how it doesn't help.

```
Didn't do it on purpose. YES - they will
pay for it, OK?
```

There, that's better. Calm and adult.
He texts back immediately.

```
All right, no need to be like that, was
just asking! Didn't say you did it on purpose!
Pls come home in better mood.
```

What? I was being nice! *Please come home in a better mood?* Is he even serious? I had a car accident today! Albeit a very small one, but still! I reach for my glass and take a big insulted gulp.

'You are correct, sir!' Pearce holds up his hand triumphantly to Kirk. I've missed another question, but Sandra is there in a flash, somehow even managing to turn a high five into something sexual. She's clearly made her selection. 'Let's line some more up shall we?'

she murmurs, looking at him seductively. 'Shots anyone?' She gets up and wiggles over to the bar, knowing full well that not only are the blokes at our table watching her, most of the men in the room are now agog, mouths open.

'Wow,' Kirk is practically panting.

'Why don't you go and ask her if you can buy her a drink?' Pearce says slyly.

Kirk stares at Sandra's neat little bottom encased in its tight pencil skirt. 'Dammit. You know what? I will. Thanks, dude.' He stands up, reaches for his wallet, takes a deep breath and staggers over to her.

'I know that was mean,' Pearce chuckles, 'seeing as it's an open bar, but it'll be fun to watch him wave his Solo card around like it's a black Amex. Having another?' He stands up.

'Yes,' I say determinedly. *Come back in a better mood?* That's outrageous. 'I am. I'll be right back.' I get to my feet. 'I'm just going to the loo.'

'I may go and rescue Sandra,' Andy says casually.

'Oh yeah? That's how rumours start.' Pearce raises an eyebrow.

'Hopefully, mate,' Andy says and stumbles off as I begin to squeeze between the table and chairs.

'Moll?'

I look up, Pearce has become serious, no hint of his earlier jauntiness. 'You all right?'

I nod, and plaster on a big bright smile. 'I'm fine. Can you keep an eye on my bag?'

Before he can say anything, I make my way unsteadily out into the foyer with the feeling he is watching me, concerned. He's so sweet – and going to be a heart-breaker when he grows up. I can see why so many of my female colleagues have already fallen for him . . . *come back in a better mood* . . . I can't believe Dan actually had the gall to send that to me. I look down at my feet, concentrating on keeping them moving one in front of the other, but unfortunately that means as I walk round the corner, I manage to walk slap bang into someone.

'Oh, I'm sorry!' I say instinctively.

'Don't be. I've been looking everywhere for you.'

I look up, and when I see who it is, I gasp out loud.

## Chapter Nine

'What are you doing here?' I'm astonished.

'I was worried about you,' Leo says. 'I came as soon as I could – I needed to make sure you were all right.'

I'm frozen to the spot, utterly thrown. Is he really standing right there in front of me?

'You look a little shocked.' He smiles. 'Shall we get you a drink?'

'I'll be right back. I've just got to—' I motion a little unsteadily up the corridor to where the loos are.

'OK – I'll be in the library bar.'

I nod and walk off, as if we've just had a perfectly normal conversation. I slam into the loos – not on purpose, I just push the door too hard – and then bang into a cubicle. Leo is here? As I sit down everything goes a bit swirly for a moment. I giggle nervously and cover my mouth with my hand. Leo is here! Oh this is not good – not good at all. Right, I have to sober up. I flush the loo and stagger back out to wash my hands carefully, before looking in the mirror, pulling a face at myself and trying to tidy my hair a bit. Urgh, if I'd have known I'd be seeing my ex for the first time in years I'd at least have put on a bit more make-up – only as a point of dignity of course, not because I want to impress him or anything. I stumble slightly as I check I have no stream of loo roll attached to my heel, or anything similarly hideous, and make my way back to the library.

Leo is standing at the bar and when he sees me come in, grins and motions to two cosy armchairs round a small table, in a tucked-away corner. I obediently walk over, sit down and then take my first proper, and extremely curious, look at him.

The very first time I laid eyes on Leo he was standing at a bar, waiting to be served, as he is now. The déjà vu makes me shiver. His effortlessly elegant suits were expensive even when he couldn't really afford them; but it was his confidence, his 'Trust me, I'm a man who has everything under control' demeanour that always put people at ease. Sure enough, on cue, he says something to the barman, who laughs. He's been here, what – less than a minute? How does he do it?

His black hair is definitely shorter, neater and just the slightest bit salt and pepper. He's also maybe a little stockier, but it suits him – he looks like a man who doesn't need to shout about his success, it's evident that it allows him to have it all.

The same relaxed capability was what attracted me back then. He hadn't needed to chat anyone up, there was no air of desperation about Leo. He was already having a really good time, which is what made it all the more flattering when the full beam of his attention turned my way. It dazzled me, made me feel special. I wanted to be wanted by him. When people look like they're having fun you want to tag along for the ride, and whatever 'it' was, Leo had in spades. Although, of course, it was the elusive indefinable something which pulled me to him in the first place that also left me with cloyingly painful withdrawal symptoms when he exited – just as abruptly as he had arrived in my life.

Getting over that man, gathering up the leftover bits of me after he'd gone, was one of the hardest things I've ever had to do.

But now? I look at him and realise that all I feel is the memory of the effect he once had on me, rather than the feeling itself. Which is both a relief and well, pretty liberating really.

'Here we are!' He places two vast whiskys on the table.

'That's not water.'

'No – it's not, that's right,' he says seriously and then his face splits like the Cheshire cat's. 'It's been God knows how many years and *that*'s what you want? Behave yourself! Now tell me – what the hell happened in the car today then?'

95

I open my mouth, but before I have a chance to speak, Pearce walks into the library looking around anxiously, clutching my handbag. He stops up short to see me sat at a table with an unfamiliar man.

'I'm so sorry,' he says politely, taking in the drinks. 'I wanted to check that you were . . . you'd been gone a long . . . but you obviously are.' He shoots a glance at Leo, who sits back in his chair with interest, holding his glass. Pearce turns back to me and gives me an oblique stare. He's met Dan before, knows what he looks like, and knows this isn't him. 'Please do excuse me for interrupting,' he says quickly, to prevent any introductions, and then passes me my bag. 'Good night.'

'Who's your boyfriend?' Leo swallows a mouthful, watches him leave. 'He looks about ten. You've got him well trained though.' He nods at the bag.

I look after Pearce worriedly, I'll have to talk to him in the morning so he doesn't get the wrong idea. 'He's not my boyfriend.' I turn back to face Leo. 'Look, how did you even—'

'Oh, come on!' he teases. 'You told me where you were going to be!'

I did? I try to remember.

'This morning? Seconds before you had your smash. I can't tell you how worried I've been about you.'

I raise my eyebrows as I pick up my drink.

He looks affronted. 'Molls, I'm not just some bloke off the street – we used to live together! OK, so we've not stayed in each other's lives, but you were a very important

96

part of mine for a long time. What would you have done if the tables had been turned? You contact me randomly out of the blue, have a car crash and then burst into tears!'

I think for a moment, about the way it must have appeared to him.

'I knew where you were going to be . . .' he shrugs. 'I *had* to make sure you were OK. You wouldn't have just ignored me, would you?'

I hesitate.

'And confession time – I actually only live twenty minutes down the road. It's no big deal . . .' he sips his drink.

Oh right. That does make it slightly more under-standable.

'Well, it's . . . very kind of you,' I say awkwardly. 'Sorry about earlier, when I hung up in the car. I think I was in shock.'

'As long as you weren't hurt, that's the main thing.'

'No – I'm fine. I am sorry though.'

He shrugs. 'Look, if I go home later knowing you're all right – and that's it for another few years, I won't consider this a wasted evening. OK? Don't sweat it.'

'You must have thought I'd gone mental, randomly messaging you like a crazy then falling apart on the phone.'

He looks at me thoughtfully. 'Actually, I was just thinking I'd forgotten how level and capable you are.'

'Level and capable?' I repeat slowly. How – dull.

'What?' he frowns. 'That's a good thing!' He looks

suddenly serious and pauses for a moment. 'Can I be honest and say it's freaking me out a bit to be sat here with you like this? You really haven't changed one bit you know.'

I meet his gaze, winter-crisp eyes staring right at me in that unnervingly direct way of his, like there is some sort of secret passing between us. It almost makes me shiver. He's wrong though – I have changed, and so has he.

'Does your wife mind that you're here?' I say lightly, in an attempt to get us back on to safe ground.

He chuckles. 'Helen? Molls, don't take this the wrong way,' he reaches for his glass, 'there are other exes she'd be irritated by my meeting, but not you.'

Oh. Ouch. What, because I am so safe? Dependable? There is a moment's pause before I smile brightly. 'Well that's good.' I take an enormous mouthful of drink.

'What I mean is—'

'You don't need to explain.'

'No, please, I do. When I first got together with Helen, Cara was still in the picture.'

I can't help bristling at that name, even after all this time.

'By that I mean she was still calling me a lot,' he shakes his head as if we *both* saw that coming . . . 'She was . . . is . . . completely mad. Anyway,' he says hastily, as I stay ominously silent, 'Helen made it very clear she wasn't having *that* . . . and in answer to your question, I doubt she'll have even noticed I've gone out. She's a very busy lady.' He trails off and stares straight ahead for a moment before turning back to me with a smile. 'So. Tell me what's been going on with you?'

'What, in general?' I ask. 'A summary of the last few years?'

'Why not? If I had to give you three words to describe them, what would they be?' He settles back into his chair and sips his drink.

'Um,' I shake my shoes off and fold my legs up underneath me as I think about that. 'Happy, settled, fun.'

'That's nice . . .'

'. . . but boring?' I finish teasingly.

He looks a bit surprised. 'No. Not at all.'

Which somehow manages to make it sound like *I* think my life is boring. I quickly reach for my drink to cover the rather awkward moment. 'And you?'

'Hmmm,' he mulls that over. 'Glass half-full.'

I wrinkle my nose. 'That doesn't tell me anything!'

'Oh I'm sorry,' he laughs, 'how about . . . Nothing lasts forever.'

I make a face. 'Really?'

'Now why would you assume that's a negative thing?' he teases. 'I might have that on my tombstone you know, apart from liking the irony—'

I roll my eyes and shake my head lightly, which makes him grin.

'—it reminds you when times are crap, it won't always be like that, but also that it's important to cherish the good things in your life while you have them.'

He looks directly at me again, just for a moment.

'So actually,' he continues cheerfully, moving straight on before I have chance to consider exactly what he means by that, 'they are three quite optimistic little words – I think.'

There is a pause.

'You mentioned you're still in corporate events then?' I say eventually.

'Yes, that's correct,' he says, trying to keep a straight face, pretending to be serious. 'I *am* still in corporate events, thank you for asking.'

I shoot him a look.

'What?' he laughs. 'You just sound very polite, that's all.'

'I haven't seen you for ages!' I exclaim. 'That's the sort of thing normal people ask, Leo, not "what three words describe your current mood".'

'Unsettled, reflective . . . intrigued.' He shoots back instantly.

'*So you're still in corporate events*?' My heart gives an extra warning thump, as I try to pretend I haven't just heard that.

'Oh OK – yes, I am!' he says good-naturedly. 'Parties, launches, lunches, exhibitions . . . still busy showing people a good time.'

'I'm sure you are,' I reply dryly and sip my drink again as he grins. 'All right, I walked straight into that one . . . but yes, it's true, my life is dedicated to the pursuit of other people's happiness.' He sighs heavily. 'It's *very* rewarding, let me tell you.'

'Oh come on. You love it.'

He shrugs. 'It's easy, that's true . . .' For him it probably is. I've seen him do small talk, deep chat – he can adapt to any social situation he finds himself in. '. . . but it's just not so much fun any more. The guest lists keep getting younger and younger. I don't like it. To be fair I haven't the patience for it these days, pretending I really love music that I hated the first time round . . . that kind of thing.'

I smile and rub my neck, which is starting to feel a bit tight.

'You all right?' he notices.

'Yes thanks. It's just a bit uncomfortable that's all.'

'Oh I don't know, we're having a nice old chat, aren't we?'

'Will you stop it?' I put my empty glass down on the table and give him another mock fierce look.

'Sorry.' He says mischievously. 'So what *did* happen in the car today then?'

'Urgh.' I think back to the woman shouting at me. 'I just wasn't concentrating, it was totally my fault.'

'Not mine for ringing you then?' he says.

'No, not at all,' I reassure him quickly. 'I had a lot on my mind, I should have been focusing.'

'Lot on your mind? In what way?'

I don't really know how to answer that.

'Tell me to mind my own business and I will,' he says gently, noting my hesitation.

'It's not that, Leo,' my tongue is loosening thanks to the booze. 'It's just . . .'

101

He says nothing, just waits patiently and I find myself compelled to fill the silence.

'You know what? I'm just managing to make a mess of everything today.'

'I'm sure that's not true.'

'Want to bet?' I sigh and sit back in my chair a little. 'Aren't things supposed to get easier as you get older?'

'What sort of things are we talking about?'

'Becoming older and wiser, that sort of thing.'

'Oh, I see. Well, I don't know that this will help very much – and you won't remember him anyway – but last week my great uncle Davy, aged eighty-two—'

'Davy? He's still alive?' I can't help my astonishment.

'Yes he is! You haven't forgotten him? Wow!' he looks pleased. 'He'll love that. Well anyway, Davy tells me he's going to split up with his girlfriend – a sweet little widower who lives on the floor above him – because it's all moving too fast. But as you've just pointed out, how slow can you afford to go at eighty-two?'

I laugh – as a very slight, young and pretty waitress appears and puts two more drinks down in front of us. When did we order them?

'Thank you,' Leo smiles charmingly at her and she blushes scarlet before discreetly withdrawing. I roll my eyes as Leo glances after her.

'What?' he says, not missing a trick.

'Maybe you're right,' I tease. 'Maybe there does come a point when perhaps you just run the risk of appearing a dirty old man.'

'Thanks,' he says, looking distinctly unamused.

Oh dear. 'I'm only joking,' I backtrack quickly. 'You were the one who blatantly checked her out!'

'I didn't check her out.' He scoffs. 'I looked to see if she was coming back with the tab for me to sign. What with my eyesight going due to extreme old age I don't see so well these days . . .' he reaches for his fresh drink. 'What do you care anyway? Cheers,' he holds it aloft expectantly. So I pick mine up and we chink.

'Cheers. And I don't care. Carry on with what you were saying before.'

He smiles, seeming to have recovered his good humour. 'I don't think we ever really hit the moment of enlightenment where it just makes sense. We're all bumbling around trying not to balls it up, hoping we're making the right decisions.'

Hmm. That does sound rather familiar actually.

'What?' he looks at me innocently.

'Nothing,' I shake my head. 'That just – sounds about the long and the short of where I am.' I shrug and take a big mouthful of drink. My head is starting to feel a bit thick.

'So I take it you're on the edge of a choice then?' he asks. 'Staring at the crossroads of life as it were?' He swirls his whisky reflectively and waits.

'I don't really know *what* I'm doing,' I say, watching the liquid spinning in the glass.

He stays diplomatically quiet, but this time, I remain discreet.

'You know,' he muses eventually. 'I was quite surprised when you mentioned you hadn't got any children yet . . . not that it's a bad thing,' he adds quickly. 'Just, I would have expected you to have them by now. Is that the big decision?'

I look at him, impressed; he always was very sharp.

'Doesn't Dan – is it? – want them?'

Or perhaps not.

'So it's automatically Dan who's not keen is it?' I say lightly. 'I see.'

He looks taken aback and I realise in being a smart-arse, I've given away more than I intended to. I gulp some more whisky.

'But when we were together you—'

I look up sharply.

'Sorry,' he says instantly. 'I didn't mean anything by that except I don't remember it being something you didn't seem to want, but hey – you're allowed to change your mind.'

'I shouldn't be talking to you about this,' I say suddenly.

'Molly, who am I going to tell?'

'That's not the point. I probably *do* want them – I just want to have some fun first, that's all.' I throw the last of my drink back, then yawn.

'So I see,' he laughs. 'I hear what you're saying though, believe me . . . Hang on a sec.'

He stands up and makes his way over to the bar again. While he's there I sneak a look at my phone. No calls from Dan. Stung, I shove the phone back in my bag and look up as Leo returns to the table with two full shot glasses. He laughs at my worried expression. 'Tequila!' he grins and passes one to me.

I blanch. 'I can't – you know what it does to me.'

He looks puzzled for a moment. 'Oh God . . . yeah – I'd forgotten it's not your best drink.'

'It's not that, I love it – it just doesn't love me.'

'Oh come on!' he says, the liquid trembling slightly in the glass. 'It's one shot! I thought you said you wanted to have fun?'

I hesitate, then reach for it and knock it back in one.

He cheers. 'There you go, you've still got it!' He sits back down and places his shot carefully on the table.

'Er, excuse me?' I nod at it.

'No way,' he pulls a face. 'I hate the stuff. You can have that one as well if you like. I'm past it, remember? The shock might kill me.'

'Just drink it,' I push it towards him and he sighs heavily and downs it, to my satisfaction, and then coughs. 'Urgh, God. You know what, the youngsters can keep it . . .'

'All right grandpa, no one likes a whinger,' I sit back in my chair.

He laughs again and then stares at me.

'What?' I squirm uncomfortably.

'Nothing,' he says quickly.

'Don't just sit there staring,' I shift again, awkwardly. 'It's rude.'

'I was just thinking how nothing fazes you.'

'Not that I've aged horrifically since you last saw me?'

I blurt, for reasons *I* don't even understand. 'Or some-thing equally as unflattering?'

He looks genuinely thrown. 'Not even slightly. You look beautiful.'

There is a very long pause.

'Right, well,' I say eventually, realising this is straying into potentially dangerous territory. 'I'm going to pretend I need the loo now,' I grab the arms of my chair to steady myself, 'so I can diffuse the tension, just in case you're thinking what I think you're thinking.'

He raises an interested eyebrow. 'Which would be . . .'

'That,' I point at him. 'Whatever you're thinking now . . . Stop it. I'll be right back, OK? *Please* can you get me some water?' I stand up and the alcohol falls down through my middle like a lift crashing to the basement. Suddenly I realise I am a lot drunker than I thought.

'You all right?' Leo's brow creases with concern as I feel my stomach swirl unpleasantly.

'I think I might need some fresh air actually,' I cover my mouth with my hand, feeling faint.

'Oh okkkayyy,' he stands up hastily and grabs my bag. 'Let's move.'

Hurriedly he leads me to a quiet terrace at the back of the hotel. I can just make out 'Love Shack' drifting across from the conference ballroom as the skin on my bare arms starts to cool my hot, drunk blood. 'I'm really sorry. I just suddenly feel really – sick and . . .' I swallow, waiting for the nausea to pass. 'I've had way too much to drink tonight.'

'It was my fault . . . that tequila probably tipped you over.'

'No, no,' I wave a hand, not wanting to even *think* tequila. 'I had a lot earlier and . . . I'm so stupid.' I shake my head.

'Oh come on. We've all done it – well, you *know* I've done it – don't beat yourself up.' He places my bag at my feet, removes a packet of cigarettes, a lighter and his phone from his jacket and then takes it off, before passing it to me. 'You'll freeze otherwise.'

I loop it over my shoulders gratefully and shiver as the warm silk lining slips over my skin. He stands there just clasping his belongings.

'Want me to take those?' I offer, making an effort to enunciate.

'Please.'

He hands them over and I slide them into his jacket pockets. A cloud of cigarette smoke drifts over to me as he lights up.

'You still smoke then?' I say, leaning back on the stone wall behind me. I am starting to feel very swirly and having to concentrate hard on the conversation so as to not make an arse of myself.

'Yeah, my skin's going to look like shoe leather in twenty years' time, between these and my crap genes.'

'So how are your mum and dad?' I ask politely, trying to think of something normal to say.

He looks at me and laughs, as if I've said something amusing, which confuses me a bit. 'Same old, still at each other's throats. You know what they're like. How are you feeling now?'

'OK.' I try to focus on the square tiles on the ground in front of us. 'Do they like having two ready-made grandchildren?'

He hesitates. 'Sort of. Helen's kids are a bit feisty—'

I try to remember the picture I saw. They just looked like two ordinary little girls to me.

'—I get a lot of "You're not my real dad" flak. He moves over to the stone balustrade in front of us and leans on it. 'But they're right, I'm not.' He shrugs his shoulders. 'It's fair enough I guess.'

'Do they still see their real dad?'

'Not really. He's just a sign-the-cheques parent. Things aren't very amicable between him and Helen and she doesn't take any prisoners. He's filthy rich but very pissed off that – as he sees it – he still has to pay for his ex-wife and her new husband, along with supporting the kids. Nice bloke.'

'Where did you meet her?'

He half-turns to face me, 'At a party.'

Of course he did. Where else?

The wind stings my face as I look out over the beginnings of a dark golf course. Feeling a vibrating in the jacket pocket I try to work out what it is. 'I think your phone is ringing.'

'Oh, thanks,' he straightens up and flicks his fag over the edge of the wall. I reach into his pocket, but drunkenly clumsy, the mobile slips from my fingers as I attempt to pass it to him and clatters to the ground.

108

'Shit!' I'm horrified, my hands rush to my mouth as I bend to pick it up. 'I'm so sorry!' The screen is displaying the name Amanda. Who is she? I wonder.

'It's OK,' he picks it up. 'Hello? Hi – yeah, it's me . . . what?' he glances at me. 'No. Not at all.' He listens intently for a moment then turns away from me, so I can't see his face. 'Anyway, you all right?'

He takes several steps away to the far side of the terrace.

'Probably, yeah.' I hear him say in a low voice. 'Yeah – I would if I were you. I'd hate to wake you. Me too.'

My eyes start to close. I am so tired. Very suddenly, I realise *I* want to be in a bed.

He hangs up and comes back over just as I yawn again.

'Am I keeping you up?' He grins. 'I should probably get going anyway.' He holds the phone aloft. 'That was the other half.'

Didn't he say that his wife's name was Helen? 'But your phone said Amanda.' I can't help myself.

'That's right,' he says quickly, 'Helen phoning on Amanda's mobile. Amanda's her daughter.' He looks at me easily. 'I expect Hel's battery was flat, she's hopeless at charging it up.'

'It's none of my business anyway,' I say quickly, thinking, wow, kids really do get mobile phones young these days. 'Sorry.'

'It's OK,' he smiles. 'You can say anything to me, you know that.'

109

There is a brief pause. He just stands there, looking at me. 'I'm sorry too, by the way.'

'What for?'

'For everything Moll, being such a cunt to you.'

There is another very long pause indeed.

'Ah, so that's why you really came here tonight?' I try to sound light, not give away my shock, and force myself to look straight at him.

'Maybe,' he says quietly. 'When I got your message . . . I – I wish it had never finished like that you know.'

'Me too,' I say. 'It was – not nice.'

'I should never have done it.' He looks ashamed. 'You were very special to me.' Bizarrely, that makes me want to laugh. I sound like a favourite pet he had to have put down.

'Don't, Leo,' I say kindly. 'It doesn't need to be said. It doesn't matter any more.' Maybe *that* was why I messaged him, because it had still somehow been unfinished for me too. Well, not any more. I offer him my hand to shake. 'We're OK, you and I.'

He reaches out and takes it. His hand is warm as he grips mine and the temperature contrast makes me shiver. 'Cold hands, warm heart,' he muses and then gives it a gentle squeeze before letting it go.

'We should go back in,' I break the moment.

'You feel all right again?'

I nod. 'Yeah – I feel much better now. Thanks.'

We walk back into the foyer, him carrying my bag for me until we reach the stairs.

'I can't tempt you to join me while I have just one more for the road?' he offers.

I grimace as I slow to a stop. 'Kind offer – but I'd actually puke.' I reach out for my bag. 'Thanks, and thank you for coming to see me too. I really mean that.'

'You're welcome,' he says. 'I'll look you up in another few years, shall I? See how you're getting on.'

'Well maybe,' I say, 'but I think we've put the world to rights tonight haven't we?'

He looks a bit surprised. 'Fair enough,' he says eventually. 'Well, in the next lifetime then.'

'Why not?' I say. 'Oh – your jacket!'

And I slip it off and hand it over to him. He takes it and as our fingers touch, he reaches out further, takes my arm gently and leans towards me. My eyes close automatically for a moment. The smell and familiar feel of him that close to me is well, not pleasant exactly, but somehow an oddly compelling sensation. It reminds me, just for a moment, of other things we've done. Things he was pretty good at. I wait to feel his kiss on my cheek but he places it very lightly *on my lips*. It lasts no more than a flicker of a second, but I almost gasp out loud before I pull back. Who does that? Who kisses people on the mouth like it is a normal and acceptable thing to do? Who? WHO? I only EVER kiss Dan like that – brief kiss or not brief kiss.

'Be good, Moll,' he says softly, and then winks at me before turning and sauntering out of the hotel, hands in his pockets.

111

That *did* just happen, didn't it? On the *lips*? The cheeky . . .

Swaying slightly, and clutching my belongings I turn to begin to walk up the stairs to my room before stopping and looking back over my shoulder, but he's vanished. In trying to right myself, I manage to trip slightly. I glance around hoping no one has noticed, but a woman in her sixties sitting in the lobby leans forward disapprovingly and whispers something to her husband, who turns stiffly in his chair to look. I decide it might be best to just remove myself to bed as quickly as possible. I am clearly still a little tipsy. Everything is starting to feel a bit lopsided . . .

So I begin my renewed attempt to get to my room. Walking up the stairs, my legs are starting to feel like lead. Oh why did I drink so much?

Back in dark, unfamiliar surroundings, I stagger over to the bed and collapse on to it as I try to take my shoes off. My limbs are suddenly incredibly heavy, it is an effort to lift them, and yet my stomach is churning ominously, aching to be rid of its contents. I've hit the tipping point and begin to wish I could go back in time and *not* have so much to drink. I roll my body sideways as my eyes close heavily, until I am in danger of being practically face down on the bed. Stupid, stupid cow. I'm going to feel like shit in the morning.

At first I think I've imagined the soft knock on the door, but through my haze, I hear it again and realise someone is on the other side, saying my name quietly.

With a superhuman effort I push myself up, force myself to my feet and stagger to the door, peering through the peephole.

It's Leo.

'I'm so sorry, I think you've still got my wallet,' he explains, as I wrench the door open, 'it's not in my pocket, did you put it in your bag by mistake?'

'Er . . . I don't . . .' I turn and look around wildly for my bag. It's next to the chair. I cross the room. Sure enough, there his wallet is, sitting on top of all the other stuff in there.

I pull it out, confused, and turn back. He is suddenly somehow right next to me.

'Thanks,' he takes it from my hand. 'Jesus – Molly! Are you OK?' He sounds very far away. 'Molly?'

'I need to sit, I need to—' I've stood up too quickly. Everything begins to slip sideways.

'It's OK,' I hear him say, 'I've got you; this way Molly.'

I take a step towards his voice. And then I simply feel myself falling.

When I open my eyes again I am lying on a bed, in a dark room, next to Dan. I instinctively move closer to him, reaching out with relief, but as I draw myself to his body sleepily, I suddenly freeze and pull back sharply. It doesn't feel like Dan at all. I try to sit up and realise I am still dressed in my work clothes, they are all twisted and clammy, clinging to me. I stare at the body next to me. It moves, turns over, and in the dim light coming

113

in under the door from the corridor, I realise it's Leo. 'Molly?' he jolts awake, peering up at me. 'Thank fuck – are you OK?'

Completely disorientated and scared, I look around the dark room. Where am I? I have no idea what time it is or how long I've been there.

'I can't . . .' I try to make sense of it all but am having huge problems getting my words out. 'What did I . . . ?' I put my hand to my head in confusion as I look around and then for the second time in twenty-four hours I burst into sudden, confused tears.

Leo sits up quickly, pulling me into his arms. 'Shhh!' he says and begins to rock me. 'Shhhh. Don't cry! You're OK.'

It is such a relief to have someone there, I cling to him and just sob.

He continues to hug me, his body warm from having just woken up. 'It's all right,' he says letting me cry, kissing the top of my head briefly and rocking me gently again. 'You're going to be all right . . . There . . . that's better,' he says. 'See? It's all going to be fine. I promise.' He tips my head up, gives me a reassuring smile and then he slowly leans forward and kisses me very lightly on the mouth.

Instantly, I have the strongest feeling of having done it before . . . but of course I have. Lots of times. He pulls back and looks at me again, searchingly. 'How could I have been so stupid?' he says in disbelief. I stare back at him, bewildered. He quickly bends and kisses me again, properly.

114

My brain isn't working fast enough and at first I simply respond to the familiarity. But after what is probably only a few seconds, some dulled reactions somewhere finally kick in and I pull my head back away from him. I try to say 'Don't,' but before I can, he kisses me for a second time. I attempt to speak again, but my mouth won't work, like trying to run in a dream. I simply can't get the words out. It is the weirdest sensation.

He does pull back, but so he can start to kiss my neck, and then slowly, he pushes me back on to the bed . . .

## Chapter Ten

I wake up to the relentless ring of the hotel phone. Dull daylight is feeding in around the edges of the cheap hotel curtains and as I move my head on the pillow to work out where the noise is coming from, it feels like it is going to split in two.

'Molly?' The sound of Pearce's voice carrying down the line makes me wince. 'Are you coming down to breakfast? I wasn't sure . . .'

'Um,' I try to think straight. 'Are you already down there then?'

'Already? We're done pal! It's a quarter to nine.'

What? I blink heavily. How . . .

'Are you OK?' Pearce says, and hesitates, lowering his voice. 'I saw you going upstairs to bed. You looked – pretty wrecked.'

I have no memory of seeing him at all.

'Oh dear,' I say, trying to sound like it's no big deal. 'That's embarrassing.'

'I was going to come and help you, but . . . Anyway,' he says quickly, trying to lighten the tone, 'do I need to order you some strong coffee?'

'Please,' I reply gratefully. 'I'll be right down.'

As I put the phone down a rhythmic whirring begins somewhere on the other side of the room. It sounds as if it's coming from my handbag. My mobile. I sit up a bit too quickly, get out of bed and wobble over to find it. It's Dan.

'Hello?' I practically whisper, holding my splitting head with my free hand as I sit down heavily on the chair – which is when I notice an empty condom wrapper on the carpet, poking out from under the bed.

My first reaction is one of disgust. Time they got a new cleaner . . .

'Morning!' Dan's obviously walking to work. 'Sorry, it's loud here. I've just got off the train. I tried to call you before I went to bed last night. Where were you?'

'I – nowhere – I was here,' I say, still staring at the wrapper.

'Oh dear,' he says sympathetically. 'You sound a bit rough. Did you overdo it?'

I swallow. 'A bit.' And then I jolt, my eyes widen. Oh my God! Leo! Leo was here last night.

'I don't blame you,' Dan says bluntly, 'the way I behaved yesterday, you probably needed a drink or two. I was a total twat; I'm sorry. I'm just – worried about money and work, and – well, you know . . . at least you weren't hurt. I'm really sorry about storming out too.' He continues. 'In the heat of the moment . . . I mean, OK, I know I get wound up sometimes, don't I?'

'Uh huh,' I try to keep my voice level, forcing myself to concentrate, to think back . . . Leo was in this room with me . . . we were in the bed . . . I kissed him.

'. . . but as a general rule,' Dan considers, 'I wouldn't say I'm a stressy person. Would you?'

*We were in the bed.*

'Hello?' Dan says. 'Moll?'

I sway slightly and nearly drop the phone. 'Yes?'

'Oh you're still there. I thought I'd lost you for a minute. Look, it doesn't matter, we can chat about it properly tonight when you get back. I just wanted to make sure you were OK. What time do you think you'll be home?'

'Er, about six-ish.'

'Oh great! I've got a meeting at three so I'll try and come straight home afterwards rather than go back into the office. I've done an online food shop,' he sounds pleased with himself, 'and I'll do tea when I get in. Have a good day won't you? And drink some water,' he teases. 'Love you.'

'I love you too.'

I hang up. Still tightly gripping my phone I am unable to take my eyes off the wrapper, now lying there accusingly. Feeling panic beginning to well up within me I

119

try to stay calm. It doesn't mean anything, it probably *is* just bad housekeeping, that's all. My mobile begins to buzz again in my hand. The vibration running through my body makes me feel sick and I answer quickly to make it stop.

'Molly? It's me. Can you talk?'

Leo. My stomach lurches instantly. 'Yes,' I answer automatically.

'Oh good,' he sounds relieved. 'Are you OK?'

'Er,' I struggle to find the right words. 'I've been better.'

'I know,' he says instantly. 'I'm sorry. In some ways not our finest hour eh? Listen, I can't be too long now – it'll be easier to talk about it later. When's good for you? About six-ish?'

What? No it isn't! 'What do we need to talk about?' I say quickly.

There's a surprised pause. 'Well, us. Last night.'

I go cold. Now trying *not* to look at the condom wrapper, I attempt to keep my voice steady. 'Us?'

'Listen, how about this? I'm just thinking; if I could ditch my plans, are you still at the hotel tonight?'

Of course I'm not! I have to go home! 'Leo – I don't—'

'I know, all this has caught me a little off-guard too,' he confesses. 'I wasn't expecting this either, not after all this time.'

That draws me up short. Expecting *what?* Oh my God – what have I done?

'Leo,' I swallow hard. 'I was pretty drunk last night.

We obviously . . .' I swallow. 'Well, we were in bed together. I don't know what we . . . what I said to you, that might have implied we should, do it again, but . . .' I trail off, because I actually *don't* know what I said to him. We had sex? Oh my God . . . oh God . . .

There is an ominous silence. 'Ah, I see,' he says, his tone changing slightly. I cringe with embarrassment and there's another horribly long pause as he seems to realise whatever he thought was going to happen again, isn't. 'Right. Well, I'd still like to speak to you later if that's OK?' he sounds more businesslike now. 'Just to make sure you're all right, once you've been to the doctor's? We don't—'

Everything grinds down and judders to a heart-stopping halt.

'The doctor's? What do I need a doctor for?' I interrupt. 'We used a condom, didn't we?' I look at the wrapper.

He hesitates.

Then a horrible thought occurs to me. 'Did it,' I close my eyes, 'come off?'

'You don't remember? It broke.'

It *what*?

'It broke?' I repeat dully.

'I know,' he says instantly, 'believe me, I know. You're still angry with me for leaving too, aren't you?' he adds. 'I can tell. You're right – I should have stayed; I just panicked, Moll. I've never cheated on Helen before. I thought if she woke up and I wasn't home . . . I'm sorry, you should have been my priority, especially after

121

what happened. Only us eh?' he laughs awkwardly. 'It will be OK though, I promise. Just do get it sorted won't you? Neither of us want *that*. Shit, I think she's just got back from the school run.' He lowers his voice furtively. 'Look – I'll text you later or something, OK? Don't panic. This is all going to be just fine, babe. I promise.'

And then he hangs up, leaving me holding the phone in shock.

I'm going to be sick . . . Utterly repulsed, I dash to the bathroom, but as I hang over the loo, nothing happens. I raise my head eventually and look in the mirror.

My eyes are bloodshot, my skin is grey and has a greasy sheen to it while my hair is clumped and matted in places. My head feels like it's going to burst. What have we done? Oh what the fuck have we done?

I walk slowly back into the bedroom and sink on to the bed as I look around and try to make some sense of it all. I had a drink with Leo. A couple of drinks. He leant me his jacket. We talked. I went to bed. He came to the room. I was drunk. I woke up next to him, we kissed . . . The rest is a blank.

I exhale slowly. We had whisky . . . and a shot didn't we? Oh – I drank tequila with him – on top of everything else I'd had with the others at the hotel bar. Then I realise I *am* actually going to be sick and have to run to the bathroom as fast as I can.

★   ★   ★

'I know she's your usual doctor, but Dr Thomas isn't in today I'm afraid,' the medical receptionist says cosily. 'Dr Hubbard has an emergency appointment today at four-thirty. It's his last one. Do you need to see a female doctor?'

'No, four-thirty is fine. Thanks.' I practically whisper, sitting on the edge of the hotel bed having showered, sick no longer in my hair, dressed in clean work clothes. Bag packed.

'And the name is?'

'Molly Greene. Mrs Molly Greene.'

I hang up and then I send Pearce a text.

Am really ill. Can you cover for me? Tell them I've got whiplash from yesterday and gone to get checked out? Know this is a big ask x

His response comes back instantly.

Sure. Got it. Wait ten minutes, we're about to start so you should be clear then. Hope you feel better soon. Call me if you need anything?

Thank God for him. I give the room one last cursory check and close the door quietly behind me. I want to get out of the place where it all happened, as quickly as I can. We are both married, what were we thinking?

Emerging out into what is a cold, blustery day, I feel a sense of disbelief that I am going home when I should be at work. It's like sneaking out of school and waiting for a teacher to see me from a classroom and shout at me to come back . . . but what I've done is horribly, disgustingly adult.

It is not my safest drive home. I am simply numb and somehow unable to comprehend that I have done something so tawdrily predictable. Booze, biology and a cheap conference hotel; this is the sort of thing that happens to other reps, not me.

When I arrive back at the house everything looks and feels just as I left it yesterday. In our bedroom Dan has made the bed, there are a couple of golfing magazines on the floor next to a pair of his dirty socks. Last night, Dan was here as usual, like nothing was wrong, while I was in a hotel, with my ex . . .

I wobble on the spot and quickly peel off my clean work clothes, changing into jogging bottoms and a hoodie, my brain pinching with every movement. The silence in the room is really beginning to get to me and all of a sudden I need to speak to someone, very badly.

Agonisingly, Bec goes straight to voicemail; she must be on an early, maybe even a long day. Her phone will be off for hours.

Joss however picks up pretty much straight away. 'Hi,' she says in hushed tones, surprise in her voice. 'I thought you were at a conference? You OK?' For a loud person, she rather bizarrely hates using mobiles when she knows other people can hear her.

'Can you talk?'

'Yup – go for it.'

'Last night . . .' I take a deep breath. 'At the conference hotel . . .'

'Yeah?' she says, doubt creeping into her voice.

'I got really drunk and I slept with someone. As in . . . had sex with.'

There is a long pause. All I can hear is background office noise, a cough and someone else's phone going off. 'OK,' she says eventually, making an enormous effort to react calmly. 'I'm just going to take this outside . . . this was with a colleague I take it?'

'No.' I pause miserably. 'With Leo.'

There is a stunned silence.

'He turned up at the hotel,' I blurt. 'I was so drunk and . . . I woke up this morning and . . . oh Joss, the condom broke.' I can barely get the words out. 'So I'm going to have to go to the doctor's today to get checked out and get the morning-after pill.'

More silence. She doesn't respond. 'Joss?' I realise I've lost her. I ring back but it goes to voicemail. She must be trying to call me. I have to wait another maddening couple of minutes to get through.

'*Leo* was at the hotel? Fuck! Of all the places . . .'

I hesitate. 'It wasn't a coincidence. He knew I was going to be there.'

There is another pause.

'How,' she says ominously, 'would he know that, unless you'd been in contact with him?'

I close my eyes and swallow. 'I sent him a message on Facebook.'

'WHAT? And more to the point *why*?'

'I sent him a message, he sent me one back, we emailed once or twice and then he ended up ringing me yesterday. While we were on the phone I bumped the car, then last night he turned up at the hotel—'

'You bumped the car?' she exclaims. 'What the . . .'

'It was nothing, I went into the back of someone because I wasn't concentrating. When he turned up I was already hammered,' I try to explain. 'We had a couple of drinks . . . I felt sick and . . . well then we said goodnight and I went up to my room, but I think he came up for some reason,' I glance over at my bag, sitting on the floor. 'Oh, that's it!' I remember. 'His wallet or his phone or something was in my handbag, so he came back to get it . . .'

'What were they doing in your bag?' Joss is icy.

'I don't remember, but then I don't remember a lot of last night. I haven't been that drunk for years.'

She sighs heavily.

'What the hell am I going to do, Joss?' I panic.

'Right, well – practicalities,' she swings into business mode. 'You have to get the morning-after pill, to be on the safe side, and I'd get some STD tests done too.'

I freeze. I haven't even considered that. How stupid and naïve am I? She's right. He might have once been

126

my boyfriend . . . but his *wife* could have had one dodgy partner in the past and that would be enough. I shudder with revulsion as I close my eyes. God knows what I might have exposed myself to.

'You can get the pill everywhere these days, you don't have to go to the doctor's.'

I pause. 'True – but the condom broke, didn't it? What if it's not all gone? – I don't want to get an infection.'

'What are you talking about?'

Then I realise the phone must have cut off before she heard everything. So I have to tell her again.

'Oh Molly. Would you like me to come to the doctor's with you?' she offers, her voice softening. 'Or have you asked Bec?'

'She doesn't know about any of this. Her phone's off. It's a really kind offer, but you're at work and everything.' I stare at the floor. How is this even happening? 'I'll be OK.'

'You sound like shit . . . I hate him so much for this,' she says, her voice tight. 'I can't even tell you . . .'

I don't know what to say.

'It's not enough for him, all that misery he put you through back then? He couldn't just fuck off and . . . Oh Moll, why would you *want* to message him? I don't understand!'

'I don't know,' I feel so ashamed. 'It didn't seem a big deal, it was silly light stuff, just—'

'Tell me,' she says, quietly, 'that this isn't you starting something up again with him?'

'NO!' I say it so vehemently she falls silent. 'Of course it isn't!'

'It's just you've always had that weird . . . blind spot . . . when it comes to him.'

'No I don't,' I insist. 'I used to love him, I'm not saying I didn't. But Dan changed everything. I can't believe I've cheated on Dan.' My eyes fill with incredulous tears at the words I've just heard myself say.

'You need to get to the doctor's, get the pill and we'll go from there.' She says firmly. 'This is going to be OK.'

'Can they do the STD tests there too?'

'Yeah, but not right away. Can you just not ask me how I know this, but you can only have most STD tests about a week after you've had a dodgy shag. I'm not sure you even can have them done at most surgeries. You have to go to the GUM clinic.'

But GUM clinics are usually based at hospitals. 'Suppose I see someone from work I know?'

'There are loads of private ones you can go to instead. You could come to one up here. I'll find you a number and text it to you, OK? And if you change your mind and want me to come with you today, call me. Remember it'll take me an hour and a bit to get back though. And definitely call when you're done. If my phone is off it's only because I'm in a meeting, I'll ring you as soon as I can. I bet you this is a more common situation that you think,' she assures me, 'and the doctor will have seen it all before. It's all going to be all night. I promise.'

\*    \*    \*

Sitting in the GP's waiting room dressed in my home clothes rather than my suit, dully watching a small, wheezing toddler sitting on the carpet as it half-heartedly bashes some building bricks, feels very wrong. I should be psyching myself up for a sales tussle. At least, thank God, the surgery isn't actually one of mine in a professional capacity. That would be unbearable. My phone buzzes with a text from Mum.

Are you OK? Dan OK? Conference good? Still coming lunch on Sunday? I've got a big chicken. Love from Mum xxx

Normally just her insistence on signing off every time makes me smile. Not today. I merely text back:

Conference OK. Dan fine. Lunch yes Xxx

Then two more arrive. The first is from Pearce.

All good. Everyone very understanding. Assume you still going to the post mortem meeting tomorrow unless hear otherwise. Take care.

That is a relief at least, and kind of him to let me know. The other is from Joss, checking I've received the clinic number she's sent me.

I have and I've already made an appointment. Then I

scroll right down and open a message Dan sent me ages ago.

```
Love you! Will txt u when on train back
home after gym. xxxx
```

I can't even remember what day that would have been. What had we done that night when he got home? Probably just sat there and ate tea watching TV perfectly happily and normally.

The receptionist calls my name just in the nick of time. Just before I lose it completely.

'So, Mrs Greene,' the slightly useless grandfatherly looking doctor glances at his notes and smiles pleasantly as I sit down in front of him. 'How can I help you today?'

I take a deep breath and do away with any pretence of pleasantries. 'During intercourse last night' – I am acutely embarrassed, it's as if we are living in the 1950s – 'the condom unfortunately broke. I just want to make sure none of it has been left . . . inside me. I don't want to get an infection.'

'Oh, I see,' the doctor doesn't seem thrown at all. 'You've had a go at finding it yourself I assume?'

I nod.

'No joy?'

I stare at him.

'Sorry. Foolish question. Why else would you be here?' He scratches his head. 'Well, it's very likely you would have got it out eventually – it's not er, a bottomless pit up there. We'll have a look anyway. Slip your things off and hop up on the couch.'

'I need the morning-after pill too,' I say awkwardly, taking my tracksuit bottoms and knickers off, wishing I'd worn a skirt as I get on the examination table. I've never felt less like 'hopping' in my whole life.

'We'll sort that out in a minute.' The doctor stands up, pulls on some latex gloves and then advances towards me. 'I need you to place your ankles together, bend you legs and just drop your knees apart please.'

'Well,' he says after an uncomfortably long time, as I focus hard on a spot on the ceiling. 'I can't find anything . . . it's probably worked its way out already.'

I wince.

'. . . Sorry . . . OK. I'm as certain as I can be that it's all gone. You can put your things back on now.' He removes the gloves. 'But even if there is a very small piece of it left, which is possible, it won't be large enough to cause a bacterial build up. The body will just flush it out, as it were.'

I nod, not trusting myself to speak.

'And here's your prescription.' The printer whizzes merrily, he whisks it out and signs with a flourish. As he passes it to me, he opens his mouth as if to say something else, but seems to change his mind as he sees me gripping my wedding ring tightly with my right hand. 'Not always the right timing is it? The sooner you take it, the more effective it is. You can collect it now from our pharmacy which,' he checks his watch, 'should still just be open.' He smiles kindly at me.

131

'Thank you,' I stand up and leave as quickly as possible.

I end up taking the pill in the car like some irresponsible teenager, burying the packet carrying my name in a random rubbish bin en route home.

When I arrive back at the house, only our end-terraced brick cottage, out of the five, is completely dark. Next door are very obviously in, the house is all lit up, every light in the place blazing away, and as I slip my key in the lock I can already hear our neighbour Mel cooing at her little toddler, repeating 'What are you doing? What are you doing?' over and over again, like a syrupy parrot.

God only knows Mel, I have no idea.

Then I hear a crash, a wail and Mel change tack immediately as she shouts fiercely, 'No! Very bad!'

He's not a dog, the poor little thing, but it actually so uncomfortably feels as if she could also be talking to me, I just want to get inside.

As I slip in noiselessly, flick the light switch, shut the front door and kick off my shoes, my phone goes with another text. Probably Joss, I haven't called her, she'll be worried. I pull my phone out, but a number shows up which I don't recognise.

`Are you all right? Have you been to the doctor's? What they say? xxx`

It's him again.

# Chapter Eleven

I don't even have to think about it – I hit delete. I want him gone, want to make him vanish without trace.

I drop my phone on the sofa as if it has burnt me and walk out of the sitting room. Upstairs in the bathroom, I pull the light on, my trousers off and then yank my top over my head. Unhooking my bra and slipping off my knickers, I climb into the bath, turn the dial and gasp as the cold water from the overhead shower stings my skin. As it begins to heat up, I get the soap and start to scrub. I rub so vigorously, with a slightly too-coarse flannel, that my inner thighs turn pink. Then I rinse and rinse myself. Over and over again until I feel sore and my fingers, clutching the showerhead, are going wrinkly. I turn off the water and climb out, shivering on the bath mat. The mirror has steamed up and as I wipe across it, my mascara-ravaged face stares back. I still don't feel clean.

I reach for some loo roll, scrape the stubborn make-up off and drop the tissue in the bin. Then I run a scalding hot, very deep bath and get in. The water rises over my shoulders and I don't look down my naked body, I just close my eyes.

But as I lie there, I remember waking up in the dark hotel bed next to Leo and *crying* . . . I think I cried and he comforted me . . . and that's when he kissed me . . .

Oh God, STOP . . . my eyes rush open and I gasp out loud as Mel bellows, in what I know is her son's bedroom, 'Time to go to sleep!' through the stupidly flimsy walls, before starting up a rousing rendition of *the wheels on the bus go round and round*, which doesn't strike me as a bedtime sort of song.

Leo is the last man who touched me. Not Dan – Leo.

I quickly rear up and out of the water, slopping it over the side as I thump first one, then the other foot down on to the bath mat and reach for my towel. I don't want to lie there any more. Wrapping my body tightly, I walk into our bedroom and pull the curtains shut. Then I dry myself off, slapping on cold body lotion and, before it sinks in properly, step into my PJ bottoms. I begin to rake a brush through my wet hair before reaching for the hairdryer.

I have been very drunk like that only once before, at university where about four hours vanished from my life after I got stupidly sunburnt, took a couple of ibuprofen to dull the pain and then had a bottle of wine before going to the end–of–term ball. I went from having a good time, to feeling drunk, to finding myself on my back, half-conscious in the toilets with several strangers' faces looming over me asking me if I was OK. I'd not been able to answer – just lain there with the vague feeling my skirt was rucked up and I probably ought to sort it out. Then Abi and Rose had appeared. I don't remember anything more about the evening than that. The morning afterwards, the whole episode was frightening enough to make me vow I'd never do it again.

My hair is almost done when I feel a change in the air within the house. Just as I switch the dryer off to listen, Dan suddenly appears in the bedroom doorway eating a packet of Wotsits, and makes me jump.

He grins. 'Didn't hear me come in then?'

I shake my head.

He crosses the room and kisses me. 'I'm a bit crispy. Sorry.' He puts the empty packet down on the chest of drawers and takes his coat off, slinging it on the bed. 'You been back long?'

'No, about half an hour.' Which, technically, is true.

He leaves the room and from the bathroom calls, 'Did the car hold up? Traffic all right?'

'It was fine.' I hurriedly put the hairdryer back on, to prevent any more discussion.

He comes back in, yanks his shirt up and begins to unbutton it before slipping his trousers off. He reaches for a T-shirt from the ironing pile and pulls on a pair of jeans last of all. As I turn the dryer off he comes round and draws me into a hug. 'I missed you,' he says and kisses the top of my head.

'I missed you too.' I close my eyes tightly and cling to him. His T-shirt smells cleanly of washing powder.

'It's been a funny old week, hasn't it?' he says. 'Still, Friday tomorrow. I thought we could do something this weekend just the two of us. That'd be nice, wouldn't it?'

'Very.'

The doorbell rings downstairs. 'Aha!' he says happily. 'That'll be Tesco's. Are you going to come down? I'll stick the kettle on.' He hastens from the room leaving me just standing there, an oily black seam of guilt opening up within me, the like of which I've never, ever experienced.

When I first met Leo, and he began bombarding me with illicit and intoxicating text messages telling me he wasn't able to stop thinking about me . . . what was he supposed to do, walk away from the love of his life knowing I was all he'd ever need? All I had to do was say the word and he'd be there for me . . . I'd felt guilty about his poor girlfriend; but not enough to ignore him. I was too breathlessly excited and absurdly flattered that he'd been so obsessed with me. When Leo falls – he falls hard and fast.

But this? This is a different kind of guilt altogether. My eyes fill with tears and I have to cover my mouth with my hand to silence myself. This is Dan; it is *us*. A drunken moment in a hotel room and the quality of light in our marriage has changed for ever.

I hate Leo for that, almost as much as I hate myself.

★　　★　　★

When we get into bed – having got through eating tea on our laps, Dan asking me painfully innocent questions about how the conference was – I shiver with the cold and he reaches out for me. 'Shall I warm you up?' He hugs me and plants a kiss on my nose. 'Arggghh!' He pulls sharply away from me. 'Your feet are freezing! OK,' he braces himself. 'Go on then, put them on me . . . FUCK!' He laughs and then his kind brown eyes search my face as if he is reminding himself of me. 'The things I do for you!' He kisses me again. 'Love you.'

'I love you too,' I mumble, trying to smile and not cry.

He kisses me again, properly, and I am now so desperate to annihilate everything else, blast it all away and make him what is real, I kiss him back with such energy he almost stops in surprise, although his hands can't help tightening round me in response to my urgency.

Afterwards, trying not to look at the condom wrapper on the floor of our bedroom because it is too horrible a reminder of earlier, I lie there in our bed listening to Dan moving around in the bathroom and clutch the duvet to me. I want to tell him everything. I desperately want to come clean . . . but that is exactly the problem; telling him will not undo what I've done. And there is no way he'd possibly be able to understand or forgive me, I am sure of that. It would only devastate him. I am going to have to learn to live alongside it, that will be my punishment.

He comes back into the room and gets back into bed.

'Moll, I know we've sort of glossed over it, but that row on Tuesday night . . .'

'I'm so sorry about that,' I say immediately.

'No – I should be apologising to you!' He exclaims. 'I flew off the handle, I let what I wanted get in the way of everything else.' He looks so genuinely worried; the guilt and the need to do something to make everything all OK overwhelms me, I just can't bear it.

'The thing is Moll,' he begins, 'I know we've said that . . .'

'Dan,' I interrupt him. 'You're right. We should have a baby. We should start trying, tomorrow in fact.'

He looks confused, 'But—'

'I really want us to.'

I don't actually have to say more than that, because he pulls me delightedly to him, and the expression on his face is all the proof I need that I have done the right thing.

## Chapter Twelve

'You're going to start trying for a baby?' Joss's voice on speakerphone echoes around the car as the road rumbles away under me. 'Are you serious?'

There's a long pause, in which I can't think of anything sensible to say.

'Do you not think,' Joss adopts an unusually careful tone, 'considering that the night before last you had sex with your ex, there's a chance this may not be the best time to make such a big decision?'

'We were always going to have kids, Joss, it was just a question of when,' I reply quickly, trying to pretend I haven't heard what she's just said. 'I know I've been putting it off but . . . look, I can't talk about this now, I'm in the car, I'm not sure where my meeting is and I'm already late.'

'All I'm saying is stop and think if this is what you actually *want*. Have you told Bec yet?'

'Told her what?'

'Well, everything. About Leo for a start.' Her voice darkens.

I shake my head emphatically. 'No, and I'm not going to. I don't want anyone to know about this. You're the only person I've told. Please Joss – it's got to stay that way.'

'But it's *Bec*.'

'The more people know, the higher the chance that it could somehow come out, and Dan must NEVER know about this. I'm ashamed enough as it is, I almost wish you didn't know to be honest. I just want to forget the whole thing ever happened.'

She snorts sadly. 'Well that I can understand.'

Thinking about it again makes me want to vomit, and I get a moment of horizontal vertigo. The car feels static, like it's the trees and other cars on the dual carriageway that are rushing past *me*. It is a horrible sensation and I know instinctively that I have to pull over for a moment.

'Moll?' Joss says. 'You still there?'

I swing on to the hard shoulder and lurch to a stop, my head thudding back lightly on the headrest. I can hear my own breathing.

'Molly! Talk to me!'

'I think I'm going to hurl, hang on a minute!'

Joss pauses. We sit there in silence, me on the road, her

140

somewhere in London. 'Is that the morning–after pill, d'you reckon?' she says. 'Bec would know.'

I ignore that. 'I didn't eat breakfast and I'm very tightly wound up. That's all.'

'You haven't actually *been* sick, because the last thing you want is . . .'

'I know,' I cut her off quickly, before she can finish that sentence. 'Trust me, I know.'

Eventually I find the dreary, anonymous roadside hotel and get out of the car. It's a thick, cold, nothing sort of day which can't really be bothered to get properly light. Everything feels leaden, even the seagull wheeling above my head is squawking lethargically like it might just fall out of the sky.

When I finally make it to the meeting room I see I'm the last to arrive. There is an empty seat between Pearce and Sandra, the only one left, so I walk round and slide into it as quietly as I can while apologising to Antony, whose flow I have broken. 'Sorry, I got stuck in traffic.'

'No problem,' he replies smoothly. 'We haven't started the debrief yet.'

Everyone waits as I place my bag down quietly, trying to avoid any further interruptions, but the bloody thing falls over and disgorges its contents on to the slightly sticky carpet. Pearce silently leans to the side, retrieves my phone and wordlessly passes it to me. I take it and our fingers touch briefly. Sandra's eyebrow shoots up obsessively, right into her blonde hairline, and she crosses

141

her arms. So that's how she and Pearce are now. That conference has got a lot to answer for.

I put my mobile in my lap for a moment while I try to scoop everything else up off the floor without causing a fuss, but unfortunately, a tinkly girly sound – which sounds like it's coming from my crotch – announces the arrival of a text message. Antony sighs pointedly.

'Sorry.' I try to get myself together and hurriedly grab the phone. 'I'm, er, waiting on an important feedback call from a GP who is about to place a large order. That's his answerphone message buzzing in I expect.' I make a show of inspecting the screen in a businesslike fashion, but stupidly open the text menu. Sandra is there like a flash. 'No, it's a text,' she cranes over my shoulder. 'Subject matter "You've not been away from my mind . . ."' she reads out loud. 'Ahhhh!' Her beautiful face contorts into a nasty smile. 'How sweet.'

'Who says that *wasn't* the GP?' Pearce jokes and everyone laughs, except me, because I know exactly who the text is from and I need to read the rest of it, but now I can't. 'Molly has them all eating out of her hand.' Sandra looks incredibly pissed off that Pearce has stood up for me in public, pursing her blow-job gob into a sulky pout.

'Yes, well let's just turn our phones off shall we?' Antony says crisply, like the school teacher who is perfectly capable of losing it, but hasn't quite hit the irritation level required yet.

Sandra hasn't given up though and tries a different line

of attack. 'I expect that's hubby checking up on you, isn't it? Are you feeling better now, Molly? You've been really poorly, haven't you? Ill *all yesterday*.' She flicks her long blonde hair back and fakes a look of concern. Everyone shifts awkwardly in their seats. Its tantamount to actually saying, 'So did you get so wasted on Wednesday night you couldn't be arsed to drag yourself out of the hotel bed?'

Antony turns to me in surprise.

'Did you manage to get to the doctor's?' Sandra asks innocently, and takes a sip of her tea.

'Yes, I did,' I say, keeping my voice steady. 'It's always sensible to get checked out after a car accident, and what with spending all afternoon in the doctor's waiting room it was just like being at work really.' Why did she have to do that? I'm no threat to her. And while it's a relief to have such a convincing excuse, its not so great to have to remind everyone I bashed up my company car the day before yesterday. She's such a bitch.

Antony looks at me worriedly. 'Right, well, if you're quite finished, Sandra? You know you might think about directing some of that concern and energy towards improving your rather low call-back rate.'

That wipes the satisfied look off her face and he launches into the conference debrief and then the territory reports. When we finally arrive at lunch, Sandra and I are the only ones still alert; me because of the text I'm dreading reading, and Sandra because she's been angrily simmering in her seat waiting for her big moment. Sure enough, she snatches her bag up dramatically and makes a show of flouncing out in a huff.

Pearce sighs and grabs his stuff. 'You OK?' he says hurriedly, to me.

I nod and he looks relieved. 'Sorry about her,' he mutters, 'I'll sort it,' and like the White Rabbit, hastily disappears after Sandra.

Antony, who has watched the little episode keenly, clears his throat. 'Molly,' he calls out. 'Can I grab a quick word?'

We wait until everyone else has drifted out of the room, staring at us curiously, trying to work out if I'm about to get a bollocking or not.

'Everything Jim Dandy?' Antony says once we are alone, half sat on the table, half off. 'Nothing I should know about?'

I shake my head.

'Look, I couldn't give a monkey's about your car mishap or you missing yesterday, as long as you're all right – but Sandra did have a point. It's not like you to be off sick full stop, and you were a bit dicky earlier this week too. Obviously, from an HR perspective, I'm not supposed to ask you if there's something I should know . . . but we've worked together so long now that if there were anything that might have a nine-month lead time . . .' He looks gloomily and pointedly at my stomach. 'I'd appreciate the nod. I suppose it's going to have to happen sooner rather than later.'

'I'm not pregnant,' I say uncomfortably. 'If that's what you mean.'

He looks very relieved. 'Thank Christ for that. My budget can't cope with any more maternity cover. Sorry, I put two and two together and . . .'

I say nothing. I like Antony a lot, he's a nice bloke and a good boss, but I just want to leave. Never in all my life have I had the level of interest in my reproductive potential as I have this week. He looks embarrassed now too.

'I hope I haven't overstepped the mark.'

We both know he has, massively.

'It's just we value you, *I* value you. So sue me for caring eh?' Antony laughs then says uneasily, 'Don't though. Please. You make us more money than most of them put together, Moll.'

'Antony, there's no problem. Honestly.' I reach for my bag. I really have to go and read that text.

'I could sack Sandra to fund a salary rise?' Antony jokes inappropriately, although that *is* a tempting offer. 'I take it her little outburst means she and Pearce are, you know,' he looks at me for confirmation and I just shrug, but don't deny it.

'Oh great,' he sighs. 'Should I say something to them, do you think?' He looks at me anxiously. 'Her particularly. I can't have her savaging every female staff member who so much as says hello to Pearce, if this is going to be an ongoing thing.'

'Ignore it and maybe it will just go away.'

He nods thoughtfully and then looks cheered. 'You're probably right. Thank goodness for you Molly.'

Walking smartly out to the car park, having switched my BlackBerry back on, it begins to update and there is the message. I take a deep breath and open it.

You've not been away from my mind, I swear. I wanted to call yesterday but Helen around literally all day, couldn't even text. Am so, so sorry. Did you go to the doctor's? Sorted? Are you OK? Can you talk? Xxx

No, I'm not, I'm not OK at all, but I definitely don't want to talk to you.

Then in amongst some random work emails a Facebook notification appears.

A message from Leo Williams, sent about an hour ago. Oh God . . .

Well Molls, I don't think grand reunions of passion are meant to be quite like that are they?! It occurred to me that perhaps email is a better way to get hold of each other than mobiles going off and prompting questions? We need to chat though, don't we? Let me know a time that works for you and I will do my absolute best to call.

```
I promise you are what is important, I just
don't want anyone else caught and hurt in
crossfire xxx
```

Grand reunions of passion? A seagull cries mournfully over my head before it wheels off in search of scraps. He's got to be joking. I just lean back heavily on my closed car door. I delete the email and then get into the driver's side and sit there quietly. I need to think.

Why does he keep going on about needing to talk to me? What more is there to say? I would have thought he'd want to forget what happened as much as I do. After all, he's clearly terrified Helen is going to find out . . . and that's several times that he's asked me now if I've been to the doctor's . . .

Oh – I get it . . . *that's* what all this interest and concern is really about; he's making sure this isn't going to come back and bite him in nine months' time; or even sooner. He's probably wetting himself. If I reassure him it's all dealt with – all over – I bet he'll not be able to vanish fast enough.

```
Been to doctor's. Am fine. Best we leave
past in the past now.
```

There. Done. I should never have disturbed it in the first place.

Back at home, Dan is incredibly cheery. It's as if his happiness from last night, when I said I wanted to have a baby, has spilled over and simply washed everything away. As if all the painful words we said to each other were only scrawled in sand. Everything feels clean and energised, ready for the new start, the new adventure.

He chatters away happily. 'So because it was a lunch meeting and they always order too much food for the clients there were two whole plates of it, just sitting there, outside the boardroom. So I walked past it a couple of times . . .'

'You scoped it out?' I laugh. I'm working on the basis that the more I force myself to joke like this the happier I WILL feel. Also, the familiarity of us laughing together as we have done many times before in the past is helping to make everything feel more normal again. 'Did you whistle carelessly in a "nothing to see here" sort of way?' I make a supreme effort to concentrate on his smile.

He chuckles. 'Yeah, pretty much. Anyway, it was still there half an hour later so I scoffed the lot and I still feel a bit sick. But I'll make some food for you anyway.' He stretches and yawns. 'What a day! You took the car into the garage this morning then?' he asks. 'I saw the hire one outside. When do we get ours back?'

'Monday.'

'Fair enough. So, what do you fancy then?' he wraps his arms round me.

'Apart from you, of course?'

'That goes without saying. For tea, I mean. Oh – I got some stuff for you today, by the way,' he becomes almost shy. 'Want to see?'

'Yeah,' I nod, my heart swelling as he happily jumps from the sofa and fetches a small plastic bag. He sits back down, pulls out a big jar of vitamins and rattles them before passing it to me and reaching into the bag again. 'And some folic acid,' he passes me another jar. 'I don't know what it's for and it sounds horrible, but apparently it's good to take if you're, er, trying for a baby.' I take it from him. 'And finally,' he looks a bit uncertain as he pulls out a pregnancy test, 'ta da! Obviously this is for *a lot* further down the line.'

I put the jars in my lap and take the test from him.

'Too much?' he says worriedly. 'I really don't want to freak you out, I know this is such a new thing and—'

I stare at it and then look up at him with a dazzling smile on my face. 'You're not freaking me out,' I insist. 'This is all good.' I take a deep breath. 'Really good. In fact I'll take one of these vitamin thingys with the cup of tea you're about to make me.'

He looks delighted and gathers the jars up. 'I'll put this little lot upstairs in the bathroom drawer, shall I?' he says.

'Please,' I say faintly.

'You've gone a bit pale,' he says in concern. 'You OK?'

'Absolutely,' I say. 'Just a long day. I feel a bit tired and achey actually, but I'll be fine. A biscuit with that tea might help.'

He chuckles, kisses me and gets up. 'I think I can manage that. So how was the regional debrief today?' he calls over his shoulder conversationally as he walks to the kitchen. 'Exciting as ever?'

'It was fine.' My BlackBerry bleeps with a text. I pick it up absently but then the expression falls from my face. Leo again. I know his number now.

```
Sorry - been in meetings. 'Best we leave
past in the past now' What? Check your
email and call me when you have! X
```

Shit. Does he mean the one I read earlier? Has he sent another since then?

As if on cue, my phone buzzes with the arrival of a new email.

```
Leo Williams sent you a message on Facebook
...
```

```
Babe, I just got your text? I understand
why you're pissed off, I really do. I can
quite see how my taking off from the hotel
opened old wounds, but I don't want to
leave the past, in the past, Molly. OK, so
the night before last was in some ways,
not the best, but in others, amazing. When
can I see you again? Call me/text me/email.
I'll wait to hear from you. Best times for
me are evening and first thing in morning
as Helen usually tied up with her kids
then. Probably best to delete this once
you've read it xxx
```

The expression just falls away from my face. When can he see me again? He seriously thinks this has restarted something? Oh no, no, no, no . . . And 'best delete this once you've read it?' You bet I'm deleting it!

My head begins to throb, in an all too familiar way, like a distant war drum beating ominously . . . I'm getting another migraine.

'I think I'm going to have to go upstairs—' I say as Dan comes back in.

'Oh really?' he replies suggestively.

'—because I'm getting a migraine.'

'Oh I see,' he looks disappointed. 'Never mind. Two in one week though – that sucks. Do you want one of the vitamins before you go up?' He reaches out for the jars and starts to peel off the tight plastic casing, concentrating so much he doesn't notice that I've gone completely mute. Something else has just occurred to me.

If Dan and I are going to start trying for a baby, how on earth am I going to explain needing to use a condom for the next seven days, until I've had the STD tests done?

'Jesus, it's like getting into Fort Knox,' Dan says, attempting to unscrew the tight jar.

We can't NOT use one – there's no way I'm putting him at any risk and moreover, if he gets something he'll know he caught it from me . . . and how would I explain *that*? For the first time ever, as I try not to panic, I am beyond grateful for my migraines, at least I have a cast-iron excuse for tonight.

But it's not going to last for a week is it? What am I going to do tomorrow, and the day after that? This is horrific . . .

I'll have to say I've come on, I'm due any day as it is. But I'm always a little irregular, what if I don't *actually* come on until Tuesday or Wednesday of next week? No one gets a period that lasts that long, except maybe an elephant.

The security plastic finally gives way with a crack and Dan says 'Aha!' triumphantly as he pulls the lid off and removes the small bit of foam from within the jar, tossing it aside. He tips a horse–pill–sized tablet into the palm of his hand and passes it to me. Sniffing it curiously – it smells of metal shavings and burnt grass – I almost gag and look at him worriedly. 'I'm not sure I can take this right now.'

His face falls. 'You're having second thoughts?' He looks so gutted that I can't bear it. I push the pill in my mouth and take a sip of hot tea – a mistake. I should have used water, the pill tastes even worse than it smells. I swallow painfully, but smile at him determinedly. 'Nope, of course not. Come on; folic acid, please.'

My mobile, lying next to me on the sofa, starts to vibrate. Terrified, I grab for it – if it's Leo again . . . but Dan gets there first. 'Your dad's ringing.'

Thank God it's only him. 'I'll talk to him later,' I say as I swallow the next pill. 'I'm going to go upstairs now.'

'Sure,' he reaches for the remote. 'I'll try and keep it down.' The bashing in my brain is getting louder.

Upstairs, sitting on the edge of our bed, I have to squint to glance at the mobile screen while I still can. Dad has left me an answerphone message and I've also got another separate, new text that arrived while I was walking upstairs.

Meet me tomorrow. Urgent. x

## Chapter Thirteen

'I'm not even sorry, so don't bother getting uppity,' Joss says defiantly, sitting back on her chair and crossing her legs.

'I thought you meant something urgent was up with you,' I look at her wearily.

'It is. One of my best friends has gone crazy.'

'Joss, I had a migraine last night, I could have done with staying in bed this morning, I feel shattered.'

'Can someone explain to me what's going on?' Bec, understandably mystified, looks between Joss and I, who are glowering at each other across the slightly grubby Starbucks table. The place is full of Saturday Christmas shoppers, and a lot of UGG-clad teenage girls screeching 'OHMIGOD! *Look* at this!' as they wave iPhones about.

Joss deliberately says nothing, just raises her eyebrows

pointedly, waits for me to speak and sucks on the straw in her iced coffee, not an awful lot unlike the girls at the next table. It's sometimes quite hard to remember that she is directly responsible for the finance team of a respectable blue-chip company.

'Dan and I have decided to start trying for a baby.'

'But that's great!' Bec looks confused. 'Am I missing something? What's the problem?'

Joss grits her teeth. She puts down her drink and eyes me unflinchingly, sending me a look that says, 'Tell her about Leo. Now.'

I stay quiet.

'Well, *I* think,' Joss says, 'that's a really big decision, one that you wouldn't want to make if you were, let's say, emotionally stressed out.'

'It's not like Dan and Molly haven't talked it through . . . and sometimes we make our biggest and bravest decisions when we're under the most pressure,' Bec suggests. 'And they turn out to be the best ones of all.'

'What?' Joss wrinkles her nose and gives her a look. 'Bec, this is going to affect the rest of her life.'

'Yes,' Bec says patiently. 'It is. And?'

'And so how about she thinks about it properly?' Joss explodes. 'Rather than just . . . doing it!'

'Joss, *most* women don't have anything more than a vague idea that having kids is the right thing to do.' Bec says. 'They just take the plunge – and it works, honestly it does. I've yet to meet a woman who regretted having her children.'

Joss says nothing, just kicks her chair back and marches off to the toilets crossly.

Bec watches her, troubled. 'She's absolutely entitled to not want them herself, but she can't go around trying to influence other people that she's right and they're wrong. That's not on.'

I wriggle awkwardly in my chair. Leaning over my mug of hot chocolate that has so much cream on it the chocolate underneath is now lukewarm, I spoon a bit off and wonder if I *should* come clean about Leo. But I just don't want to. I want to pretend it never happened. Some things are allowed to stay private mistakes surely? Even from the closest of friends.

'Anyway, *I'm* really happy for you Moll,' Bec grins. She stands up and gives me a warm and very genuine hug. 'You'll just have to tell me to back off if I get all in your face with tips and stuff once you get pregnant.' Then something occurs to her and she looks a bit alarmed. 'Please don't ask me to be your midwife though – that'd be weird.'

'I won't,' I smile.

'Phew.' She looks relieved, sits back down and takes another sip of her coffee. 'While we've got a minute on our own, can I ask you something?' Taken aback by the seriousness of her tone, I nod warily.

'I've been looking at this internet dating site. The idea is you nominate a single friend that you think is great, *you* describe them in their profile and then other people can contact them if they're interested, and I just

157

wondered,' she looks a bit embarrassed. 'Will you describe me?'

'Of course,' I say instantly. 'I'd love to!'

'Thanks,' she says gratefully. 'Here's the website,' she reaches into her bag, pulls out a pen, scribbles on a bit of paper and slides it over to me. I tuck it in my jeans pocket. 'I've finally realised I'm never going to meet anyone at work . . . not who hasn't got a pregnant wife in tow, or isn't a doctor – and I'm certainly not going down *that* route again. I don't want you to think I'm desperate for a bloke though. I'm not. I just thought it might be nice to – you know – expand my social circle a bit. That's all right, isn't it?'

'Of course it is, but,' I hesitate, thinking about the trouble the internet has landed me in over the last few days, 'it is safe, isn't it?'

She nods earnestly. 'Very. There are lots of safety tips on there. Can we keep this just between us, though?'

'Of course.'

We fall quiet as Joss comes back and sits down. No one says anything for a minute.

'So what's Dan up to today, Moll?' Bec gamely tries to restart conversation.

'Gone to watch some football with Ed.'

'Ed, as in his best man Ed?' Bec asks, and looks at Joss teasingly, but she's misjudged the moment.

'Jesus Bec, that was flipping years ago,' she says crossly. 'It was one snog for crying out loud – it's what you do at weddings – and it wasn't even a good one. He had a chin like a bum.'

'I just wonder what might have happened if you'd have let him take you out like he wanted to,' Bec muses. 'He might have surprised you.'

'What, and also had a bum like a chin?'

'Fine,' Bec sighs and turns back to me.

'He's married now anyway.' I reach for my coffee. 'Had a whirlwind romance, they've got a baby on the way now too.'

'Bully for him and Mrs Bum Chin,' Joss says shortly. 'I couldn't care less.'

'Well anyway Moll, I'm really pleased you and Dan are back on track now.' Bec decides to ignore Joss. 'I didn't like it when you two were all stressed out, it's like my mum and dad having a row. Worse actually, because I like both of you. I know it sounds a bit soppy,' she gives an embarrassed shrug, 'but you two are sort of my relationship benchmark.'

Not even Joss has the heart to take the piss at that. Bec's bleeper goes off in the silence, breaking the moment. 'Ohhhhh,' she groans. 'What now? I've just come off nights. Leave me alone! Hang on girls, I'll be right back.' She picks up her bag and walks out of the coffee shop, digging around for her phone. Joss and I watch her begin to talk animatedly on her mobile through the window.

'Remember, you're not *actually* her parents,' Joss says eventually. 'And you're only human, benchmark or not.'

'Why are you so cross with me?' I say. 'I didn't do all of this to piss you off.'

She sighs. 'I'm not pissed off, I'm worried about you.

I just don't want to see you make a decision in haste that you might repent at leisure, as my grandmother would say, if she weren't dead.'

'Honestly Joss, this is what I want.'

She just sighs again.

I'd actually really like to tell her about Leo emailing and texting yesterday, his suggestion that we meet again, but she's only just calmed down. I don't want her to get all cross and riled up – I worry about her blood pressure at the best of times given that she has a considerably more demanding job than me, and mine is stressful enough. Anyway, I suppose it's not like I don't know what to do. I'm going to ignore him, and if he contacts me again, I'll just spell it out for him.

'It would be much easier to keep quiet and not tell you what I really think,' Joss says suddenly, to my surprise. 'And Bec's wrong. I'm pretty sure if you asked my mum, she'd tell you that actually she *does* regret having had children – and I'm not saying that for the sympathy—' she holds up a hand as I open my mouth, '—I'm just telling you the truth. I'm also not saying that I'm worried that Dan's going to find out what happened between you and fuckhead and leave you in the lurch. Even if that did happen – which it won't,' she says quickly, catching sight of my face, 'you'd cope. I hate to bring her up again, but even my mum managed – twice – and second time round she had the twins, remember?' she says, referring to her half-sisters.

'Joss—' I begin.

'Hang on, let me finish. My saying all this hasn't got anything to do with selfish motivations on my part either; just because I don't want kids doesn't mean I won't be one hundred per cent behind your decision to have a baby now, if you're sure it's what you really want.' She sits up with energy. 'I just want you to know, this whole baby thing is a *choice* you're making. You don't just have to do it, OK? Not if you don't want to. Have you even asked yourself if you want children full stop? Do you not think there could be a reason why you've been putting off having kids? Because I'm not so sure that you—'

'I know this is a choice Joss.'

'But do you, really?' she looks at me seriously. 'As long as you're happy I'm happy, but there's one person you can't lie to Moll, and that's yourself.'

I'm thinking about what she said, and sort of wishing that she hadn't actually, as I get back into the car and my phone rings. To my complete horror, Leo's number flashes up. This time, he's actually calling me.

I pick up.

'Is now a good time?' he says straightaway, without even waiting for me to say hello.

'What are you playing at ringing me like this?' I say instantly. 'Suppose Dan had been with me?'

'Fair point,' he exhales. 'But – you got my email last night, right?'

'Yes I did.'

'So why haven't you mailed me back, or texted me?'

161

'I didn't want to.'

'What?' He can't keep the note of surprise from his voice. There's a pause. 'Moll, sweetheart, I can't *keep* saying sorry for buggering off. I'm here for you now though – one hundred per cent.'

Incredulously, I pull the phone away from my ear and stare at it. 'Leo, I was very drunk. I know I kissed you and I know we . . .' I trail off awkwardly but then become determined again. 'The thing is, none of it should have happened. I don't even remember most of the night.'

'Yes, I gathered that,' he says icily. 'Flattering – naturally, but I know you felt something when we were sat in the bar. You can't tell me you didn't.'

'We're both married! I can't speak for you and Helen, but Dan and I – we're happy. I don't want anything else.'

'OK,' he says quickly. 'I get that this has really upset things, I understand. But you can't pretend that there isn't something still there, Molly. There is. We both know it.' He lets the words linger. 'I have to see you again. Come and meet me now. I know it might be difficult to get away but please come. We'll talk this through.'

'Meet you now?' That completely throws me. 'What are you talking about?'

'I'm in Brighton.'

What? My eyes widen and I look around me nervously, as if I half-expect him to leap out from in between the parked cars, which is just ridiculous. 'Leo, I can't.'

'You can!' he interjects eagerly. 'I'm not asking for

162

promises, I have no expectations, I just want to talk to you, that's all.'

'I'm not meeting you! I'm not even in Brighton!' I add quickly.

There's another long pause.

'Oh?' he says sharply. 'Where are you then?'

'At a friend's in London, for lunch.' I lie.

'Well . . . that's bad luck isn't it?' he says tightly. 'You all the way up there when I've come down here.'

'But Leo, I never *asked* you to do that!' I burst. 'I wouldn't have come anyway, even if I had been here – there,' I correct myself quickly. 'I've got a husband. You've got a wife. We made a huge mistake! It should never have happened.'

'Well it has,' he says quietly. 'It has happened, and I *have* to see you again Molly, there's something very important I need to tell you.'

'What do you mean?' I'm instantly suspicious. 'Important in what way?'

'I can't do it over the phone,' he says softly. 'It wouldn't be fair. Something I told you on Wednesday which, trust me, you very clearly don't remember.'

'A bad something?'

'You need to come and meet me. I can wait until you're . . .' he gives a short sharp exhalation, 'back from London.'

'Just tell me now.' Oh my God – has he got Aids or something? 'Is it something I *need* to know? Are you ill?'

'Would you care if I was?' His voice takes on an incongruous teasing tone, which draws me up short.

'There isn't anything is there?' I say slowly.

'There is,' he insists, serious again. 'And I have to tell you in person.'

'I don't believe you.'

'No! Molly, I swear—'

'Goodbye Leo.'

I hang up, get into the car, and begin to drive home.

## Chapter Fourteen

But fuck it all to hell, just as he intended, I'm still thinking about him – what it could be that he has to tell me – when I get back home, roaring on to the drive and stopping the car with a jerk before getting out and slamming back into the empty house.

I'd forgotten this about him. How good he is at twisting things. For example, ask Leo outright if there is something going on between him and the new girl at work, Cara, who he keeps mentioning, and he'll laugh and say of course not. He'll say that she's just lonely having moved down from Cambridge, she misses her boyfriend back at home . . . Honestly – can't someone just be nice to a new colleague without getting it in the neck?

He hasn't got anything to tell me; he's bluffing. He just

wants me to go and meet him, that's all, so he can start wearing me down.

Marching into the kitchen, I yank a kitchen cupboard door open and grab a mug. Having filled the kettle, I lean against the side as I wait for it to boil.

Something he should have told me a long time ago? Something he told me on Wednesday?

He forgets that four years is a *long* time to be with someone. If it was something that vital, that important, I'd already know about it.

I cross to the fridge and get the milk out.

Why is he even doing this at all? I'm not naïve enough to believe that people who were together and separated for very good reasons, then meet up again and it's as if the intervening years never happened. That's bullshit. I'm *not* the person I was when he first met me, and on Wednesday I was so drunk I don't even remember most of the night. There's nothing romantic about that, it's just vile. He's clearly not as happy with Helen as he made out, but whatever it is that's making him think *we* should start something up again – boredom, him convincing himself he feels something again for me, or simply that he thinks he sees a chance for easy extra-marital sex – he can forget it.

To think I believed him. I actually believed he just came to see me because he was worried about me . . . *He* hasn't changed at all. How stupid would I have to be to want to revisit that ground, even supposing I wasn't happily married – which I am.

I pour the milk into the cup, but overshoot and it spills on the side. Gritting my teeth I grab for the cloth, wipe it up swiftly and throw the cloth in the sink. The bubbling hot water in the kettle grows louder until it switches itself off with a click. Something important to tell me . . . yeah, right. Important would be . . . discovering he was adopted at birth, tracing his biological family and realising Dan is his long-lost brother, which I *seriously* doubt is the case. Or perhaps a confession that he robbed a bank while we were together, and hidden in a locket he gave me is a key to hundreds of stashed millions.

And as for him having some sort of illness, something that he could have passed on, but chose to keep quiet about? I don't buy that either. Leo is many things, but he wouldn't do that to me.

I put the kettle back down and reach for a spoon. Although of course that would be the ultimate irony, all this stalling having a baby and it turns out I actually can't have one anyway, because Leo's given me chlamydia or something and made me infertile.

I pause for a moment. That wouldn't be it, the real reason why he came to the hotel on Wednesday? Surely.

I almost reach for the phone to call him—

No! That's exactly what he wants me to do! Even if I do have something, I'm getting tests done on Thursday. I'll find out then, there's no need to ring him. No need at all.

Resolve hardened, I grab my tea, break a bit off the gingerbread man I brought back for Dan from Starbucks and make my way upstairs to my office. I'm going to block Leo on Facebook, so at least he can't email me again.

It's actually easy to sort, even for someone like me who may spend a lot of their time on computers, but is not exactly technologically gifted. Thank God Dan told me not to put my email address on my profile and made me protect it from the outset. After a moment or two of tinkering, all that shows on my settings is that I've blocked Leo Williams, and if Dan were to see that – which he wouldn't anyway; he's never even shown so much as an interest in what Leo looks like – what problem would he have with me blocking an ex? None.

Anyway, Leo now won't be able to email me. Good. I'm surprised by quite how relieved that makes me feel. Next, I go through my phone and delete all of my call lists and texts, just to be on the safe side, although Dan would never dream of looking through my phone, because he trusts me implicitly.

The stab of realising how horribly I've abused that trust makes me feel so bitterly sad, I need something else to concentrate on quickly. Remembering Bec's website address in my pocket, I fumble for the piece of paper with trembling hands; trying to pretend I don't have Leo's fingerprints all over me and that I still have a right to Dan's trust – that I haven't somehow stolen from the person I love most in the world.

The dating website does actually seem fine, with some pictures of normal-looking men and women scrolling along the bottom of it. I click on a couple of blokes I could see Bec with and from reading their summary information, and what their friends have said about them, I can understand why Bec thinks she'd like to sign up. So . . . I click 'add a single friend' and start to fill in the details.

Bec is . . . thirty-three, straight, no kids, but yes definitely wants them, she's a midwife, lives in Brighton, Christian, not practising. Height . . . hmmm. Average I guess. Build? Better put slender.

Right, 'choose the attributes that best describe your friend' . . . Enthusiastic about life, a hopeless romantic and . . . pretty sexy. Perfect.

Oh – I have to add a picture of her. She didn't tell me that.

It takes a little while, but I get there eventually and move on to the limited number of characters I have to describe her.

It turns out to be the hardest bit. What I want to say is:

*Imagine you're with someone for seven years who finally decides although you're his 'best friend' he doesn't, after all, want to marry you. He then gets engaged to some random girl six months later – who your best friends assured you was just the rebound fling – and moves to Canada. He then also has a baby (which is what you want more than anything), rather than the decency to get eaten by a bear. The very least he could have done is fall off a mountain bike and break both his legs.*

*Because you're a midwife, you don't get to meet many blokes through work, except the odd random doctor; one of whom you risked dating only to discover he sucked his thumb at night. That was enough to almost tip you over the edge completely.*

*Well, this is one of my best friends, Bec; she's the loveliest, kindest, most open-hearted person you will ever meet, and the person she falls in love with is going to be the luckiest man in the world. I have to warn you though, if you're stupid enough to ever hurt her, I will hunt you down and kill you. Or worse still, I'll send Joss round.*

Hmm. Perhaps not. Threats are probably not the way forward. I sweat over it for the next forty-odd minutes, because I really want to get it right for her, and when I'm finally satisfied, I upload it, just as I hear the front door go downstairs.

'Moll?' Dan shouts.

'I'm up here!' I call and moments later he appears in the doorway, which is when I remember Bec asked me not to tell anyone about the dating site. Hastily, I pull down the screen of my laptop.

'Hello,' he says and crosses over to the desk to give me a kiss.

'Did you have a good time?' I tilt my face up to him.

'Not bad,' he kisses me. 'What are you doing? Working?'

'Yup – just finished,' I say quickly and shut the lid completely. 'Want a cup of tea?'

'Yes please.' He follows me back downstairs. 'How about you? Did you have a nice coffee with the girls?'

'Yeah, I bought you something back actually,' I say and hand over the small paper bag containing the ginger-bread man.

170

'Thanks,' he says, pleased. 'Oh, what happened to his legs?' he peers into the bag.

'They fell off.'

'In your mouth?' he smiles at me. 'Never mind.' He takes a bite. 'So, what was up with Joss then?' he asks through a mouthful. 'What was the crisis?'

'Um, a work thing,' I mumble vaguely.

'What sort of work thing? Is she OK?'

'Yeah, fine.'

My phone starts to ring upstairs. Damn, I forgot to switch it off; what if it's Leo? I make to hurry upstairs but Dan catches my arm.

'Just leave it,' he says, not unreasonably. 'I want to spend some time with you now. They'll leave a message if it's important.'

That's what I'm afraid of.

It's usually one of my favourite things in the world, cosily snuggling up on the sofa with Dan having a cup of tea and a hug, but I can't relax for being terrified about who that might have been calling me.

'How many times? *Stop chewing your nails*,' Dan says, stroking my shoulder.

I pull my finger from my mouth instantly, I wasn't aware I had been.

'You'll have nothing but stumpy nubbins left. Did you not have lunch?'

'I've snagged one of them on my jumper,' I fib. 'I'll just nip upstairs and get a file.'

But when I *do* sneak into my office and check my

phone, it's actually only a rather cross message from Mum asking me please to ring and let them know I am OK. Oh, and am I still coming to Sunday lunch?

I told her on Thursday, didn't I? I text back a yes. On the upside, I have no other texts at all and no missed calls, which is a relief. As is discovering in the loo moments later that I've come on. *Thank God.* Not only do I have a bona fide excuse not to have sex until after my tests, FAR more importantly, the morning-after pill has worked.

Things are looking up . . . assuming I don't have herpes of course.

But as I pass the study on my way back downstairs, I notice my BlackBerry is flashing with a new message. Mum has obviously remembered something else.

But it's not her.

```
What we felt when we saw each other again
was REAL. I know I didn't imagine it. I'm
not giving up on you. Just so you know x
```

## Chapter Fifteen

'You not bringing your phone?' Dan nods at it on the side, as we're about to leave the house.

I glance over – I've kept it switched off since last night – and shake my head.

He looks slightly surprised, as well he might given that I'm usually surgically attached to it. 'I just want a day off,' I explain and he nods understandingly.

'Fair enough.' He holds out a hand. 'Come on then.'

In the car on the way over to my parents' we listen to music in comfortable silence. Well, Dan does. I'm trying not to think about Leo. The only thing I felt when I saw him again at the hotel was surprised confusion. OK, I admit we had a very slightly – on my part alcohol-charged – flirty conversation. I can't deny I always used to enjoy talking to Leo, I did, it was one of the things I found most attractive about him. But our conversation certainly didn't carry the emotional weight he's given it, it was just one of those flirts you have safe in the knowledge you are in a relationship with someone else. Maybe that's the point though, maybe you can *never* flirt like that with an ex, because it's just all too loaded. I don't feel anything for Leo now, except a very real and very strong desire for him to *go away*. I cannot believe what we did. How easily it happened. It's terrifying.

'Here we are!' Dan says as we tuck on to my parents' drive behind both of my brothers' cars.

'You managed to find some room then? Hello, love,' Dad kisses me when he opens the front door. 'Why have you got a hire car?'

'I had a slight mishap,' I say as I walk past him.

'Oh dear,' he pulls a face. 'I shan't ask any more. Dan, get yourself inside, it's arctic out here.' He reaches out and puts a kind hand on Dan's shoulder, guiding him in as he simultaneously hoofs the overexcited dogs out of the way with his foot. 'We just tried to call you actually, Molly – bread sauce emergency – but your phone was off.'

'I've left it at home.' I unbutton my coat. 'I'm having the day off.'

'Very sensible. If you make yourself permanently available people will only ask you to do things. Now, what would you both like to drink?' He starts to walk up the hall to the kitchen, the dogs trotting happily after him.

As we approach the kitchen a general ruckus grows

174

louder – a crashing of saucepans, Karen asking 'Meg – shall I do all of this broccoli?' my brothers laughing and a small voice eagerly saying 'Daddy, look what I've made! Daddy, look!'

'Hi!' I give everyone a wave as I walk in to a chorus of hellos, stepping over my youngest nephew Harry so I can give Mum a kiss.

'Hello you bad girl,' she kisses me back, wipes her hands on her apron and moves over to the vegetable rack. 'Not picking up your phone on purpose. Hello, Dan! How are you?'

'Very well thanks, Meg. You?'

'Lovely, thanks,' she says cheerfully. 'Had a good week?'

'Not bad, not bad.'

'Good,' she bends down and begins to rummage around amongst some potatoes and onions.

'So what's new with you then, little sis?' my oldest brother Chris says, from his usual position on the sofa absently reading the paper.

'Absolutely nothing at all,' I say carefully, spying Lily's hair-tie on the floor and picking it up before it gets lost.

'Except we're officially trying for a baby!' Dan says eagerly.

I spring up like some reverse jack trying to climb back *into* the box, and spin to face him, aghast. Everyone shuts up completely, even the kids. I can practically hear a drop of condensation run down the steamy kitchen window over the sink.

'Well, not quite yet we haven't,' Dan corrects himself

and I close my eyes. 'But we will be. Which is – very exciting.' He trails off.

Mum, usually adept at dealing with awkward situations, has frozen in the middle of the room, holding a large cabbage in one hand and a bag of carrots in the other. Stuart stares fiercely at Dan, a little like I imagine a middle-aged male gorilla would do if a younger upstart burst into the enclosure poised to crazily start chucking bananas around everywhere, while Maria focuses carefully on a spot on the floor. Chris lowers his paper slowly, wary of moving too fast in case he triggers an accidental stampede. He gives Karen an incredulous look of 'Did he actually just say that?'

Only Dad continues like nothing has happened. 'Well that's great news, Dan,' he says kindly. 'So who's driving?' he sticks his head back round the fridge. 'You then I'm guessing, Molly?'

I nod as Dan clears his throat awkwardly, having realised he's shared a little too much.

'Okey-dokey, Diet Coke then?' Dad offers. 'Dan, red or white? We've got both on the go. Meg,' he nods at Mum, 'you've got a hole in the bottom of that carrot bag.'

Mum manages to somehow drag herself back on track. 'What? Oh well done, so I have. Karen, could I pass these to you? Will you? Thanks. The peeler's in the drawer, or the dishwasher – or somewhere,' she flusters. Only Lily is quietly minding her own business, taking advantage of the situation to scoop water from the dogs' bowls and surreptitiously force-feed one of them from the spout of a tiny plastic teapot.

176

'What time's lunch?' Dad continues calmly. 'Would it be acceptable to watch the kick-off before laying the table?' He doesn't wait for the answer. 'Anyone else want to join me?'

'I will Dad,' Stuart stands up quickly, tucking Harry under his gym-honed arm like a rugby ball. He doesn't look at Dan, just stomps past him, glaring at me en route to the living room instead, like it's somehow all my fault that he's been forced to acknowledge his little sister having sex.

'Me too,' says Chris – daddy-long-legs sensing an open window. 'Come on kids, let's get out of everyone's hair for a bit.'

Helpfully, the dogs – relieved to have a reason to escape Lily's impish hands – scramble up to follow suit and so the kids happily go trotting after them in turn. That just leaves the rest of us peeling the veg and pointlessly opening cupboards and the oven, while wracking our brains for something more socially appropriate to say.

'I might go and watch the rugby too,' Dan motions to the door, sensibly avoiding meeting my eye.

'I would,' Mum says quickly and he legs it.

Once they've all gone, Mum, Karen and Maria stop what they're doing and wait for me to say something.

'You know,' I try lightly, 'I think maybe I will have that glass of wine, after all.'

Over lunch things lighten up a little. During pudding, Oscar, who is sitting under the table happily playing with a car from the toy box, starts to sing something to himself.

'That's a nice song Os,' Chris remarks. 'What's it called?'

'It's for Christmas. I made it up. It's called "The Rat . . ."' Os pauses thoughtfully, and for dramatic effect, '". . . Is Dead."'

We all giggle and Karen shrugs, clueless, in a 'Don't ask me,' sort of way.

'Last week,' Chris confides, 'when I had to go to Paris overnight, I was on the Eurostar and these two blokes across the way were talking about how much they hated leaving for work in the morning, because their kids were all small tearful faces and 'Don't go Daddy, stay and play with me!' clinging on to their trouser legs as they were trying to get out of the door, that sort of thing. One of them was almost choking up. I was sitting there thinking 'Ahh, bless' – a bit patronising; smug older dad. Then when I got to the hotel I opened my case and someone,' he does an exaggerated motion in the direction of under the table, 'had done me a drawing. Of a daddy, a little boy with a sad face, and a big heart with a zig zag down the middle.'

'Oh!' My mother drops her fork and covers her mouth.

'I know,' Chris laughs. 'I bawled like a *baby*.'

A little voice pipes up. 'Are you talking about me, Daddy?'

Chris laughs again. 'Yes I am – trunky.' Then we hear a wail from the other room that announces Harry is no longer asleep.

'I'll go,' says Maria, standing up as Lily runs back into

the room. 'I didn't wake him up! I just touched his foot!' she insists innocently.

Dan grins at me and squeezes my hand under the table. It's a squeeze that says, 'This is going to be us!' He looks happy, really happy.

I grip his hand too and focus hard on his smile.

After lunch, Mum finally manages to pounce on me, like a wily old lioness who has been biding her time, once we're all hanging up damp tea towels and sloping off fatly to collapse in the sitting room. I realise I am the last of the pack to leave the kitchen as she grabs me firmly, hoicks me back in, and shuts the door.

'So?' she says, one hand on hip.

'What?' I shift uncomfortably, reminded of the period when she used to routinely nearly catch me having a crafty fag behind Dad's shed. I'd have just enough time to fling the cigarette over the fence into next door's garden, and fan the air desperately with the baggy sleeves of my enormous 80s jumper, while never being quite sure if she could still smell the smoke hanging in the air.

'Molly, come on.'

Who am I trying to kid? She can *always* smell the smoke in the air. The woman has the nose of a police sniffer dog. 'What's going on?'

My blood goes cold. 'What do you mean?'

'On Tuesday you were grumbling about feeling baby pressure and today Dan says you're—' she struggles for the right phrase, 'all guns blazing.'

'I don't know what you mean.'

'There's something you're not telling me,' she says, looking right at me. 'I know there is.'

I push the memory of me and Leo kissing – falling back on to the hotel bed – out of my head and hope to God Almighty her psychic mum powers don't extend to being actually able to read my mind.

'No, there isn't,' I lie defensively. I actually almost want to tell her. She's my mum, but that's exactly why I *can't*. I cannot tell my mother that, so drunk I didn't know what I was doing, I shagged Leo at a conference hotel in Windsor.

'I simply don't believe you. Something's changed. I can tell it has.'

'Yeah, me,' I say eventually, and start to pick at the edge of the tea towel. 'What I want has changed.'

'OK,' she says suddenly, 'so tell me what it was that you were wary about before, which isn't bothering you any more.'

My warning bells start to ring. I'm not falling for clever mum-psychology.

'It doesn't matter now,' I say defensively.

Before she can say anything else, the kitchen door opens and Dad comes in carrying an empty cup. 'Oscar knocked my tea over. Have you got a cloth? Karen's using the towel from the downstairs loo.' He looks between us. 'Everything all right?'

I suddenly find myself surprisingly near to tears. 'Can we please not do this? Can you just tell me you're happy for me? Whatever it is you're both thinking?'

Taken aback, they look worriedly at one another.

'It's not that we—' Mum begins, but Dad gently says 'Shhh,' and shakes his head lightly. She falls quiet and Dad puts his mug down, takes a step over towards me and wraps me in a big, comforting bear hug. He rocks me gently on the spot and kisses the top of my head, as if I am a little girl again. Then he releases me, picks up the J-cloth and ambles off into the other room without saying another word.

'I'm sorry. I didn't mean to upset you. As long as you're happy, I'm happy,' Mum says, then adds slowly, 'you are happy, aren't you Molly?'

'Yes,' I insist, 'I am.'

Which is true, because Dan is over the moon about having a baby – although I'll be having words with him later about his announcing it as a work in progress. But he's very happy – and that is all that matters.


That night, Bec calls to thank me for doing her online dating profile.

'Moll, it was really sweet! I nearly cried at all of the nice things you said. So how's your day been?'

'Not bad thanks. Listen, can I call you back? It's just I'm in the bath.'

'Oh! I've done it again! I'm so sorry! Multitasking eh?'

Something like that. Actually, I brought my phone into the safety of the locked bathroom so I could check my messages without the fear of Dan looking over my shoulder. But now I'm feeling a bit foolish for being so apparently over-cautious in keeping the phone switched off all day, because for all of his melodramatic 'I'm not giving up on you,' Leo has sent me nothing at all, and neither has he called me . . . I knew it. They were just words to him. Words he liked hearing himself say. Leo has always been the star in the movie of his own making.

Except as I'm towelling myself dry in our bedroom – once I've been lulled into a false sense of security – and Dan has walked in, that's when my phone goes off on the bed with a text; like it deliberately waited for him.

'Who's that?' he asks, climbing under the covers.

I peer at the screen, my heart having constricted to half its normal size, but then I relax. 'Pearce,' I tell him truthfully.

'Why's he texting you on a Sunday night?'

'He's read some negative stuff about MediComma in one of the Sunday papers,' I say, absently reading the text 'He was just letting me know.' I delete it.

'Oh, right.' Dan looks rather nonplussed. 'How's your tummy feeling? Still got period pains?'

'A bit,' I say, instinctively resting my hand on it. Which reminds me, I want to tell him that I'd rather not tell everyone we're trying. 'Listen, can I talk to you about what you said before lunch about us—' but before I can say anything else, my phone lights up again.

'I'm going to throw that bloody thing out of the window,' Dan says only half-joking. 'Is it Pearce again?'

'No,' I turn casually away from him so he can't see my face. 'It's just Joss. I'll turn it off now.' I stare intently at the screen.

`I'm thinking about you *right now*. Xxx`

## Chapter Sixteen

'I can't believe you barred my number from your phone,'
Leo says incredulously. 'Do you even know how that felt?
It was painful enough when I realised you'd blocked me
on Facebook. I don't understand . . . why are you doing
this?'

'I'm not doing anything!' I have to close my eyes for
a moment and swallow down my mounting frustration
as I stand on the wet street listening to him. I should
have known better than to answer a call on an unknown
number, but this is my work phone, I *have* to take calls
when they come in. 'You're doing this Leo, not me, YOU.
I just want you to leave me alone. Why can't you understand that?'

He ignores me. 'I'll buy a million more pay as you go

phones to get through to you, if that's what it takes. I'm not giving up on us.'

'What are you talking about?' I'm coming close to losing it. 'There *is* no us! You've got to stop this!'

'No. Not until you believe me. I can't stop thinking about you, I've realised that—'

'I don't have time for this Leo,' I cut across him. 'I'm late for an appointment. I have to go. Please, don't call me again. I mean it, OK?'

I hang up and with a shaking hand, slip the phone back in my bag and walk into the anonymous London clinic. He's just made an already horrible morning even worse. I'm already terrified I'm going to see someone I know here. In a lot of ways this is even worse than my trip to the doctor's. Although there's a similar sense of deep shame and embarrassment, it's the guilt that's killing me by inches. Dan left for work this morning cheerily telling me to have a good day; no idea that I was actually going to be about three trains behind him, not a clue that I would be spending my morning being tested for STD's.

Having given my name, I sit down nervously in the waiting room and turn my phone off. Leo actually bought a pay as you go phone because I had his number barred yesterday . . . I don't even know what to think about that.

On Monday while I was at the garage collecting the car, I received a text saying:

I dreamt about you last night. Xx

Tuesday morning brought:

Please, you have to let me at least tell
you what I have to say. This is important.
I'll go anywhere, anytime. Xx

Wednesday was an overused cliché that once might
have made me thrill all over, but now just made me
shudder:

I wish I had told you every day you were
mine how beautiful you are. Xx

Then an hour after that:

This is killing me. Is that what you want?
You want me to feel like this? Xx

I didn't want him to feel *anything* in relation to me at
all! That was the whole point! Each and every message
only reminded me of what I was trying to forget.

Then two hours after that came:

Am so stupid...you DO want me to feel
like this don't you? You need me to prove
that I mean what I say, that I do have
real, genuine feelings for you. You're afraid
of getting hurt again — that's why you
won't meet me, why you're doing this; well

```
I'll do whatever it takes to convince you.
I promise xx
```

He simply can't believe that I don't want him. But I don't and I have too much to lose to risk ignoring him until he gets bored and goes away. I want – need – him to stop. Which is why I had his number barred yesterday; for all the good it did me.

I run an agitated hand over my forehead, under my fingers are the lumps and bumps of a few greasy spots that have come up over the last few days, in spite of the very dry skin on my chin. I've had a much shorter than usual period and a patch of eczema is developing on the back of my left knee. . . . Maybe I should talk to IT support about changing my number completely?

'Cara Jones?' calls a nurse.

If I did that, is there anyone else he could get the new number from? I don't think there is.

'Cara Jones?' she calls again, a little louder.

Oh shit. That's me. *I'm* Cara Jones.

I grab my coat and stand up.

'Cara?' she repeats pointedly as she gives me a knowing – but not unkind – look that says 'It's a good idea to actually remember the false name you give.' 'Follow me please.'

It's all briskly efficient – the nurse runs through a list of frankly terrifying symptoms that I am very relieved to have none of, we briefly discuss the incident in question and then she tells me I can have an initial test for chlamydia and gonorrhoea, which will probably reveal the likelihood of other STDs being present anyway, or the whole shebang; HIV, syphilis and hepatitis, although it'll take another week or so at least for my body to even start making the antibodies that are detectable in an AIDS test.

'Is it possible your ex-partner could be bisexual? Would he be likely to attend,' she lowers her voice gravely, 'sex parties?'

I almost want to ask her how she manages to say things like that with a straight face. Except none of this is a joking matter.

'Activities like that would increase your risk.'

It isn't funny at all in fact . . . and the honest truth is, I have no idea about the answers to her questions. Not when he was with me, no, but that was, what – five years ago? And it's then that I realise that actually I *don't* know Leo any more, only what he was.

We decide I'll opt for the chlamydia and gonorrhoea package, the least appealing 'package' I've ever chosen – including when Joss, Bec and I went to Gran Canaria aged seventeen and it collectively cost us about £250. A urine test and £140 later and I'm back out on the street clutching my mobile tightly. They will be calling through my results within forty-eight hours.

I don't mind the £140. I don't mind the urine test, in fact that was a comparatively pleasant surprise given I had been expecting another internal examination. But I do mind within forty-eight hours. Given I thought

I'd be finding out straight away, I'm desperately disappointed to have to drag it home with me. I wanted to go back to Dan having put at least some part of all this behind us.

When I step out on to the pavement, it's raining again, so I reach hurriedly for my umbrella, before squaring my shoulders and starting back towards Bond Street tube, head down, deep in thought.

So deep in thought that at first I don't take any notice of someone shouting. I'm a stone's throw from Oxford Street after all and the wind is so blustery it's enough of a job concentrating on keeping my umbrella from blowing inside out. But then I hear someone call 'MOLLY!' and I look up to see, to my astonishment, *Leo* on the other side of the road, smiling delightedly, holding a smart black umbrella high above his head, dark grey open overcoat billowing behind him as he weaves between a black cab and a bike to get to me.

'What are you doing here?' He's clearly astonished, but seems thrilled to see me, clouds of breath forming in front of his face.

I am completely dumbstruck. I was worried about running into Dan like this, but dismissed it because what would he be doing out of the City and in the West End? It never occurred to me that it would be LEO I'd have to worry about.

'I've just been to a launch at Claridge's,' he says, motioning down the road behind him. Then he turns back to me. 'You look frozen,' he says, concerned, then reaches out and takes my arm. 'Come on, let's go and get you a coffee, get you warmed up.'

'Don't!' I shout, yanking my arm back violently at his touch, to the surprise of a random man and his girlfriend hurrying past me. The girlfriend nudges him and they both turn to give us a curious glance. I suppose we probably do look like any other couple having a row in the street. But we're not.

Leo looks a bit startled by my reaction too. 'OK,' he says slowly. 'Whatever you want BG, it's no problem.'

I freeze. BG . . . Beautiful Girl.

'Don't call me that.'

He laughs, as if now I'm just being stupid. 'Why not? It's true! Well, perhaps not at this precise moment, but you still look pretty good to me.'

He knows full well why he shouldn't call me that. Because that's what he used to call me when we were together. I was BG and he was GB – gorgeous boy. Now, it just sounds horribly twee and embarrassing. I take a step back from him, but he pretends not to notice. 'I've got to ask though, what are you doing here?' he repeats curiously. 'You work in Brighton, don't you?'

Yes, I do. I'm just up in London making sure I haven't caught a sexually transmitted disease from you.

'It's none of your business.' I'm almost rude, but it doesn't faze him in the slightest, if anything it only spurs him on.

'Fine,' he says lightly. 'Be like that then, but at least let me take you somewhere decent to wait this out,' he

191

motions up at the swollen, dark sky as if he needs to protect me from impending threat. 'We can have a coffee and you can tell me how sorry you are for barring my number.'

Even I'm astonished by his brazen lack of shame. 'I did it because I don't want you to call me, or text me.' I can hear the mounting frustration in my own voice. 'And I'm really confused by what part of that you don't understand. How many times do I have to tell you I'm *married*!'

He snorts dismissively and lightly shakes his head. 'So you keep saying. Come on, you still haven't heard what I have to tell you.' He takes a step away as if he fully expects me to just follow him . . .

. . . but I resolutely stay fixed to the spot. 'I don't want to see you again.'

He frowns. 'But I want—'

'What?' I explode. 'What is it you want, Leo? Because it's always about you isn't it? What YOU need, what YOU have to talk to me about. Tell me, *what do you want*?'

'You,' he says flatly. 'I want you.'

'No you don't!' I take a step towards him in exasperation. 'You think you do, but you don't.'

'Don't patronise me!' He is suddenly angry, and I step back again quickly. 'I do want you,' he insists stubbornly. 'You can't tell me how I feel.'

I shake my head in disbelief and then I realise that actually, I don't have to stand there and listen to this. Not any more. I turn on my heels and begin to walk smartly away from him.

'I love you!'

The words echo up the street after me and shocked, I stop and am unable to prevent myself from half turning back to face him.

We just stand there, looking at each other. Everything else keeps moving around us, cars, people impatiently navigating the two immobile idiots in the street. He doesn't break my gaze.

But I say nothing, I just turn and hasten away from him as fast as I can.

## Chapter Seventeen

He can't seriously think that is going to change everything?

'Hello?'

Dan's voice cuts into my thoughts and I make an effort
to drag myself back to our sitting room.

'I said you're quiet,' Dan repeats patiently. 'Everything
all right?'

'Yeah, I'm just tired.' I scratch my nose and wriggle
down a little deeper into the sofa as I stare at the TV.
He keeps looking at me steadily.

'And a bit worried about work,' I add. 'No one's placing
any orders at the moment. We've got an emergency
meeting tomorrow.'

That's actually true. Antony emailed me, apologising

for disturbing me on a day off, but explaining that he had no choice, the whole division are required to be present, which has the distinct whiff of redundancies about it.

'What sort of emergency meeting? A "man the boats" sort of meeting?'

'I think it might be,' I admit.

Dan sighs, then reaches out and rubs my leg consolingly. 'Well, if it happens, it happens,' he says pragmatically. 'We'll manage, don't worry. It's all going to be fine,' he looks at me sincerely and I've honestly never wanted to believe anything more in my life.

Before we go to bed, I give my emails one last check before shutting everything down. Dan comes in to find me smiling at an amusing Richard Branson one Pearce has sent me.

'What's so funny?' he smiles in the doorway.

'Something from Pearce,' I'm about to show it to him when I remember just in the nick of time what Pearce's message says above the attachment:

```
This made me laugh. Hope you had a nice
day off. Whatcha get up too? See you tomorrow
for doom day. P xxx
```

Dan of course doesn't know I've taken a day's holiday, so I have to quickly close the document.

'Oh,' he says, disappointed. 'Can't I see?'

'I've shut it down now. I'll show you tomorrow,' I say

and, before he can argue, I stand up and switch the light off.

In bed, he starts trying to kiss me while I'm reading my book.

'That's nice.' I reach my hand behind me to stroke his neck, then twist to look at him. I love him so much. He kisses my mouth and then begins to slide his hand up my leg. I know what that means and I really, really wish I could, but . . . I half smile at him apologetically. 'I can't Dan, not yet.'

He groans. 'Still? Really?'

I nod – feeling utterly ashamed of myself. *Why* couldn't they have just given me the test results today? Was that really too much to ask?

'OK,' he smiles at me ruefully, which makes me feel even worse. 'Another cold shower for me in the morning!'

I turn away and start to try and read again, but I can't concentrate. All I can think about is Leo stood there in the street holding his umbrella and shouting 'I love you!'

Five years after we've separated he tells me the one thing I cajoled, pleaded and begged him to say while we were together. I can still remember the first time I pathetically reduced myself to asking him outright if he loved me – and how it felt when he said evasively, after a pause, 'define love'.

I let my book fall from my hands in disgust and try to get comfy. I suppose it's fair to argue I should have realised if you have to ask someone that question repeatedly, the answer is probably no, they don't. I know Leo didn't love

197

me – and that's OK, no law says he had to, and of course, he turned out not to be right for me anyway . . .

Dan, having heard my book drop to the floor, stretches a hand out and turns the light off. Then he reaches out for me in the dark, pulls me into his arms and kisses my neck again. 'Love you Moll.'

. . . because that's how easy it is, when it's real. It's not a struggle, or a painful battle of wills. It's just obviously there. I really don't think Leo has actually experienced what love is, he can't have, and I'm sad for him for that. But I'm not going to let him ruin what I *know* I have with Dan, any more than he – and I – have already.

It was bad enough when I saw him running towards me earlier . . . He seemed genuinely amazed to see me, but . . . I mean, what were the chances of that happening?

Actually, what are the chances of that?

I haven't seen him for years . . . and yet I just bump into him a week after our disastrous night, when he's been texting me repeatedly asking to meet? I stare at the wall in front of me. Really?

But then I don't see how he could possibly have had any idea that I was going to be there. No one except Joss knew about that appointment, and I booked it in a false name. There's no way he could have known.

It can't have been fate – surely? The prospect of that really *is* terrifying.

By the time I'm on my way to the emergency work meeting the following afternoon I've still heard nothing from the clinic, and am becoming seriously agitated. What if I still haven't heard by the end of the day? Will they only let me know within working hours? That'll make it Monday! How am I supposed to explain that to Dan? I've also realised that I can't do anything about changing my phone number until I've got the results back through, which means every time my phone goes, I'm torn between leaping on it to see if it's the results, or ignoring it in case it's Leo again.

Of course it bleeps away unhelpfully on the passenger seat pretty much constantly for the whole journey with nothing but a succession of false starts. Dan to say he is going to take me out to dinner tonight and I'm not to worry, whatever happens at the meeting we'll deal with it together – Mum telling me to call her back, she hasn't heard from me since Sunday, am I OK? Abi to check I am still on for Saturday's baby shower – which I've forgotten about completely – Joss to see if I've had the all-clear . . . But there is still no *actual* call by the time I arrive at the roadside hotel.

In keeping with the subject matter of the meeting ahead, it's even more of a craphole venue than usual. The conference room is buried right at the back of the building, down slightly claustrophobic halls carpeted in shiny red nylon; the static crackles under the soles of my boots. The whole place smells faintly of stale chips; through the emergency exit at the end of the hall I can just glimpse the bins below the kitchen vent, which is pumping clouds of greasy steam up into the dour sky.

Peering through the glass panel in the door I can see the meeting hasn't started but pretty much everyone is here. I keep my eyes to the ground as I slip into the room and then into the seat Pearce has saved for me. Sandra leans over quickly and says in a low voice, 'Do you know anything?' I shake my head and she sits back worriedly, too preoccupied to bother with being a bitch today.

Pearce says nothing; unsurprisingly even he is quiet. Everyone looks terrified and sits up a little straighter in anticipation when Antony comes in. He puts his things down on the table and says simply, 'You will I'm sure be aware of the information that has appeared in the press recently regarding MediComma. Like many companies, the economic situation continues to have a very real effect on us. It has been considered prudent that we now adopt a new approach and create a New MediComma world that allows us to revise the shape of the company.' He says it all with no conviction whatsoever, as if he's been given a press release to read, which he probably has.

Pearce speaks up. 'So does that mean if the new "shape" is – I don't know – a circle, some of us are going to be left outside it?'

Antony gives him a direct look. 'MediComma unfortunately can't rule out redundancies at this stage.'

A ripple of fear courses through the room – Kirk looks like he's going to cry – and of course it's right at that moment that my bloody mobile starts to light up with 'number withheld'. Sod's law it's the clinic. I am just about to leave it, let it go to voicemail, when I realise they won't leave a message for me because my voicemail says I'm Molly Greene . . . not Cara Jones. Suppose I can't get them back? There's no way I can wait until Monday, no way. I stand up, and say 'Hello?' to everyone's incredulous stares, Antony included. I ignore them all, push my chair back and walk out of the room.

Shutting the door behind me I say very quietly, 'Yes, this is Cara Jones.'

I look back through the glass panel in the door. Pearce is looking at me curiously.

'Could you say that again?' I say faintly.

The broad smile of relief all over my face when I come back into the room – despite my best efforts to hide it – is, of course, wholly inappropriate under the circumstances. Sandra gives me a Disgusted of Tunbridge Wells look and shakes her head as I sit back down. Even Antony shoots me a look of quiet disbelief.

Well, so be it. I had to find out. Jobs are one thing . . . I'm not losing my marriage. Not for anything.

'So the formal announcement will be in tomorrow's press stating that we are restructuring and may be considering voluntary redundancies as a first stage but that we will be doing our best to avoid compulsory measures as we move into 2010,' Antony concludes. 'Does anyone have any questions?'

'I do. This wouldn't be one of those bad practise exercises would it?' Pearce says. 'You know, using the recession as an excuse for making employees paranoid, so they all work harder and accept whatever terms are thrown at them because they're just glad to keep their jobs?'

Antony looks at him, like he's thinking Pearce is sometimes too sharp for his own good. 'No Pearce. I don't think it is.'

'Riiight. But I suppose it's no coincidence that we were told this at,' Pearce pointedly checks his watch, 'half-four on a Friday night, when there's pretty much bugger all we can do about it?'

Antony shrugs helplessly. The poor guy looks shattered.

For once after the meeting, no one feels like going to the pub; even though it's Friday night. It doesn't seem right somehow. Instead, we all start to drift back to our cars. I'm back in mine when I get a tap on the passenger window. It's Pearce. I undo my seatbelt and lean across.

'Don't take this the wrong way,' he's trying to look cheery, 'but for someone who has just been told they might be about to lose their job, you seemed pretty smiley in there.'

'I know,' I groan. 'That was such bad timing. I was waiting for someone to call me back with some news and . . . well, I had to take the call.'

He nods. 'It was, I take it, *good* news?'

I nod emphatically. 'Very.'

'Well, that's great,' he makes an effort to look enthusiastic. 'Congratulations. Have a good weekend won't you?'

'Pearce,' I say, as he starts to straighten up. 'Are *you* OK?'

He hesitates. 'You know how sometimes you realise things aren't turning out the way you want them to? You had a plan in your mind but somehow you just sort of manage to mess it up anyway?'

I smile sadly. 'Yeah, I do.'

'I shouldn't even be doing this job, this isn't how I want to spend the rest of my life, so why am I crapping it now that I'm going to lose it? It doesn't make sense, *none* of it makes—'

'Pearce!'

He jumps and turns, revealing Sandra, just standing there, tapping her foot impatiently.

'You ready to go?' she says pointedly. It's less of a question and more a command.

He rolls his eyes, stands up and gives me a disparate wave. 'See you next week. And congratulations again.'

It's only once I've driven out of the car park I realise he probably thinks I'm pregnant. Balls. I'll have to text him later, set him straight before he ends up letting that slip to Sandra, who will take great delight in spreading it around as fast as she can.

On the spur of the moment; probably because I am so buoyed up by my all-clear and feeling equally reckless in the face of an uncertain professional future I can do nothing about, I decide to drive into the town centre and catch the last half-hour of the shops. I want to see if I can find something nice to wear to dinner with Dan, make an effort for him, and I also need to get a baby shower present for Rose.

In the changing room of a clothes shop, as I am trying to see what I look like from the back in the main mirror, a little girl of about four emerges round the edge of the curtain to the cubicle next to mine. She curiously watches me inspect myself and starts to twirl slightly on the spot, pulling on her bubbly blonde hair, before wiping a small red button nose on her sleeve. I smile at her, a social invitation which she immediately accepts.

'My mummy,' she says matter-of-factly, while gathering a bunch of the velvet curtain and twisting it, 'is forty-two.'

'Thank you,' says a rather weary voice from behind the curtain.

I try not to laugh and seconds later a woman emerges from the cubicle doing up her coat and clutching a couple of items that are slipping off hangers. She looks at me, smiles, rolls her eyes and says to the little girl, 'Come on then, Trouble,' as she holds out her hand. The little girl takes it and they disappear back into the shop. I watch them curiously as the mum hangs up the clothes. The little girl is skipping happily, bunches bouncing, asking 'Mummy, do you remember when we went to Granny's and I . . .' but I don't quite catch the end of what she's saying before they disappear out of the door. But I find myself wondering what it would be like to hold the hand of a little girl like her and have her call me Mummy. Would we be heading back home to tea? Maybe on our way to my mum and dad's – her granny and grandpa's house – before her dad got home from work?

I pay for my dress. It's not unpleasant, but a little weird to think of myself as someone's mum. I walk out of the shop carefully trying to balance the bags because one of them contains a box of cupcakes for Rose, while trying the word out for size in my mind, like I used to with Dan's surname before he proposed to me. Mummy, Mum . . . this is my daughter . . . of course it might not be a girl. It could be a boy. I think Dan would like a boy, although I've never actually asked him. I imagine Dan holding a tiny baby – me lying there shattered having just given birth, both of us crying with happiness like they do in the films. I have fleetingly imagined this scenario before, but it's the first time I have properly considered what it might really feel like to hold my and Dan's baby. I have no doubt in my mind that Dan would be a wonderful father. In fact, it's something I can only imagine doing with him *because* it's him. It's the only way I think I can imagine it would feel – right.

My thoughts are interrupted however when from my pocket, or my bag, or somewhere . . . I hear my phone bleep. I have to fumble around for it, while trying not to drop my bags.

You look incredible today. Do you even know what you do to me? X

Oh Leo . . . I look incredible today do I? Aside from the fact I am in a very ordinary black trouser suit with shoes that frankly need re-heeling and hair I've deliberately left so I can wash it before dinner, how exactly does he know what I look like? Even the cleverest cheats slip up occasionally I suppose . . . he's sent me a text meant for someone else. *That's* how much in love with me he is. I vaguely remember seeing the name Amanda flashing up on his mobile phone at the hotel. Didn't he say that was his stepdaughter's name? I'd bet good money it isn't.

I delete the message stonily. And just for a moment, I feel a flicker, a reminder of how much I used to want and wait for messages like that from him. How very stupid I was.

Well, maybe at least now I won't have to go to the bother of changing my number after all. I'm sure Little Miss 'looks incredible' will be flattered enough to respond to him. Maybe then he'll leave me alone, he's obviously got plenty of irons in the fire.

Whoever she is, I feel sorry for her.


Over dinner, Dan tells me I look very nice and I tell him truthfully so does he. I tell him about the cute little girl in the changing room and he smiles and kisses my hand. Over my second glass of champagne, I find I actually can't stop looking at him and telling him repeatedly that I love him.

'I love you too, Moll,' he says. 'So, you want to talk about what happened today yet?'

'Um,' I try to focus my thoughts on the meeting. 'Well, we got the "could be redundancies, folks" chat. At the moment, they're muttering about voluntary but . . .'

Dan listens carefully.

'. . . I don't know. You just can't tell these days can you? It could be all something and nothing . . .' I take another mouthful of drink '. . . or it could be everything.'

'We just better hurry up and get you pregnant, hadn't we?' Dan grins. 'That way you can go on maternity leave and hope it's all blown over by the time you go back!'

Hmmm. It's a bit more serious than that, Dan . . . and it's usually me that makes that sort of comment and him that reins us in. I look at him, feeling a bit unsettled and think about that sweet little girl in the changing room again. She was lovely, but really, having no job, no second income . . . that wouldn't be funny. Shit – would we even be able to get a mortgage just on Dan's salary? I suddenly see myself in our rented house with a small baby. What if the landlord severed the contract? What if we had a month to move out, or whatever it is. 'You're sure you really think now is the best time for us to start trying?' I say hesitantly, not sure if I'm saying it because I'm being sensible or if it's *me* being the baby and freaking out again. 'Should we maybe give it six months and see where we are financially then? I'm not trying to stall you Dan – honestly I'm not – and I know you say you'd look after us if I lost my job, but I don't really want to put all that pressure on you – on us. Wouldn't it be much more responsible to wait?'

Dan shakes his head firmly. 'This is the right time for us. I know the rest of the world seems to be going crazy and jobs are going left, right and centre but everyone manages, people keep on having kids. No one stopped during the Second World War, did they? They really did have something to worry about.'

I'm not really sure what to say to that. It's a point of sorts, I suppose.

'Molly, it will be OK,' Dan insists, pouring the last of the champagne into my glass. 'We might have to cut back a bit, but I will make it work, I promise. You're right to be pragmatic, but you don't need to worry. I'm not – I've never felt happier, in fact, we really should celebrate tonight, because we've actually got so much to look forward to; we're really lucky.'

That's true – we are *very* lucky. I think about getting the test results back, the completely different conversation I could be having with Dan right now, and take a very large gulp of my champagne indeed.

By the time we both fall into a taxi, much later, giggling away drunkenly together, for the first time in a while, I've pretty much stopped worrying about everything altogether. Dan's right, this is all going to be OK. It has to be.

There is no alternative.

## Chapter Eighteen

'Thank you,' croaks Dan as I stand over him, holding out a cup of tea I'm in danger of dropping because my joints are all alcohol-achy. 'Urgh. I feel rotten. We were away with the fairies last night, weren't we?' he yawns as I get back into bed. 'How come you're up already?'

'I've got Rose's baby shower in London.' I climb carefully back in next to him, trying not to spill my own drink.

'Oh really?' he sounds surprised. 'Since when?'

I twist to look at him. 'Didn't I tell you? Sorry, sweetheart, what with all the work rubbish I must have forgotten. I'm all over the place at the moment, I really am.'

'It's OK,' he says. 'I've got plenty of stuff I can do today. How are you feeling?'

'Like my head is lined with fur on the inside,' I confess and yawn again. 'It was fun last night though.' I lean over carefully and give him a quick kiss.

He smiles. 'Yeah, it was. Hey!' he sits up a bit more, suddenly excited, 'I wonder if we made a baby?'

Abi chuckles when she catches me pausing to glug another couple of mouthfuls from my bottle of water in the hotel foyer, while making her way back from the ladies. 'Ah! You've arrived! Oh I see – big night last night, was it? Why am I not surprised?'

'I don't know how you still do it,' she continues comfortably, having given me a vigorous hug. 'I'm so dead on my feet once I've got everyone through baths and into bed, one glass of wine is enough to finish me off, it's pathetic. Thank God you're still holding the side up. Rather you than me though. Was your train delayed?'

'I didn't allow enough time for the tube and the walk. I'm so sorry. Am I the last one to get here?'

'Oh don't worry about it,' she waves a hand airily. 'Actually quite a few people can't make it today after all, so . . .'

'Oh! Who can't come?' I can't help my disappointment. I was feeling cheered on the train at the thought of a nice lunch with them all.

'Eloise has come down with some grotty cold thing,' says Abi, in reference to Nula's little girl. 'She's OK, but she was very hot all last night, and really grizzly so Nula thought she'd better stay put. May's not coming because she's going through that shattered phase, when you're only a few weeks gone, she couldn't face the trek all the way from *Islington* . . .' She rolls her eyes. 'You can tell it's her first; actually that's mean of me, you do feel completely exhausted, but you just get on with it second time round because you've still got number one dashing around like a mad thing! Ha ha! Anyway, Jacquie isn't coming because, well, I'm sure she wouldn't mind me telling you but she's not in a good place right now, she just sees babies every-where at the moment, today would have been hell for her. They're going to start IVF next month.'

'Oh, I didn't realise. Poor thing.'

'Yeah, well,' Abi shrugs. 'There's a lot of it about un-fortunately. Fingers crossed it'll work out for them. So, everything all right with you?' she says as we start to walk towards where the other girls must be. 'Dan OK? Any news your end?'

'No,' I say carefully. 'Well, except . . .'

'Except what?' Abi pauses, sensing something out of the ordinary.

'We've sort of started trying.' It's strange to hear myself say it out loud, as strange as it was when Dan wondered aloud if we'd made a baby this morning. Are you meant to tell people this? Or is it something you just keep to yourself until it actually happens?

Abi lets her mouth fall open and then laughs. 'I knew it!' she exclaims. 'It catches up with all of us eventually eh? Oh Moll, that's brilliant!' She gives me a brief hug and a rather smug, knowing grin, as if all along it had just been a question of time. Just like that I'm bumped from one team to the other, with no transfer questions at all. 'Oh God, you're going to be my friend who leaves their baby in changing rooms because they forget they've got them, aren't you?'

We both laugh, although mine is less hearty than hers. 'Well, that's assuming everything is straightforward.' She doesn't really think I'd do that does she? 'Like you said, it may not happen at all.'

'Of course it will! Thirty-three is *nothing* these days, you're not exactly over the hill, love,' she says briskly, completely changing her tune from seconds earlier. 'That's really great news.' She resumes her walk to the restaurant. 'So, what are you going to do about your house? You'll start looking for somewhere to buy *now*, surely?'

'Abi,' I say urgently, grabbing her arm. 'Don't tell the others yet, will you?' That suddenly feels very important. I can't very well expect Dan not to discuss it with people but go around shooting my own mouth off. That's not fair. And today is about Rose, not me.

'Of course!' she says instantly. 'Trust me, you don't need that pressure, everyone asking how it's going all the time.' She grimaces. 'It'll really stress you out and that makes it even harder to conceive. I'll keep it zipped, promise. Come on, we're all over by the window look, there's Rose waving.'

As the last one to arrive I have to dump my stuff on a chair between two of Rose's friends I've not met before. Abi and Rose are right up at the other end of the table. Luckily though, no one has drinks or food yet, so I can't be that late . . . but all my thoughts vanish as I go to give Rose a hug, she stands up and I get the shock of my life. I haven't seen her for three months – and she's quite simply enormous. 'This is just a little something for you,' I say, handing over the wrapped present and a ribbon-clad box as I make an effort not to blurt 'Jesus Rose, have you *eaten* a baby?'

'Did you get me new ankles?' she deadpans, trying to peer into the box as everyone immediately jumps in with the obligatory 'Don't be silly! You look great!' And 'Nearly there! Not long now!'

'So how are you feeling?' I ask sympathetically.

'I'm OK,' Rose concedes. 'Tired, but OK.'

'Oh you just wait!' crows one of her friends, 'this is *nothing*!' and everyone laughs good-naturedly, me included.

'That's true Rose, you should be trying to enjoy the last few weeks or so of normality before the madness begins!' calls another. 'Trust me, I actually found doing two *marathons* easier than getting Charlie into a routine!'

'I have to confess, when my first was tiny I once went out with only one eye made up because I was so tired I forgot to do the other one,' admits Abi and everyone chuckles again.

'At least you attempted make-up, I couldn't see the point of even getting dressed in the morning, not when I'd be plastered in baby puke and sobbing by ten in the morning anyway!' says another girl. 'Mind you – my

post–natal depression was still undiagnosed at that point.'
She smiles brightly. No one knows if they should laugh
at this or not.

'Let's do the presents!' says Rose's younger sister quickly,
because Rose looks a bit like *she* wants to cry, as you
would if you'd just been told what you'd been working
towards for nearly nine months is going to be completely
shit.

The gifts are largely lotions and potions designed to
stop bits of Rose dropping off or expanding beyond repair
– 'Anything's worth a go Rose! Believe me!' – practical
things like Cook! Vouchers – 'So you can stock up the
freezer and pull something out when you're so knackered you just want to kill yourself' – or baby clothes,
over which we all coo. They are properly sweet and tiny.
I can't help but pick up an especially small cardigan to
marvel at as I sit back down. An actual real baby is going
to wear that. 'Oh! That's Baby Gap, isn't it?' says a woman
knowledgeably, looking at it.

One of Rose's friends from work swells with pride. It
must have been from her.

'They're so great for basics,' the first woman says,
'although I do find their organic cotton range a bit
limited.'

I watch as Rose's friend deflates slightly, but the
woman doesn't notice. 'What changing station did you
go for in the end Rose?' she calls up the table, turning
away.

'Still deciding – I know, I know – if this baby is early

I'm screwed – but I'll just have to make do if that happens. A friend of mine at antenatal class told me about this really great reviews site and I want to read everything on that first before I commit to a decision.'

I laugh, thinking she's joking. After all, this is the Rose who took herself off to Africa for three months on her own after we graduated and worked as a volunteer in a medical centre, bombing about all over the place in a jeep held together by prayer, rust and string.

Everyone looks at me in surprise and I realise she's not. So quickly, I make it look like I was coughing and say, 'Why not? Can't hurt to do some research can it? I don't so much as buy suntan lotion without going on Trip Advisor first.'

The first woman nods approvingly. 'You don't want to wind up like my friend, who bought the first high chair she saw. Rose, it's total crap – *it doesn't fold away* – she's gutted.'

Rose begins to open my present. I almost want to tell her to save it until later, seeing as I've bought her a girly DVD, a selection of glossy magazines and the four cupcakes; nothing baby-related at all – what the hell was I thinking? It all seemed quite fun yesterday. Now . . .

But Rose says, 'Oh great – I still haven't seen this yet. Thanks Moll. And magazines and cakes! Perfect!'

She puts it all down on the table, gets to her feet and puffs over to give me a hug. One of her chums picks up a magazine and reads out loud '"Are ripped jeans back?" Well they've never gone away in my house! Not on my lot! Ha ha!' she starts to flick through, then snorts with amusement before reading out loud, '"I take a thoughtful bath, make my first cappuccino of the morning, decide that the Marc Jacobs' will be perfect for interviewing pop's most petite princess and step out into the tinkling iciness of a delicate winter's day."' She hoots with laughter. 'Not got kids then? Who are these people? Get a life with some meaning!'

'Now, now, it's just a bit of fun. I think it's a great present Moll!' Abi says loyally.

The woman looks at me in horror and says, 'Oh God! I didn't mean that – I *love* stuff like this; magazines are the way forward.'

'That's true, Suze can't cope with actual books any more, the last full work she read was "Spot Goes to the Park",' teases the second.

'Bugger off!' grins the first. 'It's true though,' she concedes. 'And frankly even that's a little highbrow these days. Ha ha!'

'I just thought if you end up being really late or something it might be a welcome diversion,' I explain, trying to avoid looking at the Spot the Dog woman in disbelief as Rose gets to me and I lean round her bump. 'And obviously the cupcakes are just, well, for putting your feet up with.'

'When d'you last see them Rose?' someone teases. 'Sometime back in September?'

Rose grins and pats her belly as she moves back to her chair. 'I haven't been able to see anything below my

216

waist for months now which – believe me – is probably a good thing.'

Our pots of tea begin to arrive, along with proper old-fashioned silver cake stands which carry neat, dainty sandwiches on the lower level, assorted pastries and mini muffins on the next, tiny chocolately confections and fruit petit fours one up from that, and cream scones on the top. I nearly sigh with appreciation they look so good. Hurrah for afternoon tea, it should soak up some of my internal swilling champagne lake nicely. I'm happily reaching for an eclair when someone says, 'I know what you mean about not being able to see anything once you get to a certain stage, this is pretty gross but when I was pregnant I actually got to a stage where I had to get Matt to help give me a prune, down there.'

I pause, mid-éclair-en-route-to-mouth. I don't even know her name. I vaguely remember her from Rose's wedding but that's it. Do I really need to know her husband practises pubic topiary on her? I don't think I do.

No one else however seems remotely bothered by her statement, quite the opposite in fact, someone else says eagerly, 'Oh God, I know – you just can't face waxing because of the pain – and it all seems so point-less anyway . . .'

That's all it takes to quite literally open the floodgates. Horrific 'Nam Vet style stories of pregnancy and birth ensue.

'—so badly she actually needed reconstructive surgery. I know, I know.'

217

'—and halfway through they said to Jim, we've got it wrong, we're going to have to go for a c-section – but by then Milo was so far engaged they actually had to push him back up, no, I'm not even joking. I was just like, God, you can go in via my nose if you like, as long as you GET IT OUT OF ME.'

'—well no, because they don't like letting you go much beyond then, do they, so they decided to induce me, but nothing happened even after the pessaries, apart from by then of course I was just *so sore* . . . and contracting my arse off. Then the epidural didn't work either and I ended up having a ventouse delivery—'

I don't know why, but for some reason that makes me imagine a medical team with blonde plaits, dressed in lederhosen. I think I'm trying to go to a happy place.

'—seven pints in total. But you know what? It was the breastfeeding that was the worst bit . . . every time she latched on I wanted to *scream*.'

I'm starting to reel and am ready to cut my own ears off, when Abi says loudly, 'Anyway, you're going to be *just fine* Rose, and for all the other "yet to have babies" women at the table,' she winks at me with all the subtlety of a house brick flying through the air towards a greenhouse, 'I promise once it's over you forget the drama instantly and it all becomes totally worth it. Are you having a doula, Rose?'

'No, it's just the way I'm sitting,' smiles Rose and everyone chuckles. I don't get it, what's a doula?

'And have you had your last antenatal session now?'

'Yup,' Rose shifts position uncomfortably. 'Finished last week – Nathan's thrilled. He went off them after the "By the way, you might literally crap yourself" class. He was nearly sick on the spot,' she laughs. 'We had this really over-eager dad in our group, who asked questions about literally everything. We were discussing what would happen if you accidentally pooed in the birthing pool and the midwife was explaining that they have a poo sieve—'

The waiter, who has come to check we have everything we need, hears this and does a horrified about turn on the spot.

'—and over-eager dad asked if he could borrow a pen to write it down,' Rose laughs. 'I swear I saw him earnestly adding "poo sieve" to his little list – like that's something you're going to forget! Oh and this other woman asked if she could wear a *swimsuit* in the birthing pool! Yeah – just pull it to one side like you do when you go swimming and need a wee!'

'Unbelievable!' laughs the Spot the Dog mum. 'She'll learn.'

She has. And I think I'd like to go home now please.

'IF that happens, the midwives deal with it very discreetly. They just cover it up and no one is any the wiser. You'll just get Dan to stay at the head end, it'll be fine! Don't panic.' Bec pats my arm consolingly.

'It was as if they *wanted* to have had the worst possible experience.' I exhale and reach for my drink. 'And then all they could talk about was how shit everything is once you've had kids; you're knackered and everything's horrible. It can't really be as crap as they were making out, can it? If it's that bad, why does everyone do it?'

Joss snorts and immediately opens her mouth, so I turn to Bec quickly.

'Certain types of mum,' Bec says carefully, 'can be pretty self-indulgent and – a bit tedious to be honest – like they're the only person in the world to have had a baby.'

'It's not just that Bec, they were disgusting! Who wants to have that sort of conversation in public? Hello? TOO MUCH FLIPPING INFORMATION! Is it just me? Am I being weird?'

'No! Not at all. But not everyone is like them, I promise – and I'm sure if you asked even them if they'd go back to *not* having children, not a single one of them would,' Bec answers. 'You're thinking about this too much. You need to just get on with it.'

Joss's head spins like something out of *The Exorcist*. 'I'm sorry?' she demands. 'WHAT did you just say?'

'Well of course giving birth is going to hurt,' Bec says reasonably. 'People have very unrealistic expectations of pain these days, but you DO cope with it and it DOES end.'

'Oh, I thought you meant she shouldn't consider whether or not she really wants to give up a happy child-less life for something that she'll then be stuck with whether she likes it or not,' admits Joss. 'Sorry.'

220

'Thanks you two,' I bite my fingernail, 'this is really helping . . .'

I feel so confused. Yesterday, all this seemed doable, a nice thought even. Now? I feel back to square one. What if Joss is right and my decision to have a baby is nothing more than a knee-jerk reaction to what happened with Leo? Oh – he's managed to pollute everything. Everything!

'I'm *definitely* not doing it if it means I have to call my kid Milo.' I attempt a joke, trying to push all other unwelcome thoughts from my mind.

'Just because none of them talked about how wonderful having a baby is, doesn't mean it isn't,' Bec says calmly. 'Trust me, I've seen plenty of *very* normal women have babies and say it's the best thing they ever did.'

'Whacked off their tits with hormones probably,' Joss says darkly. 'Although I agree with you on the some women being over-indulgent bit. There's this girl at work who must ask me if she can leave early at least once or twice a week because she's got prenatal pogo-yogolates or some such bollocks, or she doesn't want to travel home in the rush hour, or she feels "a bit tired and dizzy". She chose to get up the duff, get on with it; everyone's bloody knackered. You don't see the blokes getting away with that kind of shit.'

'Nice that you're so understanding about it though,' Bec says. 'Lucky her.'

'Well obviously I *let* her go,' Joss replies mutinously. 'I don't have a bloody choice, do I? She'd probably sue us otherwise. You don't understand Bec . . .'

'I'm a midwife!' squeaks Bec. 'Funnily enough I *have* encountered the odd pregnant woman.'

'Can we talk about something else?' I cut in desperately.

They both stop and look at me – and then I'm pretty sure they exchange a knowing glance before Bec says soothingly, ''Course we can. Have you got time for one more hair of the dog or do you need to get back?'

I look at my watch and hesitate, but despite my still-lingering hangover, I really feel like I need one. 'Go on then.'

'Was Dan as drunk as you last night?' Bec teases as she stands up.

'I didn't get *drunk* drunk,' I say quickly, not looking at Joss. 'Just happy.'

'I didn't mean to sound like I was having a go,' Bec apologises instantly. 'You're allowed. You're not pregnant yet. Where's Dan today?'

'Gone to Chichester to help his dad throw out a wardrobe. So, what are you two going to see at the cinema later?' I determinedly change the subject.

Joss shrugs. 'Something funny I think, or we might stick around here for a bit. Nothing too mad, Bec's working tomorrow and I've got the twins coming over for Sunday lunch.'

'Oh, how are they?' I ask as Bec makes her way towards the loos.

Joss shrugs. 'OK I think. Eating crap, drinking too much, spending money like water and swearing blind that they don't have that much work to do because it's only the first year. I looked at their timetables; four hour-long lectures a week Moll – it's a joke. They don't know it yet, but tomorrow I'm going to make them sit down and plan a proper budget for the rest of this term . . . and the next one.' She drains the last of her drink smugly.

'They're so lucky to have a big sister like you,' I tease.

She grins. 'I know, they're going to hate me. But it's no joke coming out of university with all that debt these days you know.' She grows serious again.

'Are they staying at your mum's tonight then?'

Joss shakes her head. 'They're just going to get the train down tomorrow. Mum's not having a good week.'

'I'm sorry,' I say. 'Want to talk about it?'

'Nope,' she says firmly, 'I don't. Thanks though. I want to talk about you. What's up? You look stressed out of your mind. I'm not going to be cross with you, I promise, but,' she hesitates, 'is something going on I should know about?'

I shake my head. 'Nope. Nothing.'

'Have you heard from Leo again?' She looks directly at me.

I inhale. I can't lie to her. 'Yes.'

'I knew it!'

'It's not like you think!' I cut in quickly. 'Just texts.'

She says nothing, just looks at me expressionlessly, so I start to gabble. 'It's nothing to worry about Joss.'

'It's none of my business if you want to—'

'I don't.' I cut in sharply. 'I don't want to do anything with him. I was blind drunk remember?'

She sighs.

'No one would be in a hurry to repeat a night like that, would they?' I say. 'Well, apart from Leo apparently.'

Joss pulls a face. 'What?'

I shake my head tiredly. 'Don't. Anyway, I've told him where to go. He'll get the message.'

We both fall silent.

'Sorry,' she says eventually. 'I just thought . . .'

'No way,' I insist. 'Absolutely no way am I going back there . . . So, do you think Bec ordered?' I sit up and look around us. 'I could really use that drink.'

Right on cue, a waiter appears with a tray of three champagne cocktails.

'Bec's pushing the boat out a bit,' Joss exclaims. 'Are you sure these are for us?' she asks him.

'I think so,' he says, but looks a bit uncertain. 'Hang on, I'll just double check' and he hastens off to the bar.

Bec arrives back before he does. 'Oooh!'

'You didn't order these?' Joss motions at them and Bec shakes her head, as the waiter appears back alongside our table, grinning. 'With compliments from the gentleman at the bar,' he smirks, as if he doesn't get to say that often.

'*Really*?' Bec exclaims delightedly, all of us turn and peer across – and an elderly-looking Chinese man and his wife smile politely back at us. 'Oh . . .'

'Not him,' the waiter frowns. 'Hang on, my colleague

took the payment. I'll go and ask . . .' He disappears and Bec shrugs and reaches for one of the glasses.

'Whoa!' Joss says sharply. 'What are you doing?'

'Er, having a drink?' Bec looks surprised.

'Bec, you don't know who sent that, and you didn't see them make it. It could have anything in it!'

Bec puts her glass back down quickly.

'One of the twins' friends had her drink spiked in a club by some random bloke. They didn't realise – they just thought she was really drunk, but then she blacked out completely and they had to take her to A&E. I know it's—' Joss checks her watch, 'only six, but still.'

'No, you're absolutely right,' Bec says. 'Good call. Sad though isn't it? That you can't just enjoy what's probably a nice gesture.'

The waiter returns. 'Well ladies, he paid cash and he seems to have gone.'

'Sorry,' Joss says, 'but we're going to send these back. Just to be on the safe side.'

'OK,' he shrugs, not particularly bothered either way, and removes the tray.

'I'll get us some more,' Bec reaches for her purse. 'What do you want?'

But I've just had a really horrible thought.

'Actually, I'm just going to make a move,' I pick up my bag and coat suddenly. 'I'll call you both, OK?' and without stopping to kiss them both goodbye, and to their evident surprise, I make my way quickly towards the door . . .

225

## Chapter Nineteen

Back out on the cold – but still busy – street, I look up and down. There are a few groups of overdressed kids already milling around loudly and aimlessly, a long night of not being old enough to get in anywhere ahead of them; and plenty of shoppers laden down with bags making their way back to cars, strings of festive street lights twinkling above their heads. But no Leo.

And really, why would there be? I exhale, feeling suddenly very foolish indeed. It's early Saturday evening. He'll be in London with his wife, or pretending to be at a work thing while secretly skipping off to see one of the other women he regularly sex-texts. Apart from anything else, so some bloke sends over drinks – how arrogant am I to assume they're for me and not Joss or Bec? If I went back in there now I'd probably find whoever it was attempting to chat them up. I pull my coat on, tightening the belt around my waist before turning and starting to walk home, panting slightly after only a few minutes because it's all uphill. I really do need to have a stern word with myself. I am letting my imagination get the better of me and making this into something it isn't.

Firstly, Leo would never buy drinks and then just vanish; that's just not his style. He'd hang around for the glory – although Joss and Bec would never accept a drink from him, he'd *have* to do it anonymously . . . I'm starting to feel pretty hot in my coat, despite it being freezing. I should have got a taxi really . . . and, moreover, like he's going to know to show up in a random bar I would never normally be in at that time on a Saturday. So, what, now he's psychic? Oh for fuck's sake – why am I even thinking about this?

I start to speed up crossly. This is just what he wants, me thinking about him, everything revolving around him. I picture him swanning into the hotel in Windsor, buying those whiskys, that tequila. I should have done what Joss just did, sent them all straight back and—

A truly horrible thought slams into my mind; one that turns me cold and makes me stop in my tracks. I hear Joss's voice saying '. . . she blacked out completely. They had to take her to A&E'.

Leo bought the drinks at the hotel. He just turned up out of nowhere and bought me drinks. I got so drunk I went to bed with him and can't even remember it . . .

Oh. My. God . . .

I just stand there swaying on the spot, hands buried in my pockets. I let him into my room, I felt sick, I passed out and he helped me to the bed.

No! No – he wouldn't do that. He just wouldn't. Leo would never deliberately hurt me, surely? That's a very, very dangerous mind-leap too far. I *know* that I had too much to drink well before he turned up. I have only myself to blame for the effects of that, and in all honesty I do remember feeling glad that he was there when I woke up. And I did kiss him, I know I did . . . before we . . .

I tighten my coat around me again and start to walk a little faster, head down, staring at my feet as they march along the pavement. I just want to get home.

The traffic starts to lessen as I make my way into the quieter streets. My paranoid thoughts have made me feel uneasy, and I speed up to a brisk, no nonsense march. There aren't that many people around now, just an old man with a small dog out for an early-evening leg stretch, and as I glance over my shoulder, a tall teenage goth ambling along; headphones in, overcoat swinging from side to side.

I turn off on to another street – and then I'm alone entirely. All I can hear is the echo of my fast footsteps. I dig my hands more firmly into my pockets. I should have got a cab. I'm walking so quickly I'm in danger of breaking into a run, past some dark houses where no one is home, no one to hear me. 'Nearly there,' I mutter to myself under my breath. 'Nearly there.' My heart is thumping, which is ridiculous, because I'm fine. I'm *fine* . . . it's barely seven and what am I even running from?

A cough nearby makes me jump horribly – seconds before a car drives past – but when I look sharply to my left, a man is simply unloading bulging Sainsbury's bags from the boot of a Mini, the front door to his house already open and his wife with her arms crossed, shivering in the open doorway, light streaming out into the street.

Their normality, and presence, relaxes me slightly. By the time I reach the end of the street I'm a little calmer, breathing more easily and feeling very stupid for being so melodramatic. I'm a grown woman and yet I'm scaring myself silly despite being perfectly safe.

I turn into our road. A car with its lights on, indicator flashing, has pulled up on the left-hand side of the street towards the far end – but it's the one that comes up behind me so slowly I don't notice it until the last moment that makes me leap out of my skin.

'Get in.' The passenger door flings open hard enough to almost hit me in the leg.

'How many times do I have to tell you, you shouldn't walk home on your own?' Dan asks in exasperation as I clamber inside, pulling the seat belt on. 'Why didn't you ring me? I could have picked you up!'

'I thought you were still in Chichester,' I protest and we drive literally feet up the road before turning left on to our drive.

'So get a cab!' Dan says. '*Always get a cab.*'

'I'm fine,' I say, forgetting in an instant how vulnerable I felt a second ago, now that I'm safe with him.

He switches the engine off. 'I don't care how much it costs,' he says more patiently, 'it's important. Promise me next time you will?'

'I promise.'

'Good,' he says with the pleased air of having resolved a bothersome problem. 'Have we got anything to eat inside? I'm starving.'

'There's a pizza in the freezer I think.'

'That'll do,' he says cheerfully as we get out of the car.

'Can you turn the oven on?' I call down from our bedroom once we're back inside and I'm putting my feet into the furry warmth of my slippers.

'Already done it,' he calls up. 'Want a drink?'

'Yes please,' I shout, crossing the room to pull the curtains. Outside, a car is slowly reversing past the house, I just catch the end of the bonnet disappearing to my right before it's completely hidden away by the hedge. I pause for a moment. Probably just someone parking up.

Dan comes into the room. 'Is my phone charger up here?' he says, passing behind me. 'I can't find it and my battery's running low.' He glances up from beside the bedside table to see me still standing there just staring out into the street. 'What you looking at?'

The car suddenly reappears, but pulls away and drives off so sharply I don't see anything more than a pair of

231

hands holding the steering wheel before it roars off up the road.

'Nothing. Just closing the curtains.' I yank them shut quickly.

Once Dan has gone back downstairs, I check my phone. I don't want to, and I want to be wrong, but I'm not. There is a message waiting for me.

```
I love you. How many more times? How many
more ways to say it? This is starting to
hurt now. I can't stop thinking about you.
Think I need help! - think I need you. No,
I KNOW I need you. I have to see you
```

As I am deleting it with trembling fingers, telling myself that it was just a random car outside, that's all, another one comes in.

```
MUST see you. In dark place right now. Just
want this all to work out. Want us to be
happy. Want what we had. xxxxxxxxxxxxxxxx
xxxxxxxxxxxxxxxxxxxxxxxxxxxxxxxxxxxxxxxx
xxxxxxxxxxxxxxxxxxxxxxxxxxxxxxxxxxxxxxxx
xxxxxxxxxxxxxxxxxxxxxxxxxxxxxxxxxxxxxxxx
xxxxxxxxxxxxxxxxxxxxxxxxxxxxxxxxxxxxxxxx
xxxxxxxxxxxxxxxxxxxxxxxxxxxxxxxx
```

The lines of kisses just go on and on . . . and on.

# Chapter Twenty

'You're so sexy,' Dan murmurs in bed the next morning.

Much as I love Dan there is nothing sexy about any of this. The thin drizzly wail of an unwell little boy out of sorts is coming through from next door. It's all I can hear and I'm already horribly tense as it is because try as I might, I can't put Leo's text last night from my mind . . . It almost sounded pissed. Either that or he's getting carried away with his own sense of drama. I can't allow that to happen to me though – it *wasn't* him at the bar, and it was a random car outside the house. People park and reverse up and down roads, that's a normal thing.

But I still can't help glancing – for the hundredth time – at the curtains, to make sure they're still tightly shut, then at my mobile to make sure it's not somehow switched itself back on.

Urgh! I have to stop this. I'm doing this to myself and I have to stop! I'm letting this get completely out of hand; they're just text messages – that's all. So what if Leo says he's in a dark place? With a bit of luck he'll stay there.

Next door, Jack winds up for gold.

'Can they not just take him downstairs?' It's finally getting to Dan too. He stops, waits – but when the crying doesn't ease, gives up and collapses back on to his pillow, to my guilty relief. 'We *have* to move . . .' He sighs and looks at his watch. 'We should probably think about getting up anyway to be honest, it's gone nine. Should I pop out and get some croissants, do you think? Or have we got a cake or biscuits in the cupboard?'

I drag my mind back to the room and stare at him in confusion, he might as well be talking in code. 'What do we need a cake for?'

'Well, I think we ought to give them something, don't you? They'll probably have had breakfast but it's an hour's drive there and back, and that way we don't have to ask them to stay to lunch.' He looks at me and then says, 'You've forgotten, haven't you? Mum and Dad are popping over for a cup of tea. I told you last week.'

'Did you? But you only saw them yesterday . . .' I stare at him blankly, mentally running through each room in the house, seeing them through my mother-in-law's eyes; the bathroom needs cleaning, there's washing drying all over every surface in the dining room, the whole place needs hoovering and the kitchen floor is actually sticky underfoot . . .

'But they want to see you too,' he looks surprised. 'Is this because of what happened with Dad two weeks ago? Don't worry about it, he's fine. He's not even going to mention it, I promise. He's just looking forward to catching up with you. Do you want to go through the shower first or shall I?'

Mother of fuck . . . my stress levels ratchet up yet another notch as I leap from the bed, flinging the covers back. 'You can. I need to straighten up everywhere.'

'So is that yes to a cake then?' Dan calls after me.

He wanders back in about an hour later, as I'm feverishly chipping something unidentifiable but disgusting off the draining board in the kitchen, clutching the car keys and a Shell petrol station carrier bag, which – what with them not being famed for their pastry skills – doesn't bode well. 'What did you get?' I nod at the bag suspiciously.

He takes in my flushed face, tied-back mad hair and saggy T-shirt over pants and ignores my question. 'Why don't you go up and get dressed?' he says calmly, removing the knife from my hand. 'I'll finish up in here. It's only Mum and Dad . . . they've come to see us, not the draining board. I wouldn't have invited them if I'd have known it was going to stress you out this much.'

I start to pull the rubber gloves off.

'Oh, by the way, have I got any clean shirts for tomorrow?'

'I don't know, Dan!' I explode.

'Hey!' he reaches out for me in surprise as I try and blast past him, catching my arm. 'What are you flipping out for?'

I feel tears pricking at the back of my eyes. I try to look away, but I know he's seen them. 'Come here,' he pulls me to him and starts rocking me gently, but for once it doesn't help. I don't feel comforted, I actually want him to let go of me, but saying that would be very unfair to him...

'Tell me,' he says quietly. 'I can't help unless I know.'

... given none of this is his fault, it's mine.

'Are you worried about work and the money situation, like you said on Friday?'

And if I don't get a grip – fast, I'm going to be in serious danger of messing this up completely. I'm already making it all much worse than it is.

'Yeah, pretty much,' I say and pull away from him. 'I'm sorry, I shouldn't have gone off on one like that.'

'You sure there's nothing else?'

I shake my head.

'I mean it Moll. Dad'll be on his best behaviour. Go and have a shower,' he says. 'I'll finish up down here. Go on.'

Standing under the hot water I let my head hang heavily.

This whole thing is nothing more than man seeks easy repeat of sex – hardly shocking. I've bumped into him in the street once and had a few texts. End of. Get over it. There are other, far more important things I ought to be thinking about than him.

I climb out of the shower wearily and wrap myself tightly in a towel, shivering slightly on the bath mat before going through to our bedroom. I'm about to get dressed when I hesitate and cross the room to make sure the curtains are still properly drawn, only to see through the gap, my father-in-law's very shiny car pulling up outside. SHIT! I glance wildly at my watch. They are forty minutes early.

'They're here!' I yell at the top of my voice, dashing to the top of the stairs, clutching my towel about me. Dan appears at the bottom, holding the unread paper in one hand and a full mug of tea in the other. 'I thought you said they'd be here at eleven?' I say accusingly.

'Aren't you going to put some clothes on?'

No, I'm going to have coffee with your parents wearing a towel. Of course I was going to get dressed, but they are *forty minutes early.*

'You disappeared off up there ages ago. What have you been doing?'

The doorbell rings shrilly.

'I'll let them in,' he says unnecessarily, 'you just come down when you're ready. Seriously Moll, calm down . . . what's *wrong* with you today?'

Five minutes later, I appear in the sitting room ready to do the 'Sorry about that, I was just coming down when the phone rang' fib, but the words die on my lips as I see Dan has plonked a box of Jaffa Cakes and Mr Kipling bakewell tarts in the middle of the carpet, along-side a plastic milk carton and a couple of side plates.

He is happily munching a tart, and getting crumbs everywhere. Michael is busily attempting, unsuccessfully, to prize his from the foil case and Susan is delicately sitting on the edge of the sofa balancing a chipped mug on her knife-creased trousers.

I look at Dan in despair. 'What?' Dan says through a mouthful. 'They didn't have any croissants.'

'I'll just nip and get the milk jug . . .' I make a last-ditch attempt at the pretence that I have everything under control. 'Would you rather have some toast with your tea?' which is, let's face it a more normal thing to eat at twenty past ten on a Sunday morning.

'No, no, this is lovely, Molly, thank you, don't worry about the milk jug,' Susan carefully puts her tea down and stands up, giving me a very genuine smile. 'How are you?' Is it my imagination or does her warm hug last a little longer than normal?

Michael abandons his cake and gets to his feet as well. 'Hello,' he says gruffly, clearly extending an olive branch. He plants the obligatory brief kiss somewhere in the region of my left ear. But then inexplicably he pats me on the head twice too, as perhaps the Master of the hunt might do to his favourite hound. Astonished, I look at him as he sits back down, carefully negotiating not stepping on any of the boxes or the milk. It's as close to an apology as Michael will ever get, and it's big of him, especially given I was the one who was so rude.

'It's nice to see you again,' I say sincerely.

'It's lovely to see you too,' Susan says, moving things

on quickly as she picks up her mug again. 'Had a busy week Molly?'

I'm trying to think of an appropriate answer to that question, when from next door, we all hear Mel shriek 'No, Jack! Very bad. Give it to me!' followed by a thump – presumably her son flinging himself to the floor in protest – and an angry bellow a baby buffalo would be proud of. Susan stoically pretends it hasn't happened. 'Dan was just saying it looks like there are some troubled times ahead at work for you. I'm sorry to hear that.'

Michael, however, cuts across her. 'What the bloody hell is wrong with that child?'

'He must be ill,' Dan says. 'It's never normally this bad.'

'I should hope not! Good God!'

'He'll stop in a minute,' Dan says. 'Anyway, we might need them on side soon, when we have our baby.'

Susan gasps with delight, unsteadily puts her tea down and then covers her mouth with both hands. 'You're pregnant?' she turns to me, her eyes shining and dancing with excitement. She spins back to Dan. 'But you said yesterday—'

Oh? What did he say yesterday?

Dan doesn't quite meet my eye. 'I said we're trying Mum, she's not actually pregnant, yet.'

'Oh,' Susan looks visibly disappointed, but almost immediately perks up again. 'That's still wonderful news though! We were saying yesterday, Molly, my dad will be so excited about being a great-grandpa! There's only one other at his home. And I'm going to start knitting again!' she beams. 'I've actually got a pattern I bought a while ago. It's a cardigan – with such dear little socks and a hat that goes with it.'

She looks at Dan and to my huge surprise I realise her eyes are bright with tears. 'Oh, just look at me!' she says, hurriedly searching for a tissue in her sleeves but not finding one. Michael silently passes her a neatly pressed hanky from his pocket. 'Silly old woman. Good grief, what will I be like when you actually *have* your baby!' she does a high little laugh and blows her nose. 'I'm just so excited!'

'Mum was totally blown away, wasn't she?' Dan says to me later, as he flicks through the papers in bed. 'Dad's reaction I could have predicted, Mr Practical with his "Is this sensible if Molly's job is so uncertain?" You two have got more in common than you realise, but Mum, wow,' he shakes his head in disbelief then smiles at me. 'It was amazing.'

I just lie there, staring up at the ceiling. 'I didn't realise that this would be so important to other people.'

'Well, it's only because Mum doesn't have any other family bar us, Dad and Grandpa.' Dan says reasonably. 'It's probably more of a deal for her than it would be for say, your parents. I'm not saying it won't be special for them too, but they've already got your brothers' kids, haven't they? This is first time round for Mum. It's huge.'

'Was it really a good idea to tell them, do you think?' I say slowly, also thinking back to my blurting it out to Abi and wishing I hadn't.

Dan looks at me in surprise. 'Why wouldn't we tell them something like that?'

'Because it's private,' I say. 'Between you and me.'

'We told your mum and dad,' he shrugs. 'Why wouldn't we tell mine?'

'I get that you're excited, but—'

He puts the paper down. 'What's wrong? Is there something you're not telling me?'

'No! I just mean suppose it doesn't happen?' I say quickly. 'Everyone will ask questions and feel so let down and . . .'

His face relaxes. 'Oh I see. Don't worry about it Moll. It WILL happen, you're not *that* old.' He winks at me and picks up the paper again.

He sounds just like Abi.

'It'll all be fine.'

And Bec.

'Mum's just excited, that's all. She'll calm down. She would have liked a whole tribe of kids herself.' Dan says conversationally turning a page.

Yes, I got that impression.

'But I'm not sure Dad even really wanted me, he only did it for her—'

I turn to him sharply but he stays behind the paper. 'Your dad adores you.'

'I know,' he says lightly, putting the paper down, and says after a pause. 'So it turned out all right for them in the end, didn't it?'

I look up at him. He smiles hopefully back at me, his

241

words just hanging there in the air with all of their unspoken meaning.

I nod and reassured he bends and kisses me; then kisses me a little more . . . and a little more still . . . and this time there is no baby crying next door. It's just the two of us.

# Chapter Twenty-One

'Sorry, love,' shrugs the builder, 'I don't know what to say. He told us it was all systems go. We'd never have just let ourselves in like that if we'd have known you were in the dark about it.'

Yeah – well it's early enough in the morning to still practically *be* sodding dark.

'Can you just hang on a minute?' I shiver by the back gate, mobile clamped to my ear. 'I'm ringing the landlord now.'

The builder nods and shoots a look at his two mates, who sigh and rest down the scaffolding poles they have balanced on their shoulders. We all wait silently in the freezing cold for my landlord to pick up – who says Mondays can't be fun?

'Mr Landsdowne? Hello. It's Molly Greene . . . from

number 27 . . . Barcombe Road?' How many houses does he own for God's sake? 'I'm ringing because I'm stood outside with three builders who I've just found letting themselves into our back garden round through the side gate. Apparently they need access to next door to put scaffolding up because there's a problem with their roof? And you said that would be OK?' I pause and listen for a moment. 'Well yes, except you didn't tell us. I work from home and it was really frightening to find some strange men' – 'Sorry' I mouth to the builders, who shrug, unbothered – 'letting themselves into . . . well yes, I appreciate that, I'm just saying you're meant to give us notice, that's . . .' I try to keep calm as he starts to blather on about how he must have rung the wrong number by mistake – another tenant in another house. Yeah right, of course he did. 'OK, fine,' I say tiredly. 'Well, they're here now, but next time could you please let us know?'

The builders, happily sensing victory, hoist the poles back on to their shoulders and – cheeky gits – start entering the combination on the padlock, which they've obviously been given as well, before I've even hung up.

'We'll try and keep it down while we're "erecting",' says one of them, to the sniggers of the others. 'What is it you do from home then?'

'I'm a medical rep.'

'Oh right,' he says disinterestedly.

I can't say I blame him. 'I'll leave you to it then,' I reply, as if I've got any control over the situation at all, and head back into the house.

I very quickly discover that working in my office, which faces out over the garden, is not going to be an option until they've finished playing with their poles. We haven't been able to shut the window flush since we moved in, the frame obviously expanded with damp some time ago and we've not got round to sorting it out – admittedly our own fault – but it means I can hear all of their banter, and *see* it once the scaffolding goes up, because helpfully there's a platform right on eye level.

Sighing, I unplug the laptop and take it down to the sitting room with my mobile for a bit of privacy, which is much better – not to say quieter – and after a while, I begin to forget they're there. Well almost; they keep walking backwards and forwards past the window, but things could be worse.

Things could be a lot worse. Since his drunken text on Saturday, I've heard nothing from Leo. I was expecting to get a message when I switched on the phone this morning; but there wasn't a thing, which was an un-believable relief. I hadn't realised quite how stressed out by it I'd allowed myself to become.

Perhaps in the cold light of day – once he'd sobered up and re-read what he'd sent, realised how indulgent it looked – he'd felt embarrassed and now just wants to sidle off quietly. Save his male pride, pretend it never happened: 'Think I need help! – Think I need you' . . .

I snort, forgetting how scary it seemed on Saturday, when I was stood in our bedroom staring down into the dark street below. Not exactly Shakespeare, was it Leo?

I actually manage to get a lot done before and after lunch, despite the clanking around outside. I'm concentrating on how to word an email to a particularly tricky GP who likes to pick me up on every possible point he can, and have just reached out absently to switch the light on because it's getting dark outside, when the ceiling creaks above me. I've been staring at the screen with such fierce concentration I haven't noticed how quiet it's become – the builders must have gone home. It creaks again; just the usual noises a house makes from time to time – not something you'd normally notice – but on my own, it sounds like someone moving around in one of the upstairs rooms. I glance up, pause and wait a moment . . . but there's nothing, just silence. I return to the laptop . . . and then leap out of my skin at the PING! of an email arriving.

It's Pearce.

Guess what? Know it's Christmas do in two weeks?

Oh God, I'd forgotten that.

Get this - S says partners AND clients invited ... clients. CLIENTS? At xmas work do? I ASK YOU!!! World has gone mad...urgh. No fun!

Without thinking, I immediately type back:

```
You  do  know  all  email  is  probably
monitored at mo? Be more careful!

Fair point, but don't be cross with me! He
replies. Can I make it up to you at party?
Have mistletoe — will travel.
```

I'm really not sure I've got the strength for the corporate Christmas do this year. Anyway, it's hardly going to be much of a bash is it? Half of us may not even have jobs for much longer.

Another email arrives.

```
Er, Hi?
```

Pearce must be having a slow day. Although that reminds me — I don't mail back, just in case our mail IS monitored — but text him instead.

```
BTW, crossed wires. Am not pregnant. Think
you thought otherwise the other day? Just
so you know!

Not sure what to say to that! He texts back.
Congratulations? Bad luck? Call if you want
to chat! x
```

I smile, but then another sigh from the ceiling makes me frown and raise my eyes again. I put my laptop to one side, get up and cautiously make my way to the bottom of the stairs. Pausing, I stare up the dark stairwell of my own house.

'Hello?' I call out instinctively and wait. Quite what for I don't know – I'd hardly want someone to call hello back, not that anyone does of course. Then for reasons best known to myself, I reach out, not taking my eyes off the stairs, open the front door and bang it shut again – as if someone has just come in and I'm not alone – and say out loud, 'Oh, hi love! You're home early!' Then I fall silent suspiciously . . . again nothing. Not a sound.

I flick the light on and warily begin to pad upstairs. Arms tightly wrapped round myself, I stick my head first round our bedroom door, which is of course empty, pull the light switch on in the bathroom – nothing there, and then slowly push open the door to my office. It looks like it always does; my desk, a chest of drawers, the armchair by the window, but I can hear tinny music coming from somewhere . . . and then someone talking. I cross over the room and peer out on to the scaffolding. There's a small portable radio sat outside on the plat-form, aerial pertly up, but everything else has been packed away. The builders must have left it behind by mistake. I open the window to see if I can reach it – at least turn it off, and as I'm leaning out I see the side gate pulling shut, someone closing it behind them.

'Wait!' I call, feeling a bit silly that I've been shouting around randomly downstairs, not realising they were still here. 'You've forgotten your radio!' But they can't have heard me because they don't come back. By the time

I've closed the window as best I can, run downstairs and opened the front door – they've gone, because the van isn't there any more. Oh well. I'll leave it in the kitchen. They can claim it when they come back to start the roof work.

I've just sat down on the sofa again when my mobile buzzes next to me.

```
Forgive me - this isn't all talk no action,
I promise. I could leave Helen. You could
tell Dan, tell him now! We could be together
tonight! Shall we just do it?! Xxx
```

'Get a new phone, Moll,' Joss insists. 'If work really think it's going to be that much of a bitch to change your number from a client point of view, just get a new mobile for personal calls. The second it hits six each day, turn the work one off and switch your new one on – then he won't be able to get through to you apart from in working hours. It's not ideal, but it's a shitload better than him having this twenty-four hour access.'

'It seemed a good idea at the time,' I babble, 'having work cough up for my mobile bills, me just paying for whatever calls I made. I wish I'd kept it separate now, had my own.'

'Well – you still can.'

'You don't think he meant it do you? About telling his wife?'

She snorts. 'No I don't. He said he could, not he would.

This is Leo we're talking about. He's a lazy little shit. Not once did I ever see him put himself out for you when you two were together. He's just loving the drama of all this – the saddo.'

'You're not worried that . . . all the other stuff . . . you think I'm imagining it? I have to admit, hearing myself say it all out loud to you it did sound crazy.'

'You're not crazy,' Joss says immediately. 'Him texting you like this must be horrible, but even if he did come down to Brighton on Saturday hoping to bump into you, I really don't think those drinks were from him Moll, there's no way he could have known you were going to be in that bar, it was a last-minute arrangement with me and Bec. You only came in because Dan was in Chichester and you were all wound up after that baby shower. I almost wish I hadn't sent the drinks back now, because then the bloke who actually bought them for us probably would have come over and you'd have thought nothing more of it.'

'I did think that myself actually,' I admit, 'after I'd left.'

'Well there you go. As for that car outside your house; you're on edge and worried that Dan is going to find out what happened. It's making you jumpy, I get that, but if you don't chill out he's going to cotton on to something being wrong anyway. I knew something was up with you on Saturday and even Bec asked me what was going on once you'd gone.'

I fall silent. 'Did you tell her?'

'No, of course not. I said I thought you were just worried about the baby stuff.'

'So you don't think that text he sent me, the "you look nice today" one – like he'd actually seen me in person – is anything sig—'

'No, I think your first instinct was right, it probably *was* meant for someone else,' she interjects. 'He's a smarmy weasel. It's vile having him text you all the time, but that's all it is. And for the record, he's wrong – he always *has* been all talk and no action. Seriously, go out NOW and get yourself a phone. He's going to get bored and give up. Leo was never built for endurance.'

'He told me he loves me, Joss. He's never said that before – you know that.'

She snorts. 'Molly, I told the wanker with the clipboard who tried to hug me this morning that I already support Greenpeace – I didn't mean that either. They're just words.'

I take a deep breath. 'You're right. I'm sorry to ring you at work, I was just freaking out here.' I almost tell her about shouting up the stairs like a loon too, just to make her laugh, but I've taken up enough of her time.

'It's honestly not a problem. That's what friends are for.'

She sounds tired though, and I begin to wish I hadn't bothered her. 'Are *you* OK?' I ask.

'Yeah,' she says, flatly. 'We went to see Mum yesterday afternoon. The whole place was a tip, and she was off her face, it really upset the twins. I shouldn't have taken them round. You just keep thinking one day it's going to change, you know?'

There's a long pause and then she suddenly says, brisk again. 'Bloody hell, listen to us – you want to slit your wrists first or shall I? Come on Greene. Enough of this. New phone – go right now, OK?'

'OK,' I promise obediently.

'Oh! Just quickly though – what are we doing for your birthday this weekend?'

'Can I be honest? I don't really want to do anything.'

'Fair enough. No one says you have to. I've, er,' her voice suddenly becomes careless, 'actually got some stuff on this week anyway. I've a date on Thursday . . .'

'Oh?' I perk up at that. 'Who with?'

'Just a bloke from work,' she does what I think is a fake nonchalant yawn. 'But I'll speak to you before then anyway, I'm sure.'

'That'd be nice, but in case we don't, have fun Joss.'

'Pffff,' she responds dismissively, 'depends on him really, doesn't it? I'll try though. Love you.'

It's only once I've hung up that I realise I didn't tell her about bumping into Leo in London after my appointment . . . but I push away my niggling doubts, she's right. Leo's not omnipotent, he's not God. He just thinks he is.

Joss is right about the new phone. It's incredibly easy to sort. The handset will be delivered tomorrow or the day after and I'm already feeling better by the time I finally pull up outside the house, but it's quickly replaced by confusion when I see that the curtains have been pulled and the lights are on.

Dan's back? How come?

'Hello?' I call warily as I shut the front door behind me.

'I'm up here,' he calls. 'Can you come up a sec?'

I jog upstairs and appear in the doorway of my office to find him sitting in my chair, in front of my computer. 'You're back early!' I exclaim happily. 'You should have called me and let me know – I'd have come to pick you up.'

'I did, your phone was off,' he says, still frowning at the screen. 'I don't feel great, I wanted to check the swine flu symptoms but I left my laptop at work, so I thought I'd use yours.' He sits back and looks at me very directly. 'You left it on the sofa for starters where anyone could see it – and your email was open too. I want to talk to you about a message I've just read.'

All of the blood rushes from my face, I feel it just pull from the muscles. Oh my God. Oh Jesus. I just stand there, stupidly, frozen to the spot, unable to speak. Has the Facebook blocking not worked after all? Has Leo somehow found me again? Did I leave an old message on there by mistake?

'Why is Pearce emailing you and asking you not to be cross with him?'

Eh? My expression flickers. 'Pearce?'

'Yes, Pearce,' he says patiently. 'Look.' He twists the laptop round, '"Have mistletoe will travel?" I'm not happy about that, Molly,' he says. 'I'm not happy at all, and what's this supposed to mean?' – he opens another one – '"Er, Hi." Hi what? Hi, I'm sorry? Hi, how are you?

253

Hi, I'm trying it on? Because if he is, he can fuck off and hi.'

I can't help but smile at Dan's fierce tone, although mostly with relief. 'He's just mucking around. Pearce is going out with Sandra! And more to the point, since when is it OK to go snooping through my emails?'

I actually can't believe I've just said that . . . the sheer hypocrisy is breathtaking.

'I didn't snoop!' he coughs violently with indignation. 'You left it open! And if he's going out with Sandra, why does he think it's a shame that husbands and wives are invited to the Christmas do? Does he mean me? Urgh, I need a tissue.' He fumbles around in his pocket sniffing heavily.

Wow, he really did read through the mails.

'I don't like him being so over-familiar, it's not on. He clearly has a huge crush on you, but that's no excuse. Please don't encourage him, OK? Sending you email jokes he's found and texting you business updates on Sunday nights,' he grumbles. He holds out an arm to me and I walk over, bending down to kiss him as he hugs me to him. 'Cheeky little shit,' he says gruffly. 'Him that is, not you.'

'Thanks for clearing that up. Shall I go and make you a Lemsip or something?' I put my hand on his forehead. 'I don't think you've got swine flu though, you're not hot at all.'

'Story of my life,' he concedes gloomily. 'Well, you just remind Pearce you've got a husband who'll take him outside at the Christmas do if need be, give him a shiny

Rudolf nose *and* happily show him where to shove his antlers, OK?'

'You're going to come are you?' I say surprised, because Dan hates that sort of thing.

'Yup,' Dan says determinedly, glancing at the emails again. 'I am now. By the way – where did all that come from?' He motions to the scaffolding outside and I fill him in.

'Hmmm. Well, I better make sure that window is secure then,' he says – and insists on going next door to ask them if he can climb up the scaffolding, before bashing the window shut from outside so we can lock it.

'Done it,' he says, looking terrible as he comes back in from the cold and gives another hacking cough. 'I think I'm going to go to bed now.'

Which is where he stays – unusually for him – the following day. I'm awake from half-six anyway, my brain worrying away before my eyes are even open, and what with poor old Dan coughing . . . sleep is impossible.

By the time I'm up and tucking my feet under my desk ready for the start of the working day however, he's gone quiet, dozing presumably. I take a deep breath and switch my phone on . . .

And my heart thuds as the little envelope appears with a 1 next to it.

Nearly told H last night. Think we ought to discuss plan? Xx

255

My mouth falls open – just as Dan appears at the door with bed hair, dressed in tracky bottoms and an elderly zip-up fleece, looking rather sorry for himself. 'Do you want a cup of tea?' he offers, clutching a tissue.

I hit the delete button straight away and shake my head. 'No thanks. You should be in tucked up in the warm. I'll make you one if you like though.'

'Yes please,' he says weakly.

'How you feeling?'

He shrugs. 'Bit crap. I'm going to stay out of your way though, don't worry.'

'No, it's fine.' I switch my laptop on. 'In fact it's really helpful that you're here. I'm having a new phone delivered and it might arrive today. Could you listen out for it this afternoon, just in case? I won't be back from my meetings until about three.'

'OK,' he says and blows his nose. 'Is something wrong with your BlackBerry then?' he nods at it.

'No, I just thought it would make sense to get my own number and start using it now, in case I have to give my work one back in the new year . . .' I duck down and pretend to get something out of a file under the desk so he can't see my face.

'What did you get?'

'I don't know, just some bog standard thing.'

'Fair enough.' He nods.

'Get back to bed now, sicknote,' I order gently, 'and I'll bring you that cuppa.'

* * *

256

Only once I'm in the safety of the car, having left to go to my first appointment of the day, do I text Leo back furiously. I know Joss said ignore him but I can't not react to what he said, the prospect is too terrifying.

```
Am NOT telling anyone anything! No plan
needed. Leave me alone!
```

I receive no response, which is actually almost as unnerving as getting a message. It's a relief to have Dan at home when I get back – reassuring – and when he doesn't go back the following day either I'm secretly pleased.

'Your new phone's here,' he calls when I arrive back after a morning of traffic jams, a late arrival that wasn't my fault and a message from Leo.

```
Stop panicking! Know you so well! Have booked
a hotel in Brighton Friday night so we can
have dinner...we will sort this babe. Xx
```

I activate the new phone, charge it all up and by ten to six I am upstairs in my office, almost smugly waiting to switch my BlackBerry off.

But with four minutes to go, he beats me again.

```
And don't worry about having to tell them.
I'M going to do it x
```

## Chapter Twenty-Two

'You were!' I say down the phone, practically in tears I'm so frustrated and frightened, to say nothing of the fact I'm exhausted because I barely slept last night. 'You were threatening me!'

'I wasn't!' Leo insists. 'I love you! Why would I threaten you of all people? I meant that I'll make this whole thing as easy as I can for you. It's hard to get the right tone across in a text, but if you won't speak to me . . .'

'This whole thing?' I repeat. 'Leo, THERE IS NO WHOLE THING! I *don't* want to be with you, I'm *not* leaving my husband. I don't care what you do, if you stay with Helen or not, I just want you to leave me alone!'

'Don't shout,' he says quietly. 'Just because you're stressed out, you don't need to take it out on me.'

*Oh my God!* If the car window wasn't shut I'd throw the fucking phone as far away from me as I could.

'I know it's hard to think about hurting people, but we can't undo what we've done, Molly. What we know we feel.'

That's what does it. Hearing him of all people telling me how I feel. Something breaks in me like someone snapping a sharp icicle. Shivering with anger, I force my voice to try and sound as calm as humanly possible.

'I'm going to say this one last time Leo. *Leave me alone.* You want threats? Come near me again, contact me again and I won't be responsible for my actions.'

I hang up, start the car and swerve out of the lay-by back on to the road. I'm going to be late for my first meeting. I don't even know what I meant by that, telling him I wouldn't be responsible for what I'd do. What can I do? Nothing! I can't do anything at all. I am completely powerless. Whatever action I might take would involve needing to tell someone what happened in that hotel – or might result in HIM telling someone what we did, and he knows it.

I don't believe for a second that he wasn't threatening me. He was! And I know exactly how it feels when someone just steps into your life and rips your world apart like that . . . I am terrified of him doing it to Dan; the explosion it would cause.

If only Leo's stupid wallet hadn't been in my bag; he would have kept walking out of that hotel. We'd made our peace. We should have just gracefully exited each other's lives . . . and if I'd have called Dan first thing that morning and said sorry straight away, when Leo turned up, perhaps I wouldn't have been so unsettled – I'd have been more on my guard.

Surely now though, even he cannot keep acting as if we have a future, pretending that I am waiting for him to prove himself to me. I have just been as blunt as it is possible to be. Not even Leo can twist that . . . can he? Please God he will now leave me alone. I didn't want it to have to end like this, but frankly, I'll settle for any end I can get.

'I called the landlord about the scaffolding, that's how bored I am,' Dan says when he brings yet another cup of tea up to my office after lunch. 'He said it could be up for ages yet, the builders are on another job now and they can't start work on the roof anyway until the weather picks up. I don't know why they bothered putting it up in the first place.' He paces about the small room before finally sitting down on the seat in the corner. 'Do you think I should have gone in today? I do feel a bit better.'

'Well you can go back tomorrow, can't you?' I check my watch. 'Shit, I'm late.'

'Don't go!' he looks pained. 'Cancel your meeting. I've not even got any decent DVDs left now.'

I get to my feet and start to gather my stuff hurriedly. 'Sorry, I've got to – oh, I meant to say, do you mind if I go and see Bec after work? She wants to take me out for a birthday drink because she's working this weekend.'

'In town?' he blows his nose.

'Yeah, so I won't be late.'

'OK. Well, I'll probably get an early night anyway,' he shoves the tissue in his pocket, 'see the last of this off. You should definitely go – have fun.'

Once the last meeting has finished I get back into the car and put my seat belt on. It's slightly too early to switch the BlackBerry off. I better give it another half an hour, but then hopefully, after this morning, that's going to turn out to be an unnecessary precaution. I know Joss said to ignore Leo, but sometimes you have to stand up and come out of your corner fighting. Maybe it was better that I called him and let rip. OK, so he insisted I'd misunderstood, but – well, it sounded like a threat to me.

At least Bec doesn't know about all of this Leo stuff, which is great because it means she won't feel she has to ask me about it tonight and I won't waste a nice evening discussing it with her. It'll be a relief to think about something else. I check my watch . . . the antenatal class I'm picking her up from doesn't finish for another half an hour yet. Plenty of time to get there. I AM going to have a nice evening. I am . . .

The community centre smells slightly musty when I arrive and let myself in. I glance uncertainly up and down the dark corridors and notice at the far end to the right, a light shining out from under a door – that must be them.

I decide I'll nip to the loo while they finish up and

tentatively start to investigate. A door to the left pushes open to reveal a storage room containing a few yoga mats and a CD player. Another a little further on takes me into a small kitchen with some dirty teaspoons on the side, a jar of coffee and some assorted chipped mugs below a cupboard, on which someone has Sellotaped a note saying, 'Please leave this kitchen as you would like to find it!'

Heels clicking on the worn lino as I venture tentatively up the hall, I try a third door. Pulling the light cord – which makes the strip lighting flex noisily – harsh light floods the room and I jump as I catch sight of my reflection in some mirrors opposite. It's a male changing room I think, if the smell is anything to go by, but no one is around and the cubicles I find round the corner are surprisingly clean.

I've just flushed the loo when I hear the main swing door go, someone has just come in. Oh no, I hope it's not a football team piling in from outside or something, how embarrassing. I wait for a moment to hear voices, so I can work out how many people are there, but there's nothing – in fact it's eerily quiet, and inexplicably the hairs on the back of my neck stand up. I can't explain it, but something doesn't feel right . . . and I don't want to stay here a second longer. I lunge for the cubicle door and stumble back out into the main changing area, which is empty . . . Seconds later I nearly have a heart attack though, as a heavily pregnant woman bursts in clutching a mobile phone to her ear and insisting 'No, you don't understand, I'm *desperate* for the loo, I'll call you back OK?' She hangs up and holds the door ajar for me with her other hand. 'People keep ringing to see if I've had it yet!' she volunteers, looking down at her stomach and smiling.

I manage a sympathetic smile back, thank her and as I slip back out into the dark, empty corridor, a door bangs somewhere else in the building, as if someone has just gone through it. At the exact same moment, or maybe it was slightly earlier, I'm not sure, another one right at the far end of the corridor yanks open and a second pregnant lady appears together with Bec.

'Glasses should be in the top cupboard above the sink,' Bec says as she flicks a light on. Then she sees me. 'Molly!' she says. 'What are you doing skulking around in the dark? We're down here.' She beckons me enthusiastically. 'No, come in, it's fine, we're nearly done. This is my lift tonight, everyone,' she beams as I make my way into the room. The group smile back at me and wave, albeit lethargically, some of them look ready to drop then and there.

'Now Kelly, you were just about to say something about your experience of the heightened sense of smell which women often experience during pregnancy?' Bec turns back to the group confidently, as I quietly sink on to a chair, the heebie-jeebies, the prickly sensation of fear, settling back down now I'm with other people. Never mind suspecting Leo of losing his grip on reality; I'm not that far behind him.

'Yes, well, I hope you don't mind me telling people

264

this,' the woman turns to glance at her husband, who looks pretty worried, presumably because he has no idea what she is going to say, let alone if he will mind, 'but for me it was your breath. Right from day one to be honest. It wasn't bad or anything,' she explains to everyone, 'I just couldn't bear it.'

Some of the other women nod their heads wisely in agreement. 'And,' she continues, the bit firmly between her teeth, 'his trousers. Oh my God! I *hated* the smell of his work trousers,' she looks around the room. 'I had to make him take them off at the front door.'

The mental image that conjures of her poor tired husband getting back from the office clutching a brief-case and stripping to his pants while still wearing a shirt and suit jacket makes the corners of my mouth turn up and I have to look at the floor quickly before Bec meets my eye. I hear the wobble in her voice as she says, 'Well, the good news is it obviously passed as you're er . . .' she pauses and gathers herself, 'wearing trousers tonight Dave. Well done you.'

We're still laughing as we get into the car.

'I mean what are you supposed to say to something like that? Her poor husband,' Bec says. 'I don't know how he puts up with her. Guess how old she is?'

'Um, thirty-two?' I hazard.

'Yeah, actually she is,' Bec says, disappointed. 'I think she looks much older though, don't you? Well, obviously you don't. Anyway, speaking of getting older, "Happy Birthday for Saturday – Happy Birthday for Saturday",' she sings. '"Happy Birthday, dear Molly, Happy Birthday for Saturday." Here . . .' she reaches into her vast bag and pulls out a bottle of Moët and a card, which is really sweet of her. 'Thirty-four!' she says. 'You're so old!'

'Steady on there, Smugly,' I say quickly, as she pops them on the back seat. 'You're not that far behind.'

'Oh, but I am,' she says happily. 'Five months is practically half a year. I wonder where we'll be this time next year. Shit, Moll,' she says. 'By the time it gets to *my* birthday, you might be pregnant!' She pats my leg delightedly. 'Imagine that!'

What with everything else, I'd practically forgotten about the baby stuff. I shift in my seat. 'It's early days yet, Bec.'

''Course it is,' she says quickly. 'Don't worry. It's usually if nothing's happened after ten months to a year it's a good idea to get checked out. You've got loads of time yet.'

Wow, that actually is ages. 'Really?' I say. 'Ten months?'

'Oh yeah.'

Huh. I did *not* know that.

'Thanks for coming to get me,' she yawns. 'It's such a pain that my car died. I can't wait to get it back tomorrow. Anyway – to the bar, birthday girl.'

By the time we've found a free table, got a drink and Bec has filled me in on some of the men who have already responded to the devastatingly brilliant dating profile I wrote for her – one of whom she is having an online chat with tomorrow night – I'm starting to relax a bit. I am actually very pleased she and Joss are looking forward to their respective dates. We even have a toast to friends who can always take you out of yourself. Then she starts to tell me in more detail about the blokes she's been meeting online.

'Most of them seem pretty nice, to be honest,' she chatters away. 'I just liked David's smile best. There was this one guy who I think had English as his second language. His friend said, a bit ominously, that he has a "*healthy daily routine*", which sounded like regular bowel movements, although apparently it "includes running" and always walking people "back to the bus stop after dinner".'

I giggle.

'He said he wanted someone who was also "in good shape" with a "*healthy daily routine*", but who must also be able to "hold a good conversation", which I think is actually a little ambitious on his part.'

'What did he look like?' I'm intrigued.

'Oh, don't. That was the worst bit.' She laughs. 'He was dressed in full ski gear in his picture. You get internet on your BlackBerry don't you?'

'Um, I get emails. I don't ever go online with it, though.'

'Give it here, let's have a look. I'll see if I can show you what Kyle looks like.'

'Kyle?' I laugh. 'Urrgh!' I pass it to her and she fiddles around. 'Oh. You've only got maps and MySpace.'

'Maps?' I say, interested. 'Really? Where?'

'See?' She holds it up to me and shows me the icons.

I take the phone from her and click on it. Immediately a map appears with an anonymous profile box and a little arrow pointing at a street. Above it, it says MollyJo 1m ago and Brighton, UK. It's also offering me options. I peer at the screen. The arrow is pointing at the road Bec and I are on.

'Wow!' I exclaim. 'That's amazing! It's plotted where we are. How has it done that?' Bec peers over my shoulder.

I click on the options and an email address I don't recognise, but containing my name, pops up, along with options to change your status, change your photo, edit privacy and see friends. I click on 'See Friends' – but it just offers me the chance to invite others to show on my map. So I go into Privacy. It seems to be set to 'Detect Location'. Whatever that means.

'I don't get this,' I look up at Bec. 'Why would I need to know where I am when I'm already here? What's it for?'

She shrugs. 'I don't know. Why don't you ask Dan when you get home. He's the IT expert.'

'It's a free application that you can download,' Dan says. 'If you go on to . . . here . . . it'll give you traffic updates . . . here you can get directions . . . and there . . . you can add friends so you can see where they are. Say you wanted to see Joss on here. You text or email her a link asking her to be your buddy. If she says yes, she pops up on this map too. You know where she is and she knows where you are, unless you choose to withhold your location, in which case you can see her, but she can't see you.'

'But I haven't downloaded anything! You're sure it doesn't just come with the phone?'

He shakes his head. 'You have to opt into this . . . give your permission to appear,' he explains as I look at him blankly.

'Maybe work added it and forgot to tell me,' I suggest.

He doesn't say anything.

'Hang on though, you're saying this map is showing someone else where I am?' I frown.

He nods.

'Does that mean I could be saying I was at a meeting and, if it was work, they'd be able to see if I was telling the truth or not?'

'If it was your work either they would have had to have installed it on your phone before they gave it to you, or someone would have needed access to your mobile. Then they could have sent the link to your phone and agreed to it *for* you. Then the programme would just download.'

'How long would that take to do?'

'About five minutes.'

And that's when the penny drops. Well, it doesn't so much drop, it slices through the top of my head as if someone has deliberately let go of it from the top of a tall building.

'So whoever did this,' I try to keep my hands steady, 'knows that I'm in Brighton and they know what street we live on – and,' I peer at the phone, 'almost exactly *where* on the street we live?'

'Yes.'

I hand it back to him quickly. 'Delete it, please.'

He presses a few buttons. 'It's gone. What are you going to do about this?' he looks at me worriedly. 'Are you going to ring one of your colleagues? Find out if they've got it on their phone too?'

'I don't think I should do anything rash,' I take the phone back. 'I don't want to stir up some sort of storm, not the way things are at work at the moment. I didn't even know this sort of thing was possible.'

'It's not designed for snooping,' Dan says. 'It's supposed to be a social networking thing, for fun.'

'Fun?' I exclaim incredulously. 'It's outrageous!'

'Yeah,' he says quietly. 'It is.'

'Well, they can't see me now,' and I turn the phone off quickly, before Leo realises I've vanished off his nasty little map, and texts or calls.


My mind is still turning over furiously by the time Dan turns the lights off and murmurs drowsily 'try and forget about it, get some sleep. We'll sort it in the morning.'

I just lie there piecing it all together as I listen to Dan's breathing begin to slow restfully. Leo had plenty of time with my mobile in that hotel room while I was passed out on the bed – and my laptop was in there too. I didn't just bump into him in the street in London, he'd known what street I'd be on. That time he just happened to 'randomly' be in Brighton – it must have been because he knew I was there. He almost certainly *knows where I live*.

If it were a stranger doing this it'd be bad enough – worse maybe because it would be fear of the unknown – but that it's someone I once willingly shared a house with, slept with, kissed? Leo was always intense, but this? This is a different league altogether . . . This is the kind of stuff you read about in the papers. Jealous ex-boyfriends flipping out. Trailing their unsuspecting former partners . . . oh my God, this evening at that community hall . . . was it him I heard? Was he there?

He knows where we live.

He's said he's going to tell Dan.

I stare up at the ceiling, completely immobile with fear, in the dark of my own bedroom.

## Chapter Twenty-Three

'Moll, please,' begs Joss. 'Calm down. Take a deep breath.'

She waits as I try to do as I'm told.

'Good girl. That's better . . . and again, take another.'

I try to breathe out slowly, it just sounds jagged.

'OK,' she says. 'Here's what we're going to do. We're going to change your phone number . . .'

'It's too late! He doesn't need to be able to text me or phone me any more, he can just *watch* me. I know that car I saw outside the house was him, Joss, I know it was. That message he sent me? The "you look nice" one? He DID know what I looked like that day – he's been following me! Oh God, this is fucked up. Really fucked up.' I start to gabble with panic. 'I don't know what to do! He could turn up at any moment. He could tell Dan. I don't—'

'He's not going to do anything. This is going to be OK.' She cuts across me, but I can hear it in her voice, she's worried. 'Moll, I think we should call the police, I mean, really, this is harassment, people can get arrested for that, can't they?'

'But what am I going to do when they ask me about my relationship with him? I'll have to tell them I slept with him two weeks ago – or he will. Either way Dan will find out! I've already been through this, Joss – all last night. There's nothing I can do! And he knows it!'

We fall silent. 'What about telling Stuart – or Chris?' she suggests hesitantly. 'Getting them to . . . sort him out.'

I pause and think about that. Chris or Stuart walking up to Leo in an empty basement car park, like they do in films. My brothers; my nice respectable law-abiding brothers, who I love more than anything. They've got children, for God's sake. They're fathers, they have responsibilities. Suppose something were to go wrong? 'No,' I say instantly. 'I'm not asking them to do that.'

'Moll, I really, really want to help you,' she says 'but unless we tell someone . . .'

'If he finds out, Dan will leave me,' I say blankly. I can't believe this is happening. All I really want is for Joss to reassure me that of course Leo is not going to tell Dan, that I'm imagining all this, that I'm letting my mind run away with me.

'Yeah,' she admits quietly. 'I know he will. Does he suspect anything at the moment, do you think?'

274

'No – not at all. He'd ask me outright if he did. I know he would.'

'You think?' she says doubtfully. 'I don't suppose . . .' She hesitates. 'OK, you're going to think *I'm* going mad now, but you have been very jumpy and well, not your-self – at least I don't think so. There's no chance DAN could have put that tracker thing on your phone, is there?'

I know I'm prone to melodrama, and I also know that I have a habit of overreacting, not thinking things through, but I honestly think that this might be what madness feels like. I don't know what to think, or how to feel.

Dan just wouldn't do that. OK, he *is* an IT expert, but so what? If he thought something might be going on that he was worried about, he'd just ask me. In fact he did – he brought up those mails from Pearce! And who tracks their own wife? But then, as if it's been lurking in a part of my subconscious I wasn't even aware of, just waiting, I remember him holding that condom and pin.

Joss did say I'd been jumpy. Dan knows me better than anyone, better probably than I know myself. Could he have picked up on something? If it *is* Dan who has put that thing on my phone, that means Leo is – well, just bombarding me with texts and trying to get me to meet him. That's all. Unnerving, horrible even, but not a hanging offence . . . If, on the other hand, it *is* Leo's work, then my husband is innocent, but my ex is actually stalking me.

I would laugh if this whole thing weren't so completely deranged.

I simply don't know what to do. Thankfully, I have no meetings today, so I'm able to stay in the house, behind double-locked doors. I sit there all day, just staring at my computer screen unable to focus. Paralysed.

At half-past four my phone begins to ring. It's Leo.

I ignore it, trying to keep my breathing steady, and it goes to voicemail. So much for my telling him I wouldn't be responsible for my actions, that really worked. It starts to ring again, straight away. I busy-tone him. Seconds later it starts up for a third time.

Do not panic. It's just a phone – that's all. You're perfectly safe.

Beep! A text arrives:

`Pick up. Please. I know you're there xxxxxxx`

My eyes widen, and I glance at the window. The curtains are open and it's dark outside. I rush to them, look up and down the street – I can't see any sign of him. I yank the curtains shut furiously.

Beep!

`Molly? PICK UP xx`

I can't just ignore it and switch the phone off any more. What if that only provokes him?

It's a snap reaction – desperate to buy myself some time, some space to try and work out what I am going to do – anything – I text him back:

```
Let me think. Will call you on Monday. I
promise
```

Beep!

```
OK. Monday. I love you xxxxx And happy
birthday for tomorrow xxxx
```

'Have a nice day then,' the delivery man turns and heads back to his car, leaving me standing on the doorstep clutching an enormous bunch of flowers.

'Wow,' Dan appears behind me. 'Who are they from?'

'I don't know.' I close the front door and start to search around for a card, my heart thumping as I see it nestled in amongst the heavily scented roses. I slip it from the small envelope, and almost faint with relief when I realise they are from Abi, Rose, Nula and Jacquie.

'The London girls,' I say to Dan.

'That's nice,' he says. 'Can I see?'

I pass it to him wordlessly. Is he checking up on me? Doesn't he believe me? Oh shut up . . . he's your *husband*.

'Putting me to shame,' he says easily.

I manage a weak smile and hasten off to put them in some water.

'Are you sure you don't want to go out and do a cele-bratory something?' he asks for the millionth time, a few hours later through a mouthful, comforting crappy Saturday night TV blaring away in the background as we eat fish and chips. 'Wow, listen to that rain!' He lifts the edge of the curtain incredulously and looks out into the dark. 'It *is* nice being in like this, all cosy, but I feel really bad not taking you anywhere.'

'Don't,' I wait for him to let the curtain drop back down again before relaxing slightly. 'We're seeing everyone for a birthday lunch tomorrow, aren't we?'

'But didn't you want to do something with friends as well as family?'

I shake my head. 'Rose is due any day, and I left it too late for the others to sort babysitters. Anyway, I know it sounds lame but I really would rather be in with you than out on a night like this, in some bar.'

'We really are getting old, aren't we?' he gives me a rueful smile. 'Joss and Bec could have come over though . . .'

'Bec's working and Joss is on a date,' I reach for my glass of wine. 'Second date in fact.'

'Really?' he says interestedly. 'Well, well, well. By the way, did her in-house lawyer get back to you yesterday about that tracking thing on your phone?'

I tense. Why the sudden interest? But then of course he's interested, I'd be interested if he'd found that on his phone. I'd be furious in fact.

'Not yet. I'm going to monitor the situation.' Which is what *he* usually says when he's putting off dealing with something annoying in the hope it will magically sort itself out.

'OK.' He turns back to the TV. 'Well if you think that's the best thing to do.'

'Let's not talk shop on my birthday.' I reach for my

glass again and drain the remainder in one. 'Is that all the wine we've got?' I eye the centimetre left in the bottle on the floor by the sofa.

'Yeah, I only bought one. Sorry.'

I really want another drink. I pick up the empty bottle and carry it back to the kitchen. Yanking the fridge door open I find two cans of John Smith's and Bec's bottle of Moët.

Clutching the open bottle and two flutes I make my way back into the sitting room.

'Haven't you had enough, boozy Sue?' Dan says lightly, but takes one nonetheless. 'Happy birthday!' he raises the glass to me. 'I hope this year brings you more than you could ever wish for.'

To be honest, I'd settle for getting to keep what I've already got.


When we arrive at Mum and Dad's the following day, having ended up drinking most of the champagne the night before in a desperate effort to relax, I'm feeling pretty crappy. Everyone is waiting for me in the kitchen and they all burst into a rousing rendition of 'Happy birthday!' as I appear in the doorway; they've made a banner and there's a home-made cake ablaze with an awful lot of candles. Oscar and Lily are hovering very close to it, excitedly trying to resist the temptation to blow. There is a small mound of carefully wrapped presents on the side next to a chilling bottle of Prosecco and gleaming glasses.

I cover my mouth with my hands, feeling my eyes become shiny as I take in their happy, loving faces. Dan appears behind me and joins in the singing too, smiling proudly, the widest of all.

I'm overwhelmed by it all, seeing everyone I love so much all together, everything I could ever want all in one room . . .

They finish singing expectantly and wait for me to attend to the candles. How could I have risked any part of this? A tear spills over. Mum and Dad frown, and I see Stu and Chris exchange a confused look. I flap my hands quickly. 'Ignore me!' I smile through it. 'I'm just being silly. These are happy tears – I promise. Let me blow this little lot out!' I approach the cake.

'Shall I help you?' Oscar offers generously. A slightly snotty, dribbly team effort means we get there in the end. Which is somewhat of a relief all round.

'Make a wish!' calls Karen, who is sitting on Chris's knee on the sofa. I immediately wish for everything to work out OK, which is of course a totally wasted effort. Wishes have to be much more specific than that.

After lunch I come back into the kitchen to get some water, the Prosecco having done little to settle me, funnily enough. I'm glugging from my glass over the sink when I hear a sudden 'Hello' behind me. I turn round to see Mum has somehow magically appeared from nowhere and is calmly folding a tea towel. I really don't know how she does it. Was she waiting for me in the fridge?

She eyes me steadily. 'Not feeling too good?'

'I'm OK,' I try a smile. 'Just a bit thirsty.'

She walks over to the drawer, opens it and puts the tea towel in. 'What did you get up to last night, anything fun?'

I got pissed at home and for the second weekend running had sex with Dan that I don't entirely remember. Which is, Mum, becoming something of a theme for me, you'll be pleased to know . . .

'Just a quiet one, nothing dramatic.'

'What did Dan get you?' She closes the drawer.

'A massage voucher.'

'That's nice,' Mum says. 'You *have* been working very hard over the last couple of weeks.' Her face is fixed in a composed expression. 'We've hardly heard a peep from you.'

'Well, like you said, things have been busy.'

'I understand,' she says, almost too generously, and moves over to the cupboard and gets two mugs out. 'Tea?'

'No thank you,' I say, slightly annoyed at her tone. 'Mum, it's not like I've been staying away on purpose.'

'Oh I'm not saying you've done it *consciously*,' she says quickly.

And just like that, I lose it. It's a tiny, stupid comment that isn't even an accusation. It's so meaningless, so comparatively insignificant it's untrue – like sticking a pin in brickwork – but she fires straight to the bull's eye in the way only a family member can – or maybe she doesn't at all. Maybe I've just been so stressed out and on the edge I can only let myself lose it with someone

I feel really safe with, someone who will always be there, no matter what I've done.

'What exactly is that supposed to mean?' I explode. 'I'm consciously, unconsciously doing WHAT exactly? I'm just trying to get on with my fucking life! Why is that so difficult for other people to understand? *I'm doing the best I can.*'

Mum looks slightly stunned at my reaction.

'No, come on then!' I challenge hotly, putting my hands on my hips. 'Say it. Just say what you've got to say. Tell me what you really think, because clearly something's frying your arse. What have I done now? I'm such a disappointment to everyone, I really am.' As I'm saying it, I know how unfair I'm being to her, that she doesn't have a clue what I'm talking about, why I'm so angry. *I don't even know why I'm saying all this.*

Silently, she lets the words linger, like a puff of poisonous spores floating in the air that she doesn't want to breathe in.

'The only thing I'm disappointed in is the way you're behaving right now,' she says eventually, her voice maddeningly measured. 'You don't have to speak to me like that, it's very rude.'

She puts the mugs back in the cupboard and walks out of the kitchen.

I burst into tears, but not noisy, attention-seeking ones. It's more a bubbling up of frightened grief that somehow just sort of floods up from within me and pours from somewhere so deep, it scares me. I don't actually realise my Dad has come into the room until I feel his hand on my shoulder, gently turning me to face him.

'Molly?'

I wipe my eyes quickly. 'I've just had words with Mum.' I suddenly feel extremely tired, like I want to curl up on the sofa by the dogs' baskets and sleep for a thousand years, or wake up in time for tea and discover I don't have to deal with anything grown-up after all . . .

'Do you want to talk about it?'

Tears flood my eyes again and I shake my head, still looking down at the floor. I wish that I had not let myself get to a point where I was unable to look after myself in that hotel. I wish it with all my heart. I am so ashamed of what I've done, and so frightened. I just want all of this to go away, but I can't see a way out. I feel trapped, like the walls are slowly closing in on me, like it's just a matter of time . . .

'Well,' Dad says, 'OK. You know where I am if you change your mind. I'll tell the others you're on the phone and you'll be through in a minute, all right? Give you a moment to gather your thoughts.'

And he disappears off into the other room.

Dan and I watch a DVD in bed before we go to sleep. We've turned the light off and had a nice hug, and it's a relief to find I'm sleepy. But I jolt awake what feels like moments later. When I check the clock however, it's actually quarter to one in the morning. I get up to go to the bathroom, creeping around carefully in the dark because I don't want to wake Dan up.

I don't know what makes me do it, but as I'm about to get back into bed, I pause and tiptoe over to the window. Holding my breath I move the curtain the merest whisper so I can see through the gap down into the street below.

It's tipping down, raindrops are both bouncing off and dripping from the two glowing street lights. The top of the hedge which divides our little terrace of cottages from the street and lines the small drive, is bathed in their rather eerie orange fluorescent light, but everything else is cast in varying degrees of shadow, or simply hidden away completely in the dark . . . everything is very still.

I can't see any sign of life at all, but that doesn't mean it isn't out there.

## Chapter Twenty-Four

When six in the afternoon hits the following day, it feels like the moment of dead air before an explosion. Leo is waiting for me to call him, or text him – and I've done neither. What is he going to do? Will he roar up to the house, jump out of the car, march up the drive? Even though my work phone is switched off, I can't relax as the minutes tick past. I struggle to watch TV with Dan like nothing is wrong, can barely eat tea, climb into bed and lie there rigidly waiting for the doorbell to ring, the hammering on the front door to start . . .

But nothing happens.

Dan leaves for work on Tuesday morning and I hurry out of the house shortly after him. I don't actually have to leave for my first meeting until ten, but there is no way I'm staying in the house on my own. Sick with fear, I only switch my work BlackBerry on once I'm in the car and drive practically holding my breath, waiting for it to update.

But again – nothing. What's he playing at?

I stop en route for a coffee, as I'm running so early, and it actually helps just to sit in a strange cafe where no one knows me, or cares what I'm doing, what I'm thinking about. I switch off both phones – and have an hour of space. I don't come to any conclusions, no way out suddenly occurs to me, and neither do I think this is somehow all going to magically resolve itself. If anything I purposefully blank my mind and concentrate only on reading the paper, because what else can I do?

Oddly, I feel calmer as I leave and get back in the car. And when I arrive at the GP's surgery I find myself thinking that perhaps I will call Leo, say that I will meet him, try to deal with this like adults. We used to live together! Surely we can discuss this, somehow . . .

I walk into the waiting room feeling strangely detached from everything around me, and automatically adopt my wide professional smile as I approach the reception desk. I could call him once I'm done here. 'Hello!' I say warmly, as if my sanity is not in fact teetering on the brink and everything is *just fine*. 'I'm Molly Greene from MediComma. I've a meeting with the practice manager.'

'Hello,' says the slightly hassled receptionist, juggling phones. 'I'll let her know you're here. Would you like to take a seat with your colleague?'

'My colleague?' I reply in confusion, as she motions behind me.

286

I turn, somehow expecting Pearce as that's the only logical explanation, but the blood drains away from my face.

Leo stands up, dressed in an immaculate suit, holding a laptop bag. 'Hello!' he looks completely relaxed. 'Mary?' he looks over my shoulder at the receptionist and flashes her a dazzling smile, 'could you just give us a minute before you buzz Jenny? I just have to bring Molly up to speed on something.'

'Of course,' she says instantly.

'You're a doll, thanks!' he replies, eyes twinkling as he reaches for my arm and begins to guide me to a quieter corner of the waiting room. 'Don't say anything,' he says softly, still smiling away. 'She's totally bought it – just play along.'

'How did you—' I peter out, horrified.

A flash of impatience passes over his face. 'I phoned MediComma, told them I was your husband, there was a family emergency and I couldn't get hold of you, did they happen to know where you were so I could contact you? They said you'd be here – and here you are.' He looks almost smug for a moment but then his expression falls away. 'So what happened to my phonecall yesterday?'

'Leo, listen . . .'

'No, I think you should listen,' he says equably. 'I love you – you know that, and I've been happy to keep the grand expansive gestures going, as that seems to be what you want.' It occurs to me that he's really quite liking this audacious version of himself, 'but this "quest" is getting a bit boring now. All of it – this' – he motions around him – 'proves I'm serious. No more games now, Molly. Time's up. As of this afternoon I'm out of the country with work for a week. While I'm gone, decide how you want to play it. If you want to tell Dan yourself – tell him. Otherwise I'm going to sort it when I come back, OK?' He looks at me impassively. 'I'll be in touch unless I hear from you first. Be good BG. I know you're going to do the right thing.'

My mouth falls open in shock as he gives my arm another light squeeze, turns and saunters out with a cheery wave and a 'Thanks, Mary! She's on her own now, so be nice to her!'

'Molly, you have to call the police,' Joss says immediately when I finally get hold of her at about six. 'This is fucked up.'

'And say what? "I'm being stalked by someone who's out of the country right now" . . . they'll laugh in my face!'

'He's bullshitting. Give me his number. If he's genuinely abroad his mobile will have that different ring tone won't it?'

I hesitate. 'You'd have to hide your number – and promise me you'll hang up if he answers, won't you? Don't yell at him, or say anything to antagonise him, please.'

She calls me back moments later, sounding defeated. 'He *is* abroad. It did two rings and I rung off. Molly, I mean it, you really have to tell someone about this . . .'

'No!' I insist as cold fear rinses through me, 'and you can't either – you promised.'

'But—'

'You promised!'

'OK, OK—' she says uneasily, as she tries to keep me calm.

He's not bluffing. And he's given me one week.

The rest of Tuesday and Wednesday and then Thursday peel away quickly as I try to keep working and acting like nothing is wrong, burying my head in the sand one moment, and then the next being gripped by the panic of imagining sitting Dan down and coming clean, telling him what's happened and begging him to forgive me. Leo does not send me a single message, he goes completely silent, which on the one hand, allows me to pretend that this isn't really happening, but on the other, is oppressively ominous.

Friday arrives and I'm sat in the pub after work with my other colleagues feeling spaced-out and numb, while thinking, 'Should I go home and tell Dan tonight?'

I have three days left now. That's all.

Pearce is busy telling Sandra and me about the GP who insisted on helping him change a flat tyre on his car earlier in the day. 'She actually slapped the boot of the Golf like it was a horse once we'd got the wheel on and said briskly "She'll be no trouble now." She was *brilliant*!' he grins, emptying the dregs of a packet of crisps into his mouth and managing to get the crumbs all over his front. 'What a woman!'

'Dirty fat lezza more like,' Sandra says crossly, taking a sip of her Bacardi and coke.

Pearce stares at her. 'Because she knows how to change a tyre?'

'That's not normal, Pearce,' Sandra shudders distastefully. 'Trust me.'

'My mum knows how to wire a plug,' Pearce looks at her meditatively. 'Does that make her, a lesbian too?'

'Wouldn't know – haven't bloody met her, have I?' Sandra fires back acidly.

I won't be able to bear it if they start a row, I really won't. Luckily, Bec calls and gives me an excuse to get up and leave love's young dream to it.

'OK, so I'm a bit out of practice,' she says down the phone, 'but suppose you were going on a third date with a man you'd met on the internet – who *is* really nice, and you laughed loads with, and you like quite a lot – would you be worrying about what pants you're going to wear to dinner with him tonight, just in case?'

'No!' I say automatically. 'I'd be thinking, great start, this bodes well but I only met him a week ago and if he really likes me, he'll wait as long as it takes.'

'Phew,' she says, relieved. 'Thanks. Just checking – love you.' And she hangs up.

I'm walking back to the table when Joss rings. 'No developments then? You OK? Can you even talk right now?' she says quickly.

I can, but I find that I don't want to. 'Not really.'

'Understood,' she says. 'I'll call you tomorrow instead.'

'What are you up to tonight?' I ask, attempting some normality.

'I've got a date,' she says uncertainly.

'Same bloke?'

'Yup.'

'That's nice, Joss.'

'Last Saturday,' she hesitates, 'we stayed up talking literally all night. I told him about Mum, Dad – and well, everything.'

Bloody hell. I try not to react to that, I don't want to scare the horses. 'You never said . . .'

'You've got more than enough going on,' she says quickly. 'But guess what? On Monday he bought a bottle of perfume into work for me just because I happened to mention I'd dropped mine and it broke everywhere. That was nice, wasn't it?'

'Very,' I say gently. It would be lovely if someone looked after her for a change. I like this man already. 'Have fun.'

'Thanks,' she says gratefully. 'Moll? Call me if you need me, won't you? Whenever, it doesn't matter. Please think about what I said, about telling someone, won't you?'

I'm pretty sure she doesn't mean Dan though.


On Saturday Dan cheerfully announces we should go and get our Christmas tree. He takes me for breakfast first, then we go to the garden centre, get the tree home, put it up, and start to decorate it. He then nips out to buy a new set of fairy lights that actually work and while he's gone I text Leo in tears and literally beg him not to destroy my life.

Dan comes back. We pick up where we left off with the decorating and then Dan redecorates it two hours later in good humour when it falls over and all the baubles fling themselves from the branches in a dramatic fashion. I go upstairs to the loo and check my phone. Nothing. I send Leo another text, pleading with him to just walk away. I'm very careful not to incriminate myself and don't actually admit to anything. I just ask him please to find it in his heart to do what is right. That if he *really* loves me . . .

I check my phone again once we've gone to bed and Dan is asleep. Still nothing.

I'm almost out of time.

Sunday arrives. Dan gets the papers, I take him out for Sunday lunch because I cannot bear to stay trapped in the house a moment longer, and we go for a long walk across the downs.

'You know, I realised something today,' Dan reaches for my hand. 'This might be our last Christmas. Just us I mean. This time next year, we could be . . . millionaires!'

He grins at me and I have to look away quickly, pretending to inspect the view so he can't see the tears that have sprung to my eyes. We could be a lot of things, Dan.

'Parents – that's what I was really going to say. We could be parents.' He winks at me, puts an arm round me and then looks happily out over the fields spread below us.

I hesitate, and then I sway slightly as I open my mouth. 'Dan . . .'

He looks at me. 'Yeah?'

'Nothing.' I can't do it. *I can't.* 'Let's go home.'

I have nightmares that night and on Monday morning, when Dan has gone to work, I crack and call Leo. It rings – he is still abroad – but he doesn't answer, it just goes to voicemail.

I take a deep breath.

'Hi,' I begin and realise my voice is shaking. 'It's me.' I try to think what to say. 'I know you're coming back tomorrow, and what you said you were going to do.' I pause. 'I would really like . . .' My words come out a little high and I swallow painfully, trying to sound more controlled. 'Leo, I would really like—' I try again 'just to be able to talk to you as *us*. Lots have things have been said over the last few weeks. But from the bottom of my heart I never meant to hurt you and I don't think you've meant to hurt me either, but please, *please* let me . . .' I have to stop for a moment and close my eyes. 'I can't do it . . .' my voice is barely more than a whisper. 'I love him. I couldn't be more sorry for everything . . . but I don't know what more I can say. Please just let me go. Please.'

There really isn't anything more *to* say. I hang up and just sit there, hoping he's going to text or call me.

He doesn't.

★   ★   ★

293

The following morning I get dressed in a daze. He's back today.

I switch my phone on. The first call I get is from Antony, who formally invites me to consider redundancy. The day is shaping up beautifully. 'I'm so sorry to have to do this just before the Christmas party,' he says, the shame audible in his voice. I feel dreadful for him and want to tell him that really, it's the least of my worries. 'Please don't feel bad, Antony, you're only doing your job. Does everyone else know?'

'Yes they do. Pearce hasn't taken it quite as well as you,' he jokes, but sadly. 'Will you give him a ring if you get chance? Make sure he's bearing up? Listen,' he hesitates, 'I didn't say this, Molly, but don't accept the offer, all right? Trust me on this. It'll all make sense.'

Pearce doesn't pick up when I call him, so I just leave him a message saying I hope he's OK.

No need to worry about me. He texts back. Guess I have to learn to look out for number one now. Intend to be drunk and unsuitable tomorrow just so you know. Bastards.

But then, five minutes later I get:

Sorry. Didn't mean it. Shouldn't be a c**t to you. See you tomorrow. Will be on best behaviour. Promise. X

294

Poor old bloke.

Then another text arrives.

Leo.

I stop breathing and, terrified, I open it.

I've had enough of this.

'That's all it says?' Joss is as thrown as me. 'I've had enough of this'? Her silent confusion carries down the line from London. 'Is that supposed to mean he's had enough, he's on his way over – or he's had enough, the whole thing's off?'

'I don't know.' I stare at the five little words and feel the smallest glimmer of hope. 'You really think that might be what he means? He's somehow decided this is just not worth it?'

'Maybe. That'd be a very Leo thing to do, decide at the last minute that he's bored and just fancies walking away, because he can. I guess we'll just have to wait out the rest of the day and see.'

'You're sure you're all right?' Dan looks at me curiously, head resting on his pillow. 'You've just been very, I don't know – skittish tonight.'

'Skittish?' I can't help smiling.

'Are you excited about your work do tomorrow night?' he makes a face. 'If so, we need to start getting out more, it'd be too sad if this actually is a highlight on our social calendar.'

'Oh, that reminds me,' I say. 'Work – Antony called me today. Asked me to consider voluntary redundancy—'

'WHAT?!' Dan lifts his head up in shock.

'—but it's fine, he gave me the wink too.'

'Oh,' Dan relaxes back down. 'Meaning you'll be OK?'

'I assume so. That's good isn't it?' I say happily.

'Very,' he says, relieved. 'No wonder you're smiling.' He looks at me again. 'Nothing else has happened, has it?' he asks.

'No,' I allow myself a smile. 'Nothing has happened at all.'

## Chapter Twenty-Five

And nothing happens the following day either. No messages, no calls – nothing. It's like being told a devastating cyclone is heading straight for you, bracing yourself because there is nothing else you can do but wait for it to hit, only to be told it has randomly switched course at the last moment and you've been spared. I can't believe it – is it really possible, just like that, Leo could decide to walk away? Maybe what I said in my last message struck a cord with him . . . I suppose I'll never know. But I can certainly live with that.

As I'm drying my hair with forty minutes to go before we have to be at my work do – it should only take us twenty to get to the hotel – it occurs to me that Dan's cutting it a bit fine.

I'm just deciding I'll give him another five and then

I'll call him to see where he is, when I hear a thump. Immediately on guard, I switch the hairdryer off and listen, but all that reaches me is Mel next door saying warningly, 'Jack! No! Naughty!'

My hair is practically done anyway and I don't really want to put the dryer back on. Instead, I cross the room and get a pair of tights out of the drawer and sit down on the edge of the bed, threading them over my hands to check for ladders, when I *definitely* hear the front door open.

'Dan?' I shout. No answer – all I hear is feet bounding up the stairs towards me, fast.

He bursts into our bedroom to find me sat frozen on the bed in my bra and knickers, hands still buried in the tights.

'Hello!' he grins, as he marches round the bed, suit jacket tails swinging jauntily in the manner of a man who has just leapt off a Lear jet and driven at a hundred miles an hour to make it back for the ambassador's reception. 'They go on your legs, not your hands,' he nods at the tights, before leaning in to kiss me. 'Were you worried I wasn't going to make it in time? The train was late. Have I got time for a quick shower before we go?' he looks enquiringly at me. 'Doesn't matter if we haven't, I'll just put on a clean shirt.'

'I – we – have to leave in about ten minutes.' My mind has defrosted and become a blancmange in a glass box, slopping against the sides uselessly. For some stupid reason, when he didn't answer straight away, I thought it was

Leo running up the stairs – I *so* thought it was him. It's going to take me a little while to accept it's all over I think.

I reach for my dress.

'Oh, you're wearing that one are you?' Dan says, slightly disappointed, as he tucks his shirt in.

'Why, what's wrong with it?' I'm now completely thrown.

'Nothing,' he shrugs. 'It's just a bit . . . Why don't you wear your red one?'

'I haven't worn that for years!'

'I know,' he says, 'which is a shame because I really like it – go on, it's a party! Don't wear black, everyone's depressed enough at the minute without you turning up looking like a grieving widow.' He reaches into the wardrobe and fumbles about, before pulling it out triumphantly and passing it to me.

I take it doubtfully.

'Trust me,' he insists.

Moments after I've shoehorned myself into it I want to rip it off again. I've clearly added a few comfortable pounds here and there since I last wore it, so it's not so much as clinging over my boobs as hanging on for dear life, the tummy and hips aren't too bad, but – no, no, no.

'It's too booby,' I insist, 'There are clients going.'

'Too booby?' Dan looks confused. 'You've worn it to weddings and *christenings* now I think about it. You look amazing and it's a lot better than that gloomy black thing.

It's Christmas, Moll.' He peers at me more curiously. 'What's wrong? Why don't you want to wear it?'

'Fine,' I say hastily, before he can pick up on any more of my unsettled vibes. 'I'll wear it. Let's just go.'

Dan decides to drive and laughs as my tummy does an immense, audible rumble in the dark car. 'Bloody hell,' he says. 'I hope they've got food there, and a lot of it.'

I am actually inexplicably starving, but eating anything in this dress is out of the question. I should have worn the black one. I look like Jessica Rabbit's much older and fatter sister.

When we arrive at the small hotel and park at the back, Dan climbs out of the car and comes round to open my door for me, patting my bottom flirtily as I walk ahead of him towards the hotel. He's in a good mood.

A stifling, slightly sweaty warmth greets us as we step into the busy bar. I get a few mildly surprised looks at my showy dress, from blokes clutching pints, which makes me feel, quite literally, a complete tit. They're probably expecting me to get a portable CD player out and start a festive strip.

I hurriedly cross my arms over my chest – which doesn't really help matters – and practically throw myself into the private room, Dan following behind me. It's surprisingly buzzy in here too – there must be a good sixty-odd people, but it feels like more because the room is blatantly too small to accommodate everyone. I smile hello at a couple of the nicer doctors who I recognise immediately and introduce them to Dan who cheerfully begins to chat away. A waitress passes by with a tray of what looks like mulled wine, but I don't really fancy one. It smells quite nauseatingly sweet and I shake my head. Dan gives me an approving wink, but takes one himself, listening carefully to a doctor who is already in full flow.

Another client comes over to greet me – seriously, there are loads of them here, are free booze dos really that thin on the ground this year? – starting to lecture me about how he still hasn't received the order that he placed over two weeks ago; how very full of festive cheer he is. I let my eyes flicker round the room. Pearce is propping up the bar rather than mingling, oh dear. Antony is nodding thoughtfully, as a rather angular woman is waving a full glass around to make her point – which is obviously irritating Antony's capable wife as she tries to dodge splashes.

'So what do you say to that, then?' The GP asks me.

I drag my attention back to him, his breath absolutely reeks of stale coffee, but I have no idea what he's just said to me – I wasn't listening.

'I agree with you, one hundred per cent.'

He looks appalled. 'Do you think this is some kind of joke?' He reminds me a bit of Michael. I have obviously said exactly the wrong thing. 'Just make sure the order reaches me before Christmas or it'll be the last one I place.' Tetchily he shoves his glass down, gives me a final glare and marches off.

301

'All right?' Dan says appearing back by my side and places a comfortable hand on my waist.

'Yeah,' I make a face, 'although I've just said something accidentally inappropriate to a client.'

'Oh?' Dan looks amused. 'What?'

But before I can answer, Pearce comes over. To a stranger, he would look perfectly relaxed, his slow wide smile is almost sleepy and calm, but peering quickly at his very dark eyes, I can see he's actually pretty pissed.

'Hi, mate.' He is very slightly slurring but making an effort to hide it. 'Good to see you again,' he extends a hand and Dan shakes it firmly and says, 'You too.' I can't remember the last time they met. Was it this time last year?

'So, this is fun isn't it?' Pearce does a double thumbs-up and a big fake grin. 'We're probably not going to have jobs next year but hey, let's celebrate anyway!' Then he looks at me, frowns and points at my empty hands, 'And why are you without a drink Moll? Let me rectify that oversight immediately.'

'I'll do that,' Dan says briskly. 'Pearce, what can I get you?'

'Very kind of you, sir,' Pearce says elaborately. I see Dan's eyebrow flicker as he tries to work out if Pearce is taking the piss or not. 'I'll have a Jameson's, seeing as you're going that way.'

Dan says nothing and rather curtly stalks off to the bar. Pearce doesn't notice however, he's got other stuff on his mind. 'Look at him,' he says to me, lowering his voice – but not as much as he thinks he has – as he nods over at Antony. 'Acting the big happy cheesy chief. I bet he isn't going to have to apply for his own job. He makes me sick.'

'Shhhh,' I take his arm and pull him gently away from the group of clients closest to us, 'people will hear you.'

'Shhh!' Pearce whispers back elaborately. 'Because we can't have that, can we? MediComma isn't really the scum of the earth everybody.' I think a doctor overhears because he whispers something to his colleague and they both glance over at us curiously. 'Urgh. I hate my life.'

'Pearce,' I hiss. 'This isn't the time or the place. You'll get into trouble.'

'Who's in trouble?' Dan says, not missing a beat as he reappears and hands over the drinks.

'No one is,' I say quickly and look warningly at Pearce, 'everything's fine.' I take a big gulp of drink. It's pure apple juice. Great.

To my relief however, Pearce nods, takes his whisky and raises it to us. 'Your wife is a very wise woman. Cheers Dan the man . . .'

Unfortunately he stumbles slightly and jerks some of his drink over Dan's arm. 'Shit,' he exclaims in dismay. 'I'm so sorry. Let me go and get a cloth.' He weaves off. Dan just stands there, shaking his dripping arm.

'It was an accident,' I say quickly.

'I know,' he says. 'Stop looking so worried, I'm not going to deck him.'

I smile, lean over and kiss him. 'I love you.'

303

He kisses me back, mollified. 'Love you too.'

'Excuse me,' says another slightly slurred voice in front of us. I turn and see a perplexed, balding and rather useless-looking doctor standing where Pearce was moments ago, clutching a now empty wine glass. He sways very slightly as someone bumps into him on their way to the bar. 'You look very familiar to me, but I'm afraid I'm having a terrible time placing you.'

But I can't help him because I have lost the power of speech. It's all I can do to stand there clutching my drink uselessly. I know exactly who *he* is—

He's the doctor who examined me after the condom broke.

The colour must have drained from my face completely because he looks slightly taken aback and says 'I'm afraid I take so very many meetings with medical reps, you must think me very rude, I'm so sorry.' He offers a hand to Dan. 'Dr Jonathon Hubbard, pleased to meet you.'

'Dan Greene,' Dan smiles warmly, 'Molly's husband.'

'Molly Greene,' Dr Hubbard repeats, it clearly rings a distant, mulled wine dulled bell somewhere. 'This is awful. I must be going senile. Put me out of my misery, Molly, what have you sold me?' he smiles openly at me and his glass dips slightly. 'We've definitely met at my surgery, that much I'm certain of.'

'I . . .' I exhale. My breath has become jerky, my heart is thumping and crashing in my chest. I can't think of a single thing to say. 'I er . . .' I can feel my face growing hotter and hotter by the second.

304

Dr Hubbard and Dan are still waiting. Dan turns to me, bemused by my apparent struggle, and Dr Hubbard's convivial smile begins to slip slightly. He might be several glasses up, but he's realised something is not quite right. Unable to stop it happening I watch it dawn on him that he has made a mistake, I've never met him in a professional capacity, I am in fact one of his patients. Then I see him sift through a rolodex in his mind and land on a late Thursday afternoon only three and a half weeks ago. 'Ahhh!' he says and smiles generously, thinking he now understands. 'What a bumbling old fool! Now, we shan't tell anyone here I'm *your* doctor,' he attempts to whisper, reaching out and putting a comforting hand on my arm. 'You were in very recently weren't you? I remember now.'

I must look absolutely horrified, because as I begin to stutter interruptions, he then says, 'Oh, please don't be embarrassed. It happens all the time, I promise.' He gives a gentle laugh, designed, I can only suppose, to lighten the tone. 'So,' he twinkles daringly, buoyed up by the party atmosphere, 'had any more problems with rogue broken condoms then, you two?'

I go into freefall. I'm not sure if the ground is under my feet or if I'm still holding my drink.

Dan looks at Dr Hubbard, confused. 'Condoms?' he repeats. 'But we're trying for a baby.'

# Chapter Twenty-Six

Cheerful noise continues around us. I hear someone laugh. Only we three are locked in a dreadful silence. The room begins to revolve as if I am stuck on the inside of a zoetrope. We are static pictures, only beginning to flicker and appear to move like real images as the drum – and Dan's thoughts – begin to gather speed. '*Broken* condoms,' he repeats.

Dr Hubbard's empty glass looks like it's going to fall completely from his fingers, his mouth is hanging open uselessly with horror, at what he now realises was an inadvertent and foolish drunken assumption that the incident happened with my husband, but is in fact a devastating breach of patient confidentiality. I can't inhale, my lungs won't expand. Petrified, I look at Dan who is now staring at the floor, his breathing beginning to quicken with hideous realisation.

Dr Hubbard struggles to say something, 'I, I'm so sorry. I thought . . .' he grips the slipping glass so tightly it must surely break anyway. 'Forgive me,' he pleads, 'I . . .'

Dan jerks back away from the doctor's woefully inadequate words. He wobbles, then turns on his heels, and pushes urgently through a small throng of several people in conversation behind us, jogging their drinks and making them say 'Hey!' in mild surprise as, affronted, they watch him spin out of the room. I think I drop my drink on the carpet as I rush after him, clutching only my bag, leaving Dr Hubbard crushed and standing alone as he looks after us.

I slam out into the dark car park, lit only by cosy light spilling over from the bar inside. Dan's there, both hands clasped on top of his head in total disbelief, suit sleeves rucked up exposing his earlier optimistic clean shirt. He's pacing in a small tight square, clouds of breath surging around his head.

'Broken condoms,' he says again like some sort of mantra. 'Never mind we're not even using them, we've *never* broken a condom. That's the sort of thing you'd remember if it happened to you, isn't it? Especially if it was "very recently".' He turns to look at me and involuntarily I moan in distress.

I have never seen the look on his face that I can see now. His eyes are wide and frightened, anguished.

He continues to stare at me wordlessly, which is worse than shouting, worse than accusations. I can see it all in his face. He knows. The hurt and pain is so naked, I actually cry out again. My legs won't hold me up and I sink to the concrete. My breath starts to come in sharp fits and I can feel hot tears of shock streaming down my face.

'Oh God, oh God, oh God.' It's me, my voice repeating over and over again.

'Who is he?'

'I never meant—' I'm incoherent on my knees in front of him. I have no excuses, no lies that can save this; the facts are inescapable and undeniable.

'*WHO IS HE?*' he yells so loudly I wince.

Then he takes two violently fast steps to me and grabs my wrists, pulling me to my feet. 'Tell me who he is,' he cries again, so close to my face I cringe. 'And don't say it doesn't matter, because it does.'

'I'm sorry, I'm so sorry.' I sob. 'I was drunk, I was—'

'Was it at our house?'

'No, no!' I cry. 'I'd never – at the conference . . .'

'The conference,' he repeats slowly. 'Windsor? When you had that crash?'

I hear a door bang behind me. 'Everything all right out here?' calls a male stranger's voice suspiciously. 'Is he bothering you?'

I spin round, two big-bellied blokes are standing on the step clutching pint glasses. 'I'm fine,' I insist. 'He's my husband – we're OK, really.'

There's a doubtful silence and then they nod and disappear back inside. I turn back to Dan who has snatched up my handbag and is rifling through it furiously. He pulls out my work mobile, backing away warningly, staring intently at the screen. His face then scrunches up savagely. Flinging the phone to the ground he yells out with rage and shoves past me. 'What are you doing?' I cry in horror but he ignores me and absolutely pelts back in the direction of the hotel.

Confused, I grab the phone from the floor, look at the screen and my blood runs cold.

```
Sorry. Didn't mean it. Shouldn't be a c**t
to you. See you Wednesday night. Will be
on best behaviour. Promise.
```

Oh my God. Pearce.

I drop the phone again and make for the hotel, everything is jerking around, the door handle slips in my hand, I shove past people I barely notice, trying to get to the private room before it's too late.

I nearly trip in my haste, blundering to get there in time and stop it, but I'm just pushing in through the doorway when I hear a scream and the sound of a smashing glass as the room suddenly falls quiet. I elbow my way through to the bar and find a small space has already magically cleared. Dan is standing over Pearce, who is sprawled on the floor in a puddle of amber liquid, amidst glittering green chunks of a beer bottle, clutching his hand to his nose with a surprised look on his face. Sandra is looking down at her dress which is covered in red wine, it's all over her hands and dripping from the hem.

'Get up!' shouts Dan. Stunned, Pearce just lies there

and so Dan reaches out, drags him to his feet and before anyone can stop him, thumps Pearce again. There's a sickening sound of crunching knuckles, cartilage and shocked gasps as Pearce crumples to the floor. 'She's my WIFE!' Dan shouts hoarsely. 'My WIFE!'

'What the . . .' Pearce drunkenly touches his nose, which is now streaming blood. 'I haven't touched her!'

At that, Dan tries to go for him again, but by now, other people are switching back on and becoming involved. A couple of men I don't know reach out and grab Dan, pulling him back. He struggles furiously and shouts. 'So what happened at the conference in Windsor then? You lying fucker!'

'Windsor? What are you talking about? He was with me!' Sandra shrieks. 'Tell him Pearce.' She looks over at me angrily.

Before Pearce can say anything, Antony shoves in through the small crowd, desperate to stop this seedy domestic drama unfolding in front of our clients. He looks first at Pearce mumbling on the floor, waving a hand, still trying to get up, then at Dan, being restrained . . .

. . . and then straight at me, standing there between the two men, and as I drop my head in shame, thinks he instantly realises the situation. 'I understand, pal,' he says soothingly to Dan, stepping in to take control, shooting a disgusted look down at Pearce, 'but he's just not worth it. Leave it – for Molly's sake. This isn't helping anyone.'

He begins to determinedly push Dan back. 'Come on – let's get some air.'

311

'Antony,' Pearce says, voice muffled because he's holding his nose. 'You know what, on balance I've decided I *will* accept your voluntary redundancy offer.'

Antony whips round and points a warning finger at him. 'Now's not the time to get smart, sunshine, I'll talk to you tomorrow. Tessa!' he bellows grimly and his wife appears magically from nowhere.

'Oh Pearce!' she scolds lightly as if a bloody nose is no big deal at all and the stuff of a playground scuffle, nothing serious in the slightest. Antony begins to lead Dan away. 'Look at the state of you!' She gets a Kleenex out of her bag, as good as licking it before wiping his face. 'Did you know you were tonight's entertainment then? Let's clean you up shall we? What a bit of luck that we've got a lot of doctors here! I think we could all do with another drink and a little bit of music couldn't we? Thank you, oh you are kind, yes please *do* take a look at him. It *was* a bit, wasn't it?'

I follow after Dan and Antony hastily. Dan has broken free of Antony's grip and is walking determinedly ahead. He bangs out through the door but instead of making for the car, he turns left, disappears out of the car park and marches off into the freezing night. I start after him but Antony takes my arm. 'Leave him,' he instructs. 'Let him calm down.'

I turn to Antony desperately. 'What happened — it's not what you think,' I plead, 'Pearce wasn't—'

'Don't.' He can barely look at me. 'I don't want to know. Just go home, OK?'

312

I look around wildly for my bag, but I left it on the car park floor and of course now it's gone. I tell Antony and he sighs. 'Wait here.' He strides back off to the hotel.

Alone in the car park I stare desperately up at the cloudless night sky. It is bitterly cold and the stars are shining sharply. This cannot have just happened. Like this?

Antony bangs back out, incongruously clutching my bag. Miraculously, not only did someone hand it in, the keys and my purse are still in it, along with my phone, somehow still working despite Dan having hurled it at the floor.

'Right, well, we'll talk tomorrow or something,' Antony says. He pauses reluctantly, like there is more he wants to add, but thinks better of it. There's nothing either of us can say really. Nothing can make this all OK.

He gives me a final look of utter disappointment, turns and walks back into the hotel.

## Chapter Twenty-Seven

By eleven-thirty Dan has still not come home and he's not answering his mobile.

I cannot believe what has happened . . . and I thought Leo would say something, would push the button? Yet just as he cuts his losses, doesn't want to play any more – *this*.

Frozen, my joints stiff and aching, but my face puffy from crying, I eventually get off the linen box in the bedroom and come away from the window, shivering as I climb into our bed to wait.

I jolt alert a couple of times thinking I hear something, but it's wishful thinking, not Dan. It's actually gone midnight when I hear feet crunch over the gravel drive and then his key fumbling in the lock. Then nothing.

When I push open the sitting room door he is collapsed

on the sofa in the dark, shoes and suit jacket still on. I can smell the alcohol on him from where I am standing. He glances up briefly as I appear in the doorway but then looks down at the floor again.

I walk in and silently sit on the opposite sofa to him, curling my legs up and under me. I don't move to switch a lamp on, I don't try to say anything. We just sit there in semi-darkness, the only light coming in from the hall.

Eventually his eyes flicker up dully. 'I'm not pissed,' he says eventually, 'if that's what you're thinking.'

'I didn't say anything—'

'How could you?' he bleakly cuts across me before the words are properly out of my mouth. 'And don't say you were drunk, you must have had some idea what you were doing.'

My eyes fill with tears. 'I *was* drunk yes, but—'

'I went to a party tonight, perfectly happy, having a drink and then some doctor walks up to me and everything turns to shit, my whole life, and . . .' he forces his eyes tightly shut, 'you let me say hello to that bastard like some fucking stupid kid, when all the time he, and you, knew that . . .' he pauses painfully and then asks me again. 'How could you?'

I have to tell him the truth. I have to.

'Dan, it wasn't like that. It wasn't—'

'I *knew* something was wrong. I KNEW it.' He sits up and puts his head in his hands. 'I asked you about those emails and you said it was nothing.'

I feel tears of shame prick at the back of my eyes.

'I made a horrible mistake. I know that's not enough, but it didn't mean anything, I *promise* you!'

I can hear myself saying the small, useless words and realise how lame and pathetic they must sound to him, because they don't come anywhere close to capturing what that night was like. Just for a moment I remember Leo once saying them to me, how it felt to hear them, how I know Dan is feeling now.

'I knew I was right.' He repeats, barely hearing me. 'You kept shutting your computer down when I came into the room, getting texts from him. When I saw those emails . . .' He puts his hands over his head and then looks at me bleakly. 'How long has this been going on?'

I'm dumbstruck. He's been worrying and watching all this time? That thing on my mobile, might he have? . . . 'It's not what you think,' I insist.

'Don't lie to me again.' He doesn't break his gaze. 'So why did you go out and get a new phone then? I'm not stupid, Molly! You think I've not noticed you turning off your work one each night? Was it so that I wouldn't see his messages?'

'Dan, I swear to you, it happened *once*.'

'But how I can believe you?' He shouts. 'You've already lied to me!'

'Please, Dan,' I plead. 'Try not to shout. They'll hear us next door. It's not fair to them.'

'Fair?' he says incredulously. 'You're worried about what's fair?'

We both pause.

317

'You're at home all day, or at meetings fuck knows where, off at conferences – for all I know this could have been going on for ages. Is this why you've not wanted to start a family with me?' his voice cracks.

'No!' I can't believe he could think that. 'Of course not! Pearce isn't—'

'If you've been having an emotional thing with him behind my back,' he points at me warningly. 'I'm telling you now, if that's what this is—'

Any confession I might have made about Leo dies immediately on my lips. He will *never* believe that there was no emotional involvement there, I'm not entirely sure I could believe that myself. 'I was so drunk I didn't know what I was doing. It was one night,' I say quietly. 'I promise you on my life.'

We sit there silently and he drops his head to his hands exhaustedly, giving me the first proper view of the hideously swollen knuckles on his right hand. Even in the half-light, I can see the bruise has already come up and is turning violent colours, probably much like Pearce's face. Shocked, I half stand, reach out and say, 'Oh Dan! Your hand—'

'Leave it.' He says instantly, shrinking away from my approaching touch.

I try to move closer. 'But it's—'

'I said leave it.' He stands up quickly and moves to the hall doorway. 'I can't even look at you right now.' His jaw clenches. 'All I can see is that fucking bastard touching you, and you pissed and . . .' his face contorts with rage

318

then collapses into misery. He wrestles to get himself under control. 'Please, just go to bed.'

I don't know what to say. He moves aside as I go to walk past him, which breaks my heart completely because all I want to do is rush to him; kiss him, hug him, cling to him and tell him over and over how sorry I am. But none of it's enough.

'I love you so much,' I whisper.

He scrunches his eyes closed tightly as if somehow that might also block out my voice. 'Don't,' he begs. 'Please don't. I can't do this right now. Please, just leave me alone.'

Hugging my knees to my chest, sat on our cold bed as I rock on the spot, my face wet with tears, I listen to him slowly getting the sofa bed out downstairs.

If I was frightened before, now, I'm terrified.

## Chapter Twenty-Eight

I jerk awake at about half-six having had snatches of confused dreams that I am back with the boyfriend I had before Leo, that we've moved into a house together. He was holding my hands and trying to kiss me – and while it was a relief not to be with Leo, I kept pulling back in total confusion thinking, 'This isn't right, how did I end up with *you*? I'm sure there was someone else who I was much happier with, someone who . . .'

Then everything that happened last night rushes back to me, and I crane to hear some evidence of that person moving around downstairs. Everything is silent. I creep down the stairs, peer round the door and feel physically sick with relief to see the outline of his body still on the sofa bed. Disappearing back upstairs, I lie quietly in our bed waiting for him to wake up, but by half-seven – a quarter of an hour later than he normally gets up – he hasn't moved.

'Dan?' I say tentatively, going back down five minutes after that. He shifts and peers at me standing over him before turning his face away and closing his eyes again, as if he wishes I wasn't. A waft of stale booze mixes powerfully with the pine fresh Christmas tree.

'Are you going into work today?'

He shakes his head almost imperceptibly and moves again, his bashed-up hand comes into view and rests redundantly on the duvet cover.

I wince. 'Your hand . . .'

'I can move my fingers,' he mutters. 'I'll be fine.'

'You don't think you should see a doctor?' I say it without thinking. He opens his eyes and shoots me a quick look before closing them again.

Desperate for something normal and useful to do, I walk over to the Christmas tree and switch the lights on. It begins to merrily twinkle, but as I'm stepping away from it, I trip over one of Dan's shoes which I haven't noticed sticking out from under the edge of the sofa bed, stumble and shoot a hand out to the nearest thing that will steady me, but there's nothing there, only the tree. It topples over sideways and lands in a crash of baubles and flurry of needles. Dan jerks his head up and stares at me in disbelief before saying 'What are you *doing*?' It's enough to make me burst into tears, standing there foolishly in my pyjamas, everything crashing down around me.

He picks the tree up while I get the hoover out. Once

I'm finished, and everything is almost as it was, the sound of Mel bellowing 'Jingle Bells' at Jack filters in from next door.

Dan glowers at the wall silently, but says nothing, just rubs his face tiredly with his good hand. 'Have you got meetings this morning?' he says quietly as I sink on to the edge of the sofa.

I shake my head. I don't even know if I have a job after last night. 'I'm going to call Antony in a bit.'

'You know what one of the worst bits of this is?' he says suddenly. 'Knowing that you kept all this from me.'

'I wanted to tell you Dan. I SO wanted to tell you.'

Mel's front door bangs and we hear her shout 'Come on then! Let's get in the car. No – the car! Don't put that in your mouth, it's dirty.' Then car doors slam, the engine starts and the tyres crunch on the gravel before leaving us in absolute silence.

Dan closes his eyes and whispers, 'I wanted to kill him. I actually wanted to kill him. I have never felt so much hatred for another person in my whole life.'

I look at the floor.

'Do you have any idea how it feels, Molly, to think about you . . . drunk and . . .' he closes both of his eyes tightly again, like he's trying to shut it out. 'Don't you understand? *Anyone* that hurts you . . . and yet I'm just supposed to . . . FUCK!' he shouts, darting a hand out and hurling the lamp from the small table across the room so fast I don't even realise he's done it until the base explodes on the wall.

'I'm so sorry,' I begin to cry quietly. 'I'm so, so sorry, Dan.'

'You should have stopped it!' he shouts. 'Why didn't you stop it?'

'I was too out of it to know what I was doing.' I'm so bitterly ashamed the words are no more than a whisper.

He gets up and walks out of the room, slamming the door behind him. There's nothing more I can do than sink to the floor and begin to slowly pick up the shattered pieces of the lamp.

When he comes back down, showered and dressed in home clothes, it's just as I'm putting my mobile down. 'Who were you calling?' he says sharply.

'Antony rang me. He's told me to cancel my meetings. We're going to talk in about an hour.'

He doesn't say anything to that, just sits back down. 'Has *he* tried to call you?'

'No.'

'Did it really only happen once?' He asks me outright.

'Yes.'

'That's the absolute truth?'

'On my life.'

He stares at the floor, and trying to work out what he's thinking, what those questions mean, I begin to babble.

'I love you,' I say. 'I made a mistake; a huge error of judgement that I will regret for ever. I—'

'Stop,' he says quickly. 'I don't want to hear any more.'

I don't know what more I can say anyway.

We sit there for what feels like hours, opposite each other.

'Who else have you told?'

'Joss.'

'Anyone else?'

'No one.'

'Because the only way I can even consider doing this,' he says quickly, 'is if no one knows. None of our families, friends . . . especially not about last night. I can't handle anyone pitying me, I won't be able to deal with that.'

'I understand—' I begin.

'I want it to be like it never happened. You have to promise me,' he says fiercely.

'I promise, of course I promise.'

'And you have to leave your job.' He looks at me defiantly, almost daring me to say no. 'As soon as possible.'

I think back to the humiliation of last night, all of my clients standing there looking at me, Pearce sprawled on the floor, Antony not able to look at me. I'd give pretty much anything not to have to deal with the aftermath of that, and have a fresh start somewhere else.

'The thought of you being in the same room as him . . .' Dan clenches his jaw. 'All the time you work for the same company he can email you and phone you, get news about you. Every day I'd be going off to work worrying that you were going to see him, imagining you talking to him. I knew that something was going on and

I can't spend every day from here on in worrying that it's starting up again. That'll kill me. I don't even care about the money. You just have to leave. Effective from today.'

Today? I look at him uncertainly. 'Well – I'll try, when Antony calls but . . .'

'You'll have to just make it happen somehow.' He says defiantly, sensing my reservations. 'It's a job, not a prison sentence. You don't HAVE to do it. I want you to clear your work email down by the end of today too, and give that phone back. I'll drive it over to their offices myself.'

'Dan, it's not that simple—'

'My hand is fine,' he insists, misunderstanding me.

'No, I mean the car is theirs too.'

He pauses, he'd obviously forgotten that. 'Well, we'll have to arrange for that to go back as well. And I want to get you a new phone.'

'But I've just got one!'

He shakes his head determinedly. 'He's got that number too, for all I know.'

'He hasn't – I promise you.'

'It's the only way this can be,' he insists, warningly.

'OK, OK.' I agree hastily. 'I'll go and get dressed and then we'll . . . get sorted.'

He just nods.

I get up, make my way to the doorway and then pause there for a moment, and look back at him.

'I can't promise anything,' he says. 'But I'll try. That's

326

the best I can do.' He looks at the floor again and mutters, 'I knew I wasn't going mad. I knew it.'

'Dan—'

'I think I'd just like to be on my own again for a bit please.'

Defeated, I leave the room. He keeps saying that; he knew. Joss was right, I must have let myself get so over-wrought I gave it all away without even realising it. I almost want to ask him about the tracking application but the last time I made a wild accusation like that . . . and I honestly think if I question the trust between us again right now that will be it.

And anyway, arguably he had good reason to do it. He was right, I did cheat. Whether it was acceptable or not for him to track my movements is neither here nor there. In all honesty, the only person who has fucked up from beginning to end here – is me.

# Chapter Twenty-Nine

'Mum, where would I have found anywhere on Christmas Eve selling double cream – even if I had got your message?'

'Double cream?' Dad repeats as he comes into the kitchen and looks between me and Mum. 'What on earth do you want more double cream for Meg? There's a dairy's worth out in the big fridge.'

'I know, but,' Mum frowns at the tray of mince pies on the table, slapping Chris's hand away as he breaks from present wrapping and tries to sneak one, which makes Karen grin. 'I've still got the trifle to do and . . . I expect you're right though. We'll manage.'

Dad rolls his eyes and then says 'Aha!' happily, as he spies his glasses on the table, picks them up and purposefully strides back out again.

'I *keep* using your *old* new phone number Molly, it's

329

so annoying,' Mum sighs. 'I'd only just learnt it, and now I've got to un-learn it all over again.'

'Sorry,' I try to keep my voice relaxed, pretending to read a magazine. I don't look at Dan. 'I didn't lose it on purpose.'

'You'd think someone would have handed your phone in, wouldn't you?' Mum continues. 'Especially seeing as you knew everyone at that silly party. I still don't understand why you had to change the number though.'

'It's an identity fraud protection thing,' I say vaguely.

'*Really?*' Mum says, fascinated. 'They can clone you just from having your phone? Well I think that's horrid. It's Christmas for goodness' sake.'

'What difference does that make?' Chris looks up from biting off a piece of Sellotape that immediately doubles back and sticks to his fingers.

'Were you drunk?' Mum frowns at me. 'Is that why you lost it? That's not very good for your ovaries you know.'

Yeah, because they're at the top of my worry list. 'No Mum,' I reply shortly, shooting a nervous glance at Dan who is focusing on leafing through a Christmas gifts catalogue. 'I wasn't drunk.'

'It's a harsh *slur*, Mum,' Chris says lightly. 'Get it?'

No one except me notices as Dan gets up and walks out of the room. Worriedly, I look down at my magazine again. Should I go after him or leave him alone?

'Chris,' Karen interrupts, reaching out and taking the Sellotape from him as Dan abruptly stands up, 'if you put any more tape on that present Oscar's going to need a hacksaw.'

'And do NOT eat any of these while I get the cake from the garage,' Mum points at Chris severely as she steps away from the mince pies.

'Every man's dream,' Chris muses. 'Wife in one ear, mother in the other.'

'You all right Moll?' Karen remarks as she measures a piece of wrapping paper. 'You're quiet tonight.'

'Just tired.' I try to smile. Chris reaches out, grabs a mince pie and stuffs it whole into his mouth.

'Probably knackered from all that baby-making you and Dan have been doing,' Karen teases.

Chris gives her a look of dismay. 'Do you mind?' he says through a flurry of pastry crumbs. 'That's my sister. I don't want to hear about stuff like that.'

'Them having sex you mean?' Karen says innocently.

'Seriously, stop it,' Chris insists but she just laughs.

He needn't worry. For two weeks now Dan has barely kissed me on the cheek, let alone anything else. To the outsider things may appear normal, but behind closed doors . . . I sit next to Dan and I feel him shrink away. If I deliberately move closer, even boldly put his arm round me, it just lies there lifelessly and after a moment or two he removes it. Last Sunday night, the weekend before Christmas, when usually we would be out seeing friends, we stayed in because Dan didn't want to see anyone. I quietly wrapped some presents and he watched a couple of movies back to back, silently stretched out

331

on the sofa. During the last, I crept over and sat down next to him on the floor. That was as close as I got. The idea of sex is laughable; we can't even hold hands.

'So have you got all of next week off Moll? When do you go back to work?' Karen enquires as she starts to wrap a fairy wand for Lily.

'Um, not sure yet,' I say, trying to sound light and upbeat, while wishing I could snatch the wand from her, wave it and make everything magically OK. 'Everything's a bit up in the air at the moment.'

Chris, still chewing, frowns. 'What do you mean?'

They both look at me curiously as Mum staggers back in carrying a vast Christmas cake which makes such a heavy thud when she puts it down I almost expect it to go right through the table top. 'Oh Chris!' she scolds, looking at the pies. 'I told you not to—'

'Mum, shut up!' Chris instructs. 'What are you talking about? How can your job be up in the air?'

'I've left actually,' I confess.

'WHAT?' they all exclaim in unison.

'Well, technically I was made redundant.'

'Mark!' yells Mum.

'Why haven't you said anything?' exclaims Chris.

Dad comes in, patiently clutching the crossword and a pen. 'Did you know about this?' Mum nods at me accusingly, like it's his fault.

'I haven't a clue what you're talking about.' He crosses over to the sofa, sinks on to the arm and says calmly. 'What's the drama, Molly Malone?'

'There isn't one,' I mumble as they all wait for me to elaborate. I notice Dan has silently appeared in the doorway, hands in pockets, and is looking at me intently. 'They warned us it was probably going to have to happen and it did. I've taken voluntary redundancy, I had some holiday owing too – so . . .' I shrug and try to smile brightly.

'But, you shouldn't have taken voluntary, Moll,' Karen says with concern. 'You should have hung on. You're trying to get pregnant anyway, you could have gone straight on maternity leave and they couldn't have made you redundant then.'

Oh Karen, leave it. Please.

'Have you had the letter from them yet?' she persists. 'Until they've written to you and you've written back, it's not legally binding, you could change your mind. Have you?' She looks at me anxiously.

'It's all done. I've left.'

I think back to my conversation with Antony.

'So that's it? You ring me up and tell me just like that you're off?' he'd said gruffly. 'You'll get bugger all money if you resign, you do know that?'

'You could have sacked me for what happened last night Antony. We both know *that*.'

He didn't disagree.

'Technically, it was on company time, in front of everyone. You can't keep me on now and I wouldn't expect you to, it's not fair.'

'I don't need to discuss what happened again,' he said

333

brusquely. There was a pause and then he said, 'You really don't have to do this.'

I'd watched Dan walk past the door to the kitchen, shoulders slumped.

'Yes,' I said firmly. 'I do.'

He sighed heavily. 'Right then . . . Molly, I owe you an apology. I neglected to tell you that your notice period started on Monday, when you told me you wanted to accept the offer of voluntary redundancy, which I'm sure you remember, I accepted.'

'What?' I said, completely confused.

He ploughed on. 'Which with the holiday you're owed means you can leave immediately and of course you'll get your redundancy pay.'

I finally realised what he was doing for me. 'Thank you, Antony,' I said quietly. 'That's very kind of you.'

'You'll be missed,' he said sadly.

I didn't see him when I returned everything back to the offices while Dan waited in the car park for me. I only had just enough time to text Pearce as I walked along the corridor to the HR department – madness really but I HAD to say how sorry I was for everything.

He texted me back immediately.

No – I owe you one! I have accepted redundancy too – finish after Christmas – and S dumped me! Sleeping with you was the best thing I never did! Would say stay in

'It's all final – done and dusted,' I insist and Karen sighs heavily. 'I wish you'd have said, I could have got one of my friends to help you out with some advice.'

'That's very sweet of you, but I could have asked Joss if there was any need. She's very clued-up on that sort of thing.'

'What's she said about it then?' Mum asks.

Nothing, I haven't told her. She'd smell a rat. She was so great when I was worrying that Leo was going to turn up and blast everything wide open, phoning to check I was OK, listening to me panicking, sharing my jubilance when he threw in the towel . . . she deserves a break from me. She, like Bec, is completely loved up right now. In their own separate ways they each spend so much time looking after other people they've earned the right to just enjoy having some fun without distractions. And what could she do anyway? The only people that can fix this are Dan and me. No one else.

'I just want to move on,' I say truthfully to my family, briefly meeting Dan's gaze before he looks away, 'have a brand new start. I'll get another job. Who knows – maybe I'll do something completely different!'

'Everything happens for a reason,' Mum smiles kindly.

Yeah, you have a one-night stand with your ex, then your doctor tells your husband at a party. That's the reason,

335

Mum. If it weren't for Dan, I'd have Dr Hubbard struck off.

'Well, you're being remarkably cool about it,' Chris says. 'Dan,' he turns to the door, 'your company is stable isn't it?'

'I think so,' Dan says flatly. 'You never know for sure, but we'll be all right.'

My heart lifts hopefully, we will? Or does he mean his company will be all right?

Mum smiles at him. 'Of course you will!'

The dogs bark and scramble to their feet at the sound of the doorbell.

'And that'll be Stu and Maria!' Mum says. 'I think,' she adds firmly, taking my hand and squeezing it, 'we should see if we can make this the best Christmas ever, don't you? Dan, would you get the door? I must just nip to the loo.'

He obediently vanishes just as two small and very overexcited people appear in his place wearing their pyjamas. 'Lily can't get to sleep,' Oscar explains helpfully and Chris stands up and says 'Oh yeah? Just Lily eh? Come on you two. Yeah – don't worry, Mum's coming too.' Karen's chair scrapes back, the dogs are still woofing madly and I can hear enthusiastic hellos happening in the hall.

Only Dad is sitting still, looking at me carefully.

'Molly . . .' he begins.

'Don't, Dad,' I get up quickly, determined not to be forced into breaking the promise I made Dan. 'Not now. Please.' And I rush out of the room before he has the chance to say another word.

# Chapter Thirty

When we get back home at about ten at night, having assured my family that we will be back bright and early in the morning for Christmas breakfast, our front door is slightly ajar. My heart sinks. I was the last one out. 'Oh look, Father Christmas has been already,' I try gamely.

'Shit!' Dan flings his seat belt back. 'You can't have shut it properly behind you when we left!'

'I was carrying the presents,' I call after him, to excuse myself. 'I didn't do it on purpose.'

He ignores me and vanishes into the house.

Miraculously, however, inside everything is just as we left it. The tree lights are still twinkling away, everything is tidy, neat and still.

'Well, thank God for that.' He throws the car keys on

the side in relief and makes his way into the kitchen, as I go upstairs to the bathroom and shut the door behind me. I can't believe I left the front door open. That's what it's come to?

I'm just flushing the loo when I see, under the edge of the bathroom door, Dan's shadow outside. 'Fancy putting the kettle on if you're going back down?' I call. He doesn't answer, I just hear his feet on the stairs, which makes me sigh heavily. I know he's trying and I know it's only been two weeks and we've got a long, long way to go yet. I also have no right to any expectations at all, but God, this is tough.

When I get back down he's in the kitchen putting a fresh bag in the bin. 'Did you make me a tea?' I ask.

He looks up in surprise. 'No.'

'It doesn't matter if you didn't,' I say quickly. 'I can do it myself.'

'Look, I'll do it,' he goes to get up, 'but I didn't know you wanted one.'

'I said, upstairs.'

'I didn't hear you – I was putting the rubbish out.'

'Just now!' I exclaim. 'I said could you— Oh you know what, Dan?' I'm suddenly too tired to do this. It's Christmas Eve for goodness' sake. 'It doesn't matter. Really it doesn't.'

I make us tea and we take it into the sitting room, both of us shivering slightly because the house is still so cold. He doesn't move away at least, when I sit down next to him on the sofa, which is something I suppose.

And Christmas Day is a bit better still. In amongst the kids' Christmas excitement – the general noise of everyone mucking in together, not only is there safety in numbers, it also allows us to mask everything. Someone else is always there, chattering away, preventing Dan and I from noticing the silence between us. Mum and Dad do all the caring, plying us with more food or drink, activities and distractions are provided by the boys and the kids; there is a walk outside with the dogs and persistent requests to play another round of Hungry Hippos. If anyone notices Dan and I are quiet, they tactfully say nothing, no doubt attributing it to my sudden joblessness. We are gratefully swept up by the family tide and it really helps. It doesn't make it all go away of course, but it shouts it down a little. Dan even abruptly kisses me, when we find ourselves alone for a moment in the kitchen. 'Happy Christmas.'

'Happy Christmas to you too.'

We just stand there for a moment, opposite each other. He reaches out and I think he's about to hug me, only Chris walks into the room clutching some empty glasses. 'All right?'

'Yes thanks,' Dan says. 'Fat, but all right.'

Chris laughs. 'I know. I keep thinking I can't eat another thing and then having just *one* more chocolate.'

Dan allows himself a smile and turns to me. 'I'm going to go and sit down in the other room. Coming?'

Chris watches him leave and then says casually, as I'm about to follow. 'You OK, little sis?'

Am I? I think on balance I am. We're hanging on in there.

I'm still feeling optimistic the following day. It's a crisp, cold and clear Boxing Day morning – the sky a pale icy blue as we drive to Dan's parents. I find a radio station playing carols, and when we arrive Susan has prepared a lovely light lunch, the fire is blazing away in the beautifully decorated sitting room . . . it's like stepping into a Christmas card.

Apart from Michael. He and Susan spent Christmas at one of her friends' in Oxford. Being away from the golf club irritated him, not having his home comforts irritated him – and he wants everyone to know how he has suffered. Like every good vintage, he does not travel well.

'Bloody mattress crucified me. Imagine sleeping on a collection of cast iron springs, each of which has been wrapped in a very worn sock. No, it really was that bad,' he grumbles as Susan gives him a look. 'Then they had this God-awful Christmas morning breakfast of *bagels*,' he says distastefully, 'and cream cheese. Then nothing more until about three!' he shakes his head as if he can't believe what the world is coming to. 'By then my stomach had virtually eaten itself and she hadn't done enough of everything as it was anyway. I had three sprouts. Three! I ask you? What's the bloody point? Never again. Never again,' he grips the arms of his chair fiercely.

I say nothing, having made a mental note the moment we arrived to keep my mouth zipped, whatever he says. I am determined to learn from my mistakes.

'And after lunch we all had to sit and play Monopoly! You can't say no because apparently that's what they do "every year".' He tuts furiously. 'Well, from now on, what I do "every year" is stay here.'

'Michael,' Susan says, with just a hint of warning. But for once he's too carried away to notice. 'And who was that idiot Laura's daughter brought along with her?'

'Her new boyfriend.' Susan pours herself another drink. 'I thought he was very nice.'

'He was an imbecile,' Michael retorts. 'Trousers halfway down his arse.'

'He's an artist.'

Michael snorts. 'Oh well, that's all right then. When you say artist do you mean he glues one lavatory roll to another one and calls it sculpture, or do you mean he can actually use a paintbrush?'

Susan ignores him and turns to me. 'Would you like some more tea, Molly?'

'What did the first husband do? The one that left her?' Michael demands.

'He was a hairdresser.'

'A hairdresser?' Michael repeats in disbelief, as if Susan has just said he was an Olympic gerbil trainer or something equally ridiculous. 'Well she certainly knows how to pick them. I suppose he turned out to be batting for the other side?'

341

'Actually he was having an affair with one of his assistants,' Susan replies.

Oh no. I look down at the untouched sherry in my hands.

'Don't you remember? They tried to sack her because Lydia – that's Laura's daughter,' Susan explains helpfully to me, 'didn't want her around once it all came out, but the girl brought an unfair dismissal case. It was all very unpleasant, too much for them to cope with and he walked out.'

'He left her even though *he'd* been the one playing away from home?' Michael snorts derisively.

'Hmmm. He actually ended up with the girl he'd had an affair with,' Susan pulls a face. 'They've got a baby now.'

Dan, that is not going to happen to us. We are in no way similar to this couple at all. I look at him beseechingly but he's staring at the fire.

'Meanwhile poor old Lydia's wound up with that bloody artist bloke! Dear oh dear,' Michael chuckles. 'Just goes to show, doesn't it?'

'What?' explodes Dan, making us all jump. 'What does it go to show, Dad?'

Susan and Michael look at him in surprise.

'You don't know what it's like to be either of them,' Dan insists. 'Maybe Lydia really loved her husband and wanted to try and work through it rather than just give up.'

Oh Dan . . . I feel my heart break all over again for my husband.

'Well I can tell you now putting up with it was her first mistake,' Michael retorts defensively.

'Oh just shut up!' Dan slams his drink down and gets to his feet. 'At least she tried. Which is more than can be said for *you*,' he jabs a finger at Michael, who, all of the wind taken out of his sails, collapses back in his chair in shock. 'Sitting there passing judgement like you're bloody perfect.'

'Dan!' says Susan, taken aback by the uncharacteristic outburst.

'I'm sorry Mum, but enough's enough.' Dan is so angry he's shaking. 'It's Christmas, everyone's trying to be cheerful, and all he does is sit there and mouth off like he knows it all. You're a miserable old fucker Dad. Excuse my language Grandpa,' he turns to Susan's father who is sitting on the sofa quietly.

'He won't have heard you,' Michael retorts, but with considerably less bluster.

'I'd like to go outside please,' says Grandpa suddenly. 'Could you help me up, Daniel?'

We watch as Dan heaves him out of the sofa. He leans heavily on his stick and begins to shuffle towards the door. 'Come on, lad,' he plucks at Dan's sleeve with thin, birdlike fingers and silently Dan follows him out of the room.

Susan, Michael and I just sit there. No one really knows what to say.

'What the hell has rattled your father's cage?' Michael says defensively.

'Oh, because it's always someone else's fault Michael, isn't it?' Susan suddenly whirls round on him. 'You're a stupid old fool!'

My eyes widen.

'Sorry Molly.' She gets swiftly to her feet and sweeps out of the room after Dan and her dad.

Michael coughs awkwardly and grabs the arms of the chair before uselessly releasing them again. 'Well, that told me,' he says eventually.

I glance over at him; he looks tired and sad. An old man really, who ought to know better but just keeps managing to stuff it up regardless. 'I always seem to say the wrong thing somehow.' He scratches his head uncomfortably, looking very worried. 'I didn't mean to upset him. I never mean to upset him. I'm a bit of a disappointment to your husband, I think.' He tries to do a gruff laugh but it doesn't quite come off. 'And quite possibly my wife.' For the first time perhaps ever, I feel rather sorry for him.

In the car on the way home though, my compassion somewhat evaporates. Unintentional though Michael's comments were, they have hugely upset Dan. I want to talk to him about it, particularly the bit where Michael said that woman made a mistake in taking her husband back in the first place – but I don't know where to begin. Like Michael I suppose, I never usually have a problem finding words, it tends to be more of an issue *stopping* myself from talking, but this time I don't want to make a bad situation worse.

We go virtually the whole way home in silence, he only asks, 'Have we got anything at home we can eat?' and all I venture is, 'I'm sure we'll have something in the freezer.'

I kick my shoes off as we get in through the front door and make my way across the sitting room towards the kitchen. 'I'll go and see what we've got that I could do quickly.' Thank God for the tree, at least it's not totally devoid of Christmas cheer.

'Molly,' says Dan suddenly, just as I reach the door. The tone of his voice makes me stop immediately. I turn and look at him. He's standing by the front door still holding the keys.

We just stare at each other.

'What?' I practically whisper.

'I think we need to . . .' he says eventually and then tries to start again. 'I can't . . .'

I feel myself wobble and say quickly. 'You can. You can do it, you *are* doing it. Please Dan.'

He says nothing.

'I'm begging you,' I say, tears filling my eyes. 'I know we can do this.'

'We don't feel like us any more.'

'We are us!' I insist desperately. 'We *are*. You and me . . .'

He closes his eyes and swallows painfully. 'I keep seeing him touching you. I can't get it out of my mind.'

'But, it didn't—'

'—mean anything,' he finishes. 'I know. You said. But now I can't stop thinking that he's going to try and get

345

in contact with you again. That he'll . . .' he peters out, exhausted. 'I just can't do this. It's too much.'

'I love you Dan,' my voice crumples. 'Don't you love me?'

'You know I do!' he cries. 'You *know* I do! Why would I be doing even this if I didn't? I just — it's just too fucking much!' He pushes past me suddenly and takes the stairs two at a time.

I rush up after him to find he's grabbed a bag, into which he is shoving things wildly.

'You're *packing*?' I say in disbelief — it's utterly, utterly incomprehensible. 'You're leaving me?'

His eyes fill with tears at that, he throws the bag away from him and then he breaks down completely.

I scramble round the bed, horrified. I've never seen him cry, except at the odd soppy movie. I try to wrap my arms round him and just for a second he lets me — but then he gently pushes me off, not unkindly, but as if my touching him is unbearable. 'Please don't,' he says. 'Please.'

He picks up the bag again and slowly begins to put some bits and pieces in it. I stay on the floor, just watching him, unable to believe what I am seeing. All sense of time starts to slip, it is both the longest and shortest moment of my life.

He closes the bag and straightens up.

I have no feeling in my arms and legs, nothing. Everything falls away around us as he takes a step towards the door.

'Please don't do this,' I say, barely able to see him through my own tears. 'Let's just talk about it.'

346

'But I don't know what more there is to say. I thought I could do it, but . . .' He shakes his head.

Neither of us move, we just look at each other and then, to the sound of me collapsing into sobs, he disappears round the door and is gone.

*Chapter Thirty-One*

Bec and Joss rock me in their arms as I do great heaving, gulping sobs. Bec was completely horrified when it all came out – every last horrible detail – and I can tell she's also very hurt indeed that she knew nothing about any of it, although she assures me it's OK, when I put a desperate hand on her arm and try to justify my reasons.

Both of them gasp out loud when I tell them about the doctor at the party. Dan punching Pearce. That I've left my job – what our last two weeks have been like.

'He's going to come back,' says Joss fiercely, arms round me, 'because he loves you. And when he does, I'm going to kill him.'

I look at her exhaustedly through red eyes and blow my nose. 'It's not his fault Joss. He really has tried – he can't even touch me. It's eating him up and it's *my* fault. I brought the whole thing on myself.'

'Molly!' Bec looks appalled. 'You were so drunk you don't even remember half the night! Leo should never have taken—'

'Bec,' Joss says quietly. 'Don't. It's not going to help. He's irrelevant now.'

'I'm so sorry.' I scramble around for a tissue. 'You should be with your families, not here with me, I've ruined everything.'

Joss snorts. 'You're all right. The twins and I were about to murder each other. My flat is *way* too small for all three of us.'

'And I hate turkey curry, you know I do,' Bec tries to make me smile. 'Anyway, you need us. End of.'

'But your blokes – you might have wanted to see them today.'

'Er, hello weirdo, I've been dating him less than a month,' Joss says. 'Why the fuck would I be seeing him on Boxing Day?'

'And I've dumped mine,' Bec shrugs. 'Turns out he wasn't that funny after all. Let's just say he found himself unable to reach the required standard.' She hesitates. 'Molly. I've got something to tell you. I wasn't going to mention it because it upset you enough when I told you he turned up on Facebook, but you know that internet dating site I was on?'

I nod, as Joss looks at us both blankly.

'Leo contacted me through it. I didn't think anything

of it at the time, he just asked after you, said did I have an email address or home phone number for you? I didn't give them to him, but if I'd have known what was going on, I'd have told you, I promise.'

'So he's been surfing around internet dating sites too?' Joss shakes her head in disbelief. 'What a nice guy – he really has had each of his bases covered, hasn't he?'

We're silent for a moment before she speaks up again. 'And I can't believe what else has happened over the last two weeks – that you didn't say anything to either of us?'

'I promised Dan.' I shrug, and can't help starting to cry again.


Both of the girls insist on staying the night, taking turns to pop home and collect their stuff while the other sits with me. I hear them whispering while I'm sat on the loo, staring into space as I get an uncomfortable lower abdominal twinge. Staring dully down at the packet of Tampax I keep by the loo, I reach out for it automatically.

Joss looks up from the magazine she's found as I come back in to the bedroom and says, 'Finally! We thought you'd fallen in!'

'I've just come on.'

She gives me a sympathetic look. 'I'd send today back if I were you,' she tries. 'Get a refund.'

'I've made you some hot chocolate.' Bec comes back in clutching a mug. 'You should try and drink some, it'll help you sleep.'

351

'I'm going to kip on the sofa bed,' Joss gets up. 'You two can stay in here.'

'No, *I'll* sleep downstairs,' Bec volunteers. 'I don't mind. Plus I snore.'

It doesn't matter to me in the slightest which of them I get, although Bec is right, she does snore. I lie silently next to her, on Dan's side, getting tears in my ears as I smell his aftershave on the pillow and wish with all my heart that it could be him lying next to me instead.

'Did you manage to sleep at all?' Bec asks me the next morning as she stretches.

'A bit,' I lie, getting up stiffly. 'I'm just going to the loo.'

When I come back in she's sitting up in bed and yawning.

'Do you think you could drive me over to my mum and dad's?' I ask her, feeling dazed. 'In a bit?'

'Of course,' she rubs her face, trying to wake herself up. 'Would you rather be there than here?'

I nod.

'I understand totally,' she says and swings her legs out of bed. 'I'll wake Joss up and we'll get on the move, OK?'

In the car they both chatter away earnestly as I numbly stare out of the window. 'I honestly think Moll, that he'll come back,' says Joss, 'really I do. You just need to give him some time.'

'I know you're in shock now,' says Bec, looking at me in the rear-view mirror, 'but I promise you – you're going to survive this. Trust me. You think you won't but you do. Look at me, I did – and I'm happy Moll, really happy.'

'And we're going to be here for you every step of the way,' Joss grips my hand tightly. Which is lucky, because she actually does have to help me out of the car when we arrive.

'Girls! What a lovely surprise!' Mum exclaims happily, swinging the front door open as the dogs barge out into the crisp air, barking excitedly. Her smile falls away as soon she sees my face. 'Molly? What's wrong? What's happened?'

It feels like my legs are giving way under me at the sight of her, I can't hold it together a moment longer. The dogs, sensing drama, leap up around us madly – nearly knocking Bec over. 'Is someone hurt?' Mum helps to prop me up as I stumble. 'Has there been an accident? Is it Dan?'

Once we're inside and the girls have gone, my parents are amazing. They ask me no questions, just tuck me up on the sofa and wait until I am ready to talk. I manage to tell them that Dan has left me, and why – although I don't discuss the circumstances, or disclose that it was Leo.

They are incredibly kind and pass no judgement. Neither do they say things like 'He'll come back,' because they have never lied to me before, and they're not going to start now.

But what I haven't told them is that this morning, when I went to the loo, I discovered I hadn't come on at all. Which was really confusing, because I'd had that weird crampy feeling the night before, as well as other signs – my boobs were massive . . . I was certainly due on . . . In fact, I was more than due on. I was pretty late.

If it hadn't have been for the fact that I knew the test Dan had bought me was right there in the bottom drawer, less than three feet away from me, I probably would have just dismissed it as a skipped period entirely due to stress overload and not given it much more thought. But it *was* there. So I did it.

And it came up positive.

I'm pregnant.

## Chapter Thirty-Two

Dad comes back into the living room. 'Are you warm enough love?' he asks kindly. 'You didn't have much at tea? You've got to eat. Shall I make you a snack?' He tucks the blanket in round my feet like I'm an invalid as I shake my head, silently doing myself up in knots.

'Mum's just putting some clean sheets on the bed for you.' He sits back down comfortably in his chair.

Despite knowing that I could ring Dan *right now*, as I clutch my phone, something is stopping me. How horribly emotionally manipulative would that be? I may have the one thing that could bring him back to me – a baby – but can I really do that to him? Can I pull him back when I *know* how hard he's struggled with the knowledge of what I've done, how impossible he's found it? I *know* that infidelity can kill relationships. If he never knows about this pregnancy he'll be free, free to eventually get over all of this hurt.

But then a baby is also the one thing he's wanted more than anything. Doesn't he have a right to make the decision, to come back or not, himself?

And then again, what about me? What sort of person would bring a child into the world just to glue their marriage back together? Now that the chips are really down, and I'm really thinking about it, I can't honestly say all I've ever wanted is a baby. I don't *not* want it – but they are hardly one and the same thing, are they?

But do I even have a right to make THAT decision full stop? Of course I know the arguments for and against abortion, both scientific and religious – which I can't pretend I am especially – but I've never properly considered them in relation to myself, never questioned what I would *really* do. Until now. What AM I going to do? What on earth am I going to do? I feel absolutely numb. I'm pregnant. Actually pregnant . . .

I let out a shaky breath and Dad looks up from the TV. 'You all right?'

I nod.

'Are you sure? Have you got—' but before he can finish the dogs suddenly sit up, on alert. Then they both woof and jump to their feet.

'Shhh! Silly old things!' Dad scolds. 'There's no one there!'

But they both rush over to the French windows and

start whining, sticking their noses under the curtain edge and barking imperiously.

'What?' Dad says. 'Heard a fox, have you?'

He wanders over to the window, pulls back the curtain and stares out into the garden. I let my eyes flicker back to the TV.

'What the . . . ?' Dad says suddenly and then he quickly starts to fumble with the door lock.

'What is it?' I sit up slightly, but he doesn't answer, just slides the door back furiously, upon which the dogs burst out; barking madly, disappearing off into the dark. Dad hastens after them.

I get up and move to the window, waiting on the threshold, the freezing air snapping at me. I can't see anything, all I can hear are the dogs. 'Dad?' I call.

A moment or two later, he reappears out of the gloom, clouds of breath forming around his head, as he walks stiffly up the garden back towards the lit-up sitting room, dogs trotting at his heels.

'So silly,' he puffs, wiping his brow, 'but for a moment, I thought I saw—' he tries to catch his breath . . . 'Hang on a minute . . .' He stops, bends slightly, and rests his hands on his knees. 'That's better,' he straightens up and smiles at me, but then the colour simply drains from his face like someone emptying out a sink and he sits down very heavily and suddenly on the grass.

'Dad!' I rush out. The dogs are prancing around him, confused, barking crazily again. 'Are you all right?'

357

He tries to swallow and puts a hand out to me. It's all clammy. 'I feel a bit funny,' he says, blinking, and still breathless.

'Don't move,' I say, trying to stay calm. Shit – shit! I dash back into the house and shriek 'MUM!' at the top of my voice, then grabbing my mobile from the sofa, I stumble back out.

I take his hand in mine and he sways slightly. I can hear his breath coming in short, fast little gasps. 'Please don't try and move, Dad!' I plead, dialling 999.

Mum appears by my side as I'm giving the operator our details and, eyes widening with fear, she takes off her cardigan and bunches it up on the grass as she kneels down next to him. 'Lie back darling,' she says. 'We're just going to wait for the ambulance together.' I dash inside to get my blanket and tuck it over him as he did moments ago for me.

He stares up at the sky and tries to steady his breathing. I'm clasping one hand and Mum is holding the other. The dogs have gone quiet and the only sound is the sharp effort of his breath.

Then, without moving his head, he looks first at me and then at Mum, and barely squeezes our hands as he says in between gasps, his gaze flickering between us, 'I – love – you.'

'We love you too, my sweetheart!' my mum tries to smile but her voice has gone all high and frightened. 'Just try to rest Mark, they're on their way.'

## Chapter Thirty-Three

Sitting on the swing in my parents' back garden, on which I have seen Dad push Oscar and Lily countless times, I grip the cold rope with my hand and fix unseeing eyes on a tuft of grass, blades blowing in the fresh wind. I glance at the kitchen window across the lawn. Even though it's early morning, they've had to put the kitchen light on and I can see Mum, Chris and Stu moving around inside. Mum is getting cups out of the cupboard. She glances up at me briefly and I think I see her say something to one of my brothers.

I turn away and stare at a couple of the bare trees against the grey heavy sky, my feet pushing automatically into the damp ground as I swing very lightly, looking at the spot where she and I were kneeling last night.

What are we going to do without him? Who is going

359

to listen to me when I have things I want to ask, that won't make sense to anyone but him? Who is going to kiss the top of my head and say things like 'What's the drama, Molly Malone?' And where is he right now? Why can't I feel him here?

I think about Mum, tiny, sitting in the hospital surrounded by us, smiling through tears as she clutched a very small piece of tissue to her. 'He really was very calm you know.' She reached out and firmly clasped Stu's hand as he gave way. 'I promise. Wasn't he Moll?' Everyone looked at me as I stood there rigid and silent. 'He just closed his eyes. He wasn't frightened.'

I don't want him to not be here, he's always been here. I'm not ready for this. I'm not ready at all. And I don't want him to be on his own without us.

I've got things I want to tell him, things I need to talk to him about. I close my eyes and I can see myself as a little girl, lying in bed giggling with delight as he tells me and the boys stories with funny voices. Him holding me over water and letting me dip my toes in rushing waves, but I can't remember that really, can I? I'd have been far too young. Maybe it's just something I've imagined from seeing photos . . . Then I see him doing his speech at our wedding. You can't bloody die Dad; I need you! You've got too much to do, too much to see.

How? How can this be? And why am I not crying? My eyes are completely dry and I find myself wondering, almost abstractly, how weird that is. My dad has just died. Cry. You should be crying.

I hear the back door close and one of the dogs bursts into the garden, gambolling around happily. Mum follows, walking slowly in my direction, smiling but teary as she holds out open arms to me.

I stand up automatically to go to her. My head falls on to her shoulder and she holds me to her. We both just stand there rocking lightly on the spot, the cold wind blowing around us. 'I want my Dad,' I blurt, stunned to hear myself say the words and voice cracking she says 'Oh my darling girl, I know. I want him too' as she strokes my hair.

'I shouldn't have let him run out there like that, I should have—'

She pulls back sharply and takes my shoulders. 'There was *nothing* you could have done to stop this. It could have happened at any time.'

'He thought he saw something and, then—'

'Molly, this was not your fault. The aneurysm was there, we just didn't know it.'

I don't know what to say. I can't think straight, I feel hollow, like there's a gap where my middle used to be and my head is floating in space.

At the hospital, they told me Dad's body was just a shell, that I needn't be afraid, what was him had gone . . . that I might find it reassuring to see him, it might help me say goodbye.

But I didn't want my last picture of my Dad to be him lying in a hospital covered by a sheet. And I don't want to say goodbye.

'Molly, please come inside,' Mum says. 'It's so cold out here. Come on.' She tries to take my hand. 'You're shaking. Please sweetheart.'

I look at her. She's devastated, completely overwhelmed – shattered. I should be looking after her. I suddenly want to tell her about the baby, but she will only worry – she knows about Dan leaving. It will be yet more load and I can't do that to her. So I say nothing, just follow her into the house obediently.

I simply want to make it all go away. Make it all un-happen.

# Chapter Thirty-Four

In the last two days I have learnt that if someone dies within twenty-four hours of admission into a hospital there may be a post-mortem. That the post mortem can take up to three weeks, depending on how busy the coroner is. Also, that the middle of winter is not a good time to die, because it's busy. Lots of elderly succumbing to flu, which will mean the funeral directors – once the post mortem is done and the body released to the relatives – will be busy too.

I also learn that *if you decide to have an abortion you will attend the clinic in person to meet with one of our fully qualified and non-judgemental healthcare professionals, who will talk you through the right procedure for you. We accept unwanted pregnancies occur and believe that women have the right to choose for themselves how to deal with the situation. Please use our pregnancy calculator to determine which treatments may be suitable for you should you decide to go ahead.*

I click on the link.

*Please enter into the required fields, the information which will help us determine how advanced your pregnancy is.*

I enter my postcode, the first day of my last period and . . . click

*We estimate, from the information provided, that you are four weeks pregnant.*

That means the procedure most suitable for me is the abortion pill, *available up to nine weeks, which will induce an early miscarriage.* Or I can have a *surgical abortion; gentle suction to remove the pregnancy.* I suppose they describe it as gentle so it doesn't frighten people.

Either way I have to make an appointment to discuss my options. They call me back very promptly and from the list my postcode search threw up, the closest clinic that has the first available appointment – is in London.

'Will you be bringing a nominated companion with you?' the woman asks me. She's kind and I'm grateful for that. 'A partner? A friend or relative?'

'No.'

She doesn't seem surprised. Or if she is, she keeps it to herself.

I don't want to tell anyone. Everyone will have opinions, advice . . . and we can't even bury my dad yet, we have a funeral to arrange. I want *none* of this to be real – none of it. I want it all to go away. I keep seeing Dad in my mind over and over again, sinking to the grass, the confusion on his face . . . I'm not sleeping, I can't eat. I still can't cry. I am well, nothing really. I've just confirmed the time of the appointment and hung up when there is a soft knock at my bedroom door.

'Molly?' It pushes open and Joss puts her head round. 'Is it OK to come in? Karen said I should just come up.'

She comes into the room tentatively, dressed in work clothes.

'Isn't it a bank holiday today?' I'm confused, laptop resting across my outstretched legs, back propped uncomfortably against the wall.

She gives a slight shake of her head and sits down on the edge of the bed. 'That was yesterday. How are you?'

I don't know really, so I just shrug as I close the screen and she says quickly. 'I'm sorry, that was a really stupid question.'

I shake my head. 'It wasn't. It wasn't at all.'

She pauses. 'I don't know what to say to you.'

I look at her and she reaches a hand out to me. I take it and she grips it fiercely.

We just sit there quietly for a moment.

'I'm so sorry.' Her eyes fill with tears.

'Thank you.' I squeeze her hand lightly before pulling mine away.

'I wish I could make it all go away for you.'

'I know you do.'

We fall quiet again.

'I can't even begin to imagine what you must be feeling like.'

I think she probably has a rough idea. Joss has lived most of her adult life dreading someone in a hospital saying 'We did all we could'. Every time her mum doesn't pick up the phone, every time she does but she's slurring, every time she rings Joss and is excitedly high as a kite because she's decided tomorrow is the day she's stopping drinking *for good*. Every time, Joss is dreading the worst and in it on her own. She knows better than anyone. How does she stay so brave all of the time?

I reach my hand back out and she takes it again.

'How's Bec?' I say eventually. 'She called me yesterday. When you see her will you say sorry I didn't pick up? I'd fallen asleep. I don't want her to think I don't want to speak to her.'

'She doesn't think that,' Joss says quickly. 'Not at all. She just wants – we both want – to do whatever we can.'

'That's really kind,' I say automatically. 'I appreciate that. So how are things going with that new man of yours?'

Slightly thrown, she hesitates for a moment. 'They're good – really good, but we don't have to talk about—'

'I'm looking forward to meeting him. We must sort something out.'

'OK,' she says slowly. 'That'd be nice. He'd like that . . . Moll, Bec wondered if she could come and see you tomorrow? We didn't want to come together tonight, in case it was too much.'

'No, no – I'd love to see her.' But then I remember

366

the appointment I have. 'Do you think she'd be able to come after six?' I take my hand back and scratch my head worriedly. 'Would that be all right, do you think?'

'Of course!' Joss gives me a troubled look. 'It's whatever *you* want.'

'After six would work for me.'

'OK,' she says carefully. 'Well I'll tell her then.'

'Thanks.'

Another moment passes and she takes a deep breath. 'So, have you heard from—'

'Joss do you mind if I have a little nap?' I say quickly. She's going to ask me about Dan, and no I haven't heard from him, I don't even know where he is. 'It's just I haven't been sleeping and I'm suddenly really tired. Is that OK?'

She looks a bit startled but recovers herself well. 'Absolutely it is. I'll pop off home. Can I ring you tomorrow? Is that OK?'

'Yeah I'll be here.'

Oh. Except I won't. Well, I'll deal with that then.

'Do you need anything from your house?' she asks as she gets up.

'No thanks.' I can't even think about that now, that I have a house somewhere else, full of stuff. It feels like it belongs to a different lifetime.

She looks at me, concerned.

'Thanks for coming over.' I deliberately stonewall her, and she knows it, so instead she just leans over and in a most un-Josslike way, gently kisses the top of my head.

It says everything, but nonetheless, when she reaches the door she turns back, just to be on the safe side. 'I'll be here when you want me, you can ring me any time of the day or night. I'll keep my phone on.'

I know she will, and I am so grateful, I really am. I'm not being mean – I just . . . I want to say it all to her, but I don't know how to. I am actually very tired – I seem to have no energy at all. I just want to be left alone. So I just nod instead and she slips from the room quietly, closing the door behind her.

# Chapter Thirty-Five

'You're sure you'll be OK?' I say to Mum, wrapping a scarf around my neck. 'I won't be late.'

'I'll be fine,' Mum smiles tiredly. She looks shattered. Underneath her eyes has gone the colour of dusty blueberries and her skin appears paper-thin. But she's wearing neatly pressed trousers and when I get up from the table, she picks up our lunch plates and scrapes the crusts into the bin before carrying them over to the sink, like normal. 'You don't want a coffee, do you? You'll have one with Joss I expect?'

'I should think so, yes,' I button my coat up evasively.

'It'll do you good to go out,' Mum says, turning the hot tap on and reaching for the washing-up liquid.

I look at my watch. 'I thought you said Maria was coming over? Shouldn't she be here by now?'

'She will be soon,' Mum reassures me. 'Go on, you go.'

'But I don't want to leave you on your own.'

She turns to face me. 'Please don't be upset by this, but I'd actually really like it, just for a bit. I'm so, so pleased that you're staying here my darling, but it would be nice to have five minutes space to hear myself think. You understand, don't you?'

I walk up to her and give her a quick kiss. 'See you later.'

She turns back to the sink and calls over her shoulder, 'Take care my love.'


Take care. Her words are still bouncing around my hollow head as I stand outside the clinic on the pavement looking up at the front of the building. There's no sign, just a number on the door. It appears to be an expensive townhouse in a smart area of London. It could be any number of things; a barrister's office, an embassy, a private members' club . . . a place to end pregnancies.

I shiver and stare at the glossy door. I must look very odd, just standing here. I should go in. It's only a door, a building. I'm going for an appointment. One step at a time.

I swallow, close my eyes and wobble on the spot a bit. Taking a deep breath and a step forward, I feel a wave of nausea woosh up within me. Just as quickly I turn and face away from the door again. My heart is beating very fast. Am I really going to do this? I scrunch my eyes up tightly and exhale, trying to calm my mounting sense of panic, but my throat starts to tighten, I gulp painfully and then I start to shake, really properly shake. Fumbling in my bag I scrabble around for my phone and pull it out, staring wildly at it for a moment, but I know exactly who I want to call.

Standing there shaking in the middle of the pavement, I listen as it rings. I know he's not going to pick up, but somehow even hearing him on his answerphone will be better than—

'Hello'

Oh! It's *him* . . . and the sound of his voice . . . It simply releases something in me; my eyes flood with tears, everything rushes up from somewhere within me so suddenly and I am crying, crying and crying as I hold the phone tightly as I can, as close to my ear as possible.

'Molly?' I hear him say in confusion. 'Molly? What is it?'

I can just hear myself sobbing like my heart is going to break with grief but all I can think is don't tell him, it would be so cruel, so manipulative. Don't tell him about Dad either. Don't. Don't do that to him. But oh . . . my dad. My dad . . .

'Molly, please – talk to me!' he says desperately. 'Are you hurt?'

And that just makes me just collapse from the inside out. My eyes are open but I can't see through them the tears are so thick. 'I can't—' I hear myself gulping. 'I'm—'

'Where are you?'

371

I can't get words out, it feels like a physical pain. 'I'm—Great Portland Street, I can't— I'm so sorry, I didn't mean to call, to upset you.' I hear my voice go very high. 'I'm so sorry, Dan.' And I hang up quickly.

I can't cope. I can't cope with this, hearing his voice, knowing that – I just wanted to . . . I just wanted to what? Make everything *even worse* than it already is? Nothing has changed, Dad is still . . . and I'm . . . Oh shit! Before I can think about it a moment longer I wipe my eyes furiously, whirl round on the spot and ring the buzzer. Then the door unlocks. I push it open, and go in.

# Chapter Thirty-Six

'Now, although the pregnancy test we've just done is positive, one of our doctors needs to determine what stage of pregnancy you're at,' explains the counsellor. 'Then we can talk through your options. You'll see another doctor and after that, you and I will talk again, to see if it's something you still want to go ahead with, OK?'

I nod. This is all happening very fast. I feel numb. Did I really even speak to Dan? His voice echoes around in my head '*Where are you?*'

'I'm going to take you through to the first consultation now, OK?'

'So Molly . . .' says the doctor, pushing the gel around on my tummy and looking at a monitor that is turned away from me. 'You think you are only about four weeks? Hmm. I don't think I'll be able to . . . oh – hang on . . .'

My heart gives an involuntary thud.

'Right, I can see there is a pregnancy, it's very early, but it's there. I think you're more likely nearly six weeks' actually.'

'Six?' I'm astonished. 'But the first day of my last period was . . .' I try to remember 'the thirteenth or fourteenth of November?'

She pauses. 'So, yeah – coming up to six. Give or take a day or two.'

So it was pretty much literally first time – lucky?

'Can I look?' My voice is shaky.

'Of course,' she says gently, and turns the monitor towards me. 'But *you* won't be able to see anything, it's too early. It is there though.'

Silently, I stare at the screen, transfixed, not able to say a thing. She's right, I can't see anything of note at all – just grainy, indistinct blurs, but my eyes fill with tears all the same and I cover my mouth with my hand. I cannot stop staring. She's seen it – it *is* there – and I know instantly that I absolutely cannot do this. I simply can't.

It doesn't matter what I thought I wanted, or didn't want, what anyone else thinks, it's completely irrelevant to me now. Everything has changed, again.

All I know is right here, right now; how I am feeling *now*. And I have never been more sure of anything in my life. There is no choice to make.

374

So I tell her, I explain everything, and she's incredibly kind and understanding, offering me more counselling if I would like it and telling me that she will do a referral letter with my permission, for the antenatal care I'm going to need.

I've just finished slowly dressing, trying to take it all in, start to get used to how this feels to me, think about how things are going to be, when a knock at the door interrupts us. A younger woman half-slips into the room and murmurs something discreetly to the doctor while I'm reaching for my coat, then melts away.

'Molly, I need to let you know that your husband arrived, asking for you.' The doctor's voice is deliberately neutral and calm.

'Dan was here?' I say in disbelief and my heart leaps. 'Just now?'

'He won't have been told anything, no one will have confirmed whether you are here or not, so if you would like to wait and not leave immediately . . .'

'No, no, you don't understand—' I reach out and place an urgent hand on her arm. 'I *want* to see him!'

'He won't have been allowed in, I'm afraid, it's to protect your right to confidentiality . . .'

I'm one step ahead of her. I grab my bag and rush from the room, running down the corridor, becoming lighter with every step, through the anonymous reception area, into the corridor, before pushing out through the heavy door on to the cold London street. I look left and then right, I can't see him! Where is he? I start to hurry up the road.

Then across the street, right at the far end, coming out of a newsagent, fingers fumbling desperately with a packet of cigarettes, I see a very familiar face. He looks up and notices me at the exact same time . . . my muscles lock, my heart starts to pound and frightened heavy breath begins to suck in and out of my lungs.

I step backwards with shock . . . I turn, and I start to run . . .

# Chapter Thirty-Seven

'Molly! Wait!'

I look over my shoulder as Leo drops the fag packet and goes to rush over the road, but a white van turns the corner, going too fast to stop and gets in his way. He vanishes out of sight behind it, and reaching the door to the clinic, I frantically press on the intercom button for all I'm worth. 'Please, let me in,' I plead, frantically looking back up the street, he's dodging a car, weaving across the road. 'It's Molly Greene, he's coming! I need to—'

The door buzzes, I push on it, hearing him yell 'No!' – he's sprinting towards me, but the door doesn't move, the lock buzzes redundantly again and again, *why won't it open?* FUCK – because it's a pull . . .

I've realised too late. He reaches out and grabs my

arm, making me yelp with fright, and wrenches me back from the door.

'Shhh!' he hisses. 'I'm not going to hurt you! Stop it!' he looks up at the door and for the first time I notice a security camera. 'They'll be watching us. Calm down.'

I look at him, terrified. How could I have thought it was Dan? All I told him was Great Portland Street. He might not even be in London for all I know. He could be anywhere.

'Don't make a scene,' Leo instructs, still holding my arm and marching me away.

'How did you know I was here?'

'Just come away from the door,' he pulls me further up the street and I yank my arm free. 'How did you know?' I stare at him, my mind swirling.

He hesitates.

I try to think. 'That tracking thing, it *was* you, wasn't it?'

He laughs derisively and looks away, scratching his neck irritably. 'What are you talking about?'

'But I took it off the phone.' I ignore his dismissive tone. 'Have you . . .' my voice drops to a disbelieving whisper. 'Have you been following me since then? All this time I thought you'd—'

'You thought I'd what?' he snaps, frowning. 'So what if I have been keeping an eye on things? You've not exactly been keeping me in the fucking loop, have you? I come to yours the Wednesday I get back to sort it all because you're still dithering around – only to find you've apparently already told him! One minute you're ringing me and crying down the phone to, quote "let you live your life" . . . the next you're in tears at the window, he gets back and I hear arguing! Then the next few days you are getting rid of the car, you are both off work . . . OK – I think – they're splitting up. At last. Give her some space to get it all done . . . but then *still* you don't call. And *still* he doesn't actually go. I mean, what the fuck? How do you think that made me feel?' He leans in towards me and instinctively I jerk back. 'I tried to call you countless times and you didn't pick up.'

'I had to give my phone back. I lost my job,' I say, dazed.

'Yeah, I worked that out eventually, thanks,' he says irritably. '*Two weeks* I wait for you to contact me and tell me what we are going to do. I'm not saying I wasn't pleased that you told him, but I've been going out of my mind Molly. I honestly don't remember you being this unpredictable, you've changed, you really have. I've got responsibilities! I know they're not my kids, but Daisy and Millie are my stepkids, and Christmas is a big deal to them. I didn't know whether I was going to be there or not, or what! On Christmas Eve I had to tell Helen I had to work late so I could come and check on you – *Christmas Eve*! She went fucking mental, do you know how hard that was for me to pull off?'

I stare at him open mouthed, I'm simply stunned by what I'm hearing . . . hang on, didn't he say one of her daughters was called Amanda?

'I get to your house and your bloody front door is

379

wide open. I was terrified, I thought he'd done you in or something! I'm checking your house over and then you get back with him like there's nothing wrong and it's all happy families again! Do you even know what that did to me? Hearing you two like that?'

He is starting to look very angry indeed and some instinct tells me to stay completely quiet.

'I go all the way home again,' he gestures violently, 'give the kids Christmas . . . the day after Boxing Day, I drive *all* the way back down again – and it's all gone off! You've being taken to your mum's by Joss and Bec, he's nowhere to be seen . . . I ring the bell at your parents' and your dad tells me it's "not a good time right now" for you . . .' He snorts incredulously. 'Oh, but I'M just having a peachy one Mr Baxter, don't you FUCKING worry about me! . . . You know what I resorted to then?' He challenges me and I give a frightened shake of my head.

'I'm *thirty-five years old* Molly and I climbed into your parents' garden to try and get to your bedroom window so I could throw some stones up and get your attention. Can you even hear how ridiculous that sounds? But the best bit is your dad coming charging out with some pack of bloody baying wolves! I had to leg it before he called the police! I know I love you but Jesus Christ, woman!' he shouts.

My hands fly to my mouth.

'Exactly. Beginning to get it now?' he says, completely misunderstanding my reaction. 'I've practically *lived* in my car in Brighton for the last month – all this, for you.'

'It was you?' Tears rise to my eyes as I stare at him. 'You were at my mum and dad's house. You bastard!' I shriek and fly at him, raining a flurry of fists down on him.

Thrown, he has to quickly scramble to catch my arms, holding on around my wrists.

'My dad had an aneurysm. He *died*!' I cry.

Leo pales. 'That's not funny.'

My legs give way and my body weight dragging down nearly pulls him over with me, one of my wrists slips away from him. 'Stand up,' he orders quickly under his breath. 'People are looking. Stand up NOW!'

'Do you even know what you've done?' I pull my other arm free. 'Get away from me!'

He swallows worriedly. 'He really died? I'm sorry.'

'You're *sorry*?' I can barely whisper.

'But aneurysms are just there, aren't they? Anything can set them off.' He runs his fingers through his hair in agitation. 'I was trying to make sure you were all right, I was trying to look after you.' He takes a small pace left, then back to me. 'That's what all of this has been about. You need someone to take care of you. We're meant for each other Molly. You must see that now, surely?' He bites his lip anxiously.

We're meant for each other are we? So who was Amanda and why was he fishing around on that dating website? I realise that I was just the unlucky one whose

381

number came up, the most promising lead . . . I left the door wide open and he sauntered on in and began to wind everything tighter and tighter.

'You're mad,' I say slowly. 'You need help Leo. This is obsessive, it's—'

'No it's *not*,' he says, instantly irritable again, stopping dead still and facing me. 'If you don't think we're meant to be together why did you contact me out of the blue like that?'

'It was just one of those random things! One of those stupid things you do!'

He flushes angrily. 'There's no such thing as random. Every action has a reaction. Everything happens for a reason.' I can't tell if he really believes that or not, or if he's just told himself that's how it is.

'I'm sorry.' I realise I'm only making him more irate. 'I should never have done it. If I gave you the wrong idea, I'm sorry. But Leo, I don't want to be with you! I've lost everything and I still don't, can't you see that?'

He doesn't seem to hear me. 'Talking of actions, I take it you've done it?' he nods back towards the clinic. 'You've got rid of it?'

I gasp.

'I Googled the address,' he says simply, 'when I saw you go in. I know what you were there for. Have you done it? They wouldn't tell me . . . it's sensible though. That would be an unnecessary complication too far, to say the very least. You can't – as you quite rightly said to me at the hotel – have much fun with babies in tow.

Particularly when,' he concludes acidly, 'they're someone else's.'

And it's that which makes me think I can see a way out of all of this. It occurs to me in a split second and I seize it.

'What makes you think it's not yours?' I say quickly, taking a step back away from him. 'And what makes you think I've "got rid of it".' A baby is the last thing he wants. I know it is.

'Oh?' he says dangerously. 'It's mine, is it?'

'Yes – it is,' I say determinedly. 'And you know what Leo? Like I said, I've got nothing else to lose now, and I still don't want you. But you know what?' I pause and try to think quickly . . . 'If you don't swear to me that I will never lay eyes on you again, if you don't walk away from me right now, I'll come and I'll find you. I'll tell Helen about this baby – and then you'll lose everything too. You'll be left with *nothing*.'

A muscle begins to flex furiously in his jaw as he looks at me in silence. Trying to weigh up if I'm serious or not? Well I am.

'From what you told me at the hotel, I seem to remember Helen is rather practised at getting her pound of flesh from ex-husbands – and good for her.'

'So it's definitely my baby then, is it?' he says, eyes glinting. He seems not to have heard what I just said. 'You're really, really sure about that, are you?' His voice is getting louder. It throws me for a moment. 'Yes, of course I am!' I say, more bravely than I feel.

'Well, that's So. Very. Interesting,' he pretends to look as if he's pondering a real puzzler, while clearly simmering with repressed rage. 'I wonder how *that* happened, seeing as we last had sex five years ago.'

Everything just stops.

I can see his chest rising and falling he's breathing so hard. He's gone bright red in the face but looks utterly triumphant. I can see him thinking how much smarter he is than *everyone else*. In his complete arrogance, all he can think is how dare I be mad enough to try and get one over on HIM?

'But at the hotel . . .' I feel like I'm being sucked into a huge whirlpool. I saw the wrapper, we talked on the phone . . .

Oooooooooohhhhhh my God . . . that's the reason I can't remember it?

Nothing actually happened?

'You made it up?' I whisper. 'You made the whole thing up?'

'What kind of man would have sex with a woman who's unconscious?' he spits back, dodging my question.

What kind of man? I think of going to the doctor's, the morning-after pill, the GUM clinic, the constant fear, the tears, the work do where Dan hit Pearce, losing my job, Dan's face in the car park when he shouted 'Who is he?', my DAD! None of it needed to happen. None of it.

'You blackmailed me with something that never happened?' It's all too much to take in. 'Why?'

He just shrugs. 'You were freaking out, acting like we

384

were never going to see each other again. I had to do something to buy some time. That's not blackmail.'

He is crazed. And suddenly I even begin to doubt that he had nothing to do with my passing out completely at the hotel. 'Did you give me something? Something that made me unconscious?'

He laughs, looks back at me blankly and shrugs, like maybe, maybe not, but he can't be bothered to tell me.

'You set it all up, you made me believe that we'd had sex – you emotionally blackmailed me!' I can barely get my words out. 'Do you have any idea of how serious that is? I should go to the police!'

'Police?' he scoffs. 'What are you talking about? For the last time, that's *not* blackmail!'

'I've still got your texts,' I lie quickly. 'All of them. The doctor I saw the day after? That's all documented. I have plenty of evidence.'

'It would be your word against mine.' He sounds a little less sure though.

'Except you've been following me too. Somewhere, someone will have got you on a camera. It looks like you're on that one right now.' I point up, it has swivelled right round and is watching us intently. 'How could you do this to me?' I'm actually asking him. I'm stunned. I really do not know this man any more.

He hesitates, and as he does, there is a screech of tyres further up the street that makes us both glance in the direction of the noise. The door to a black cab flings open and Dan, dressed in work clothes, jumps out.

He thrusts something through the driver's window and then looks around him frantically. He sees me and shouts, 'Molly!' He's come to me, for no other reason than I called him and I needed him.

'Shit!' I hear Leo mutter and I turn to look at him. He's just staring at Dan running towards us, then he looks right back at me and his gaze suddenly seems to turn blank, his face becomes completely vacant. He takes a step closer to me and I see him reach his hand into his pocket, but then we both jump as a very sudden and loud siren wails. A police car has turned into the road and is roaring up to us. It jerks to a stop, the doors open and two uniformed men jump out, rushing straight up to Leo. It all happens very fast. 'Sir, I'm going to need to ask you who you are,' one of them is saying. 'Can I see some identification please?'

Dan is next to me, gathering me into his arms, almost pulling me completely off my feet. 'You're all right! Thank God.' He looks sick with relief. 'I thought you'd been hurt – I had to get to you. Oh thank God.' He squeezes me again. 'I've never heard you cry like that – it was horrible. What's going on?' He continues worriedly. 'Who's that bloke,' he nods at Leo, 'and why are the police here?'

'Do I have to give you my name?' Leo is saying, looking first at Dan then at me, I think attempting a tacit acceptance of my now expired deal. I cannot believe what he has done, it's barely sinking in, the enormity of it all.

The officer frowns. 'Well, could you explain what you're doing here, please?'

'I—' Leo exhales tightly. 'I saw this woman,' he motions to me, 'on the street in some distress. I came up to ask her if she was OK and she fainted.' He looks at me and waits. I am too numb to say a thing.

'Right,' says the officer as he glances up at the clinic security camera. I think he's about to ask me if that's all true, but in fact he turns back to Leo. 'Sir, I'm going to have to ask you to turn out your pockets please.'

Leo says nothing, but looks straight at me – not breaking his gaze once – as he turns out his wallet, his phone and a weird-looking plastic handle.

Dan protectively pulls me to him again although I don't understand why. I can feel his heart thudding.

*None of it happened?* Can I even believe that? Leo might have drugged me. Am I ever going to know what really happened in that hotel room?

The other police officer has already stepped forward and taken the thick bit of plastic from Leo and then I hear the first say, 'Sir, I am arresting you for carrying an offensive weapon. You do not have to say anything, but it may harm your defence if you do not mention when questioned something you may later rely on in court. Anything you do say may be given in evidence. Do you understand?'

Leo says nothing. They start to take him over to the police car.

'Dan?' I'm completely confused and don't really understand what is happening. 'It was just a handle.'

'Molly, it was a flick knife. You push a button and the blade springs out.'

I whip back round in horror and look at the police car door closing on Leo.

He was carrying a knife? He knew I was pregnant and he was *carrying a knife*?

My ex – the one who nearly was.

'Shit!' Dan is clearly shaken. He hasn't let go of me and I don't think he's going to either. 'He just walked up to you in the street?'

I swallow, beginning to feel lightheaded. 'Dan . . . there're some things I need to tell you . . .'

He looks almost as panicked as I feel – for a moment – but then seems to steel himself. 'Good or bad?' he says bravely.

I'm not sure how to answer that. 'Some really good stuff and some . . . not so nice' which is a huge under-statement. I'm pregnant. With a baby that we pretty much conceived, I think, because I felt guilty for something I never did, but I now know I want, for all of the right reasons . . . in fact arguably I'm pregnant because of Leo. I never had an affair . . . my dad . . . 'I'm not sure where to start,' my voice starts to shake, 'there's so much to say.' And as I look at him I can't help but feel incredibly frightened. I don't want to be without him ever again. Will he believe me? Will he still want me – us?

But he reaches for my hand and he holds it very tightly. 'Well I'm not going anywhere. Why don't we just start at the beginning?'

# Book Club Questions

1. Molly wants to keep what happened with Leo a secret from Bec, one of her closest friends. Do you think we are all pressured these days to disclose too much about ourselves?

2. Can you ever stay friends with an ex? Or is there always an agenda? Is it possible to completely get over an ex?

3. Does Dan behave honourably throughout or does Molly have cause to doubt him?

4. If you could have one night with an ex and you knew that no one would ever find out – would you do it?

5. Did you feel for Molly when she realised she was having doubts about having children and why that might be, or did you think her reasons were selfish and indulgent?

6. Molly, Joss and Bec all have very different ideas on having children. Who did you most closely identify with?

7. Dan and Molly are very happy apart from the one issue that threatens to shatter their marriage: having children. If one person wants them, and the other doesn't, can there ever be a way through that?

8. Is it ever acceptable for someone to 'track' someone else?

9. *'If only Leo's stupid wallet hadn't been in my bag; he would have kept walking out of that hotel. We'd just made our peace. We should have just gracefully exited each other's lives . . . and if I'd have called Dan first thing that morning and said sorry straight away, when Leo turned up, perhaps I wouldn't have been so unsettled, I'd have been more on my guard.'*

   Molly seems to believe here that everything snowballed as a result of bad luck and circumstance. Do you think that's true, or did flattery blind Molly to what experience had taught her about Leo?

10. What do you think really happened in that hotel room? Could you live with not ever really knowing?

11. Do you think Molly got her happy ending?